SHILOH WALKER

HUNTERS INTERLUDE

ELLORA'S CAVE
ROMANTICA PUBLISHING

THE HUNTERS: INTERLUDE
An Ellora's Cave Publication, April 2005

Ellora's Cave Publishing, Inc.
1337 Commerce Drive Suite #13
Stow, Ohio 44224

ISBN #1419950665

Edited by: *Pamela Campbell*
Cover art by: *Syneca*

Warning:

The following material contains graphic sexual content meant for mature readers. *The Hunters Interlude: Bryon and Kit & Jonathan and Lori* has been rated *E-rotic* by a minimum of three independent reviewers.

Ellora's Cave Publishing offers three levels of Romantica™ reading entertainment: S (S-ensuous), E (E-rotic), and X (X-treme).

S-*ensuous* love scenes are explicit and leave nothing to the imagination.

E-*rotic* love scenes are explicit, leave nothing to the imagination, and are high in volume per the overall word count. In addition, some E-rated titles might contain fantasy material that some readers find objectionable, such as bondage, submission, same sex encounters, forced seductions, etc. E-rated titles are the most graphic titles we carry; it is common, for instance, for an author to use words such as "fucking", "cock", "pussy", etc., within their work of literature.

X-*treme* titles differ from E-rated titles only in plot premise and storyline execution. Unlike E-rated titles, stories designated with the letter X tend to contain controversial subject matter not for the faint of heart.

Also by Shiloh Walker:

CONTENTS

BRYON AND KIT

Dedication

To my editor Pam, the Wondrous One.

To my kids Cam and Jess — my world revolves around you two. I love you both.

And to my husband Jerry. My real life fantasy… I love you.

Prologue

Byron stared down at the pain-racked body of Kristof Beauchamp and wasn't sure if he could fight off his rage much longer. The man responsible was in this house and Byron would see to it that he paid. But his duty, through friendship, was here, by his dying friend's side.

"Katrine...will you take care of her? So young, she is, and now alone..."

Byron held tight to Kristof's hand and broke a promise. The Inherent was so battered in body, so injured — the vampire doubted the shifter would even notice. As Byron slid inside and separated the pain from the man, Kris was able to breathe and think without the pain caused by the silver and poison.

"I'll take care of the girl as though she were my own," Byron promised, smoothing back Kris's sweat-tangled hair. The air stank of the poison that was eating through Kris's body and Byron shoved his fury under control again. Wolfsbane...the poison served only one purpose, and it was exactly what it sounded like. It had been put inside a hollow silver bullet that had exploded on impact with Kris's body and even now was eating away at him like acid.

"She will not be a girl always. What then?" Kris asked, his accent thick with his weariness.

"I'll see to it that Kit has everything her heart desires," Byron promised. "She will want for nothing."

Kris laughed, and when he did blood leaked from his mouth. "My Bella is telling me...da, you had best remember that. Kit will want what she wants. Da." His combined French and Russian upbringing made his accent, at times, difficult to understand. Bella? The lady had died in childbirth three years earlier. "Ah, my Bella. I see you now. But Katrine. To leave her, my *bebè*, my heart breaks."

"Go to Bella," Byron whispered roughly, feeling tears sting his eyes. He could hear the baby crying. The hearing of an Inherent child was sharp, and she had heard her father. One of his people should have taken her away. They'd be lucky if heads didn't roll for letting the baby be upset this way.

"I will take care of Kit, I promise. I will do everything in my power to see her happy."

Chapter One
Twenty-four years later...

Kit tapped her pen on the table and stared at the disheveled woman in front of her. "I warned you, Melissa. Byron doesn't like women placing themselves naked in his bed unless he invites them. He chooses his women and his feeding companions. If he sent you away, then it is your fault. I am not intervening for you," Kit said wearily.

How many times before had she done this? Of course, Byron didn't exactly help much. He had been known to walk into a room and just take one of the women by the hand and lead her away without even speaking a word. The sexual pull a vampire exuded was always intensified after he'd touched one particular woman, and for a little while Melissa had been his favorite. Byron's call seemed to be rather strong for a vampire who was just over a century old, but then, Kit had only known a few. She was very drawn to Byron, so maybe she wasn't the best of judges.

Melissa sat staring at Kit with heartbroken eyes.

Kit hated her. Not for any particular reason. Melissa was nice, pretty, she had a sweet heart, she was sharp, and she had been through a rough time, otherwise she wouldn't be here.

A Hunter's home tended to be a fortress on the outside, but the inside where the Hunter brought people when he wasn't sure what else to do with them, held a veritable enclave of wounded souls.

Enclave—that was what they were—an enclave. Made up of the warriors who surrounded the outside and protected the vampire during the day while he slept, and those who acted as food and sex partners while he was awake.

Byron had brought Melissa here three years ago. For a year, she hadn't been able to even look at another person without fear in her eyes. She had moved past that. In the second year, she had learned that she could take care of herself, and in the third, Byron had taken her into his bed.

That was why Kit hated her.

And Byron, being the bastard he was, had even made sure Kit saw it. She had walked into his office thinking he had business to discuss, and instead she had been audience to a blowjob. Granted, somebody had given her the wrong fucking time. He had wanted to talk to her in a couple of hours, but for crying out loud.

Well, it really wasn't his fault.

She could still remember it, how Melissa had sucked on Byron's cock, and how much Kit wanted to be the one doing it. Byron had opened his eyes—he had known she was there—and glared at her. "Do you mind, Kit?"

"Not at all, Byron. I like to watch," she had drawled. Well, she hadn't ever really watched anything like that before, but she hadn't really been able to leave either. Her eyes were drawn to the length of his cock as Melissa slid her lips up and down, pulling back to stare at Kit with wide eyes before resuming what looked to be a very pleasant task.

His fangs flashed and she suspected part of him wanted to tell her to get the fuck out. But another part was aroused. He had gripped Melissa head's tightly and started to rock his hips faster, forcing his cock further and harder into her mouth until he came. Kit's sharp sense of smell caught it in the air and she stared at him, so hot she burned.

He'd made his human pass out. "That's the bad thing about humans, Byron. They just can't handle as much," Kit said, tsking a little, clucking false sympathy.

That was when things had started to change, at least on his end.

Things had been changing on her end for a long time. Byron was her soul mate. She knew it. She had told him so when she was nineteen, which had been a mistake. Apparently. He had taken her for a love-struck kid and he had laughed, patted her on the head, and sent her off to college. Six years ago. And she still felt the same.

After her little peep show, Byron had gone out of his way to antagonize her, and she couldn't figure out if he was angry at her or trying to tease her. He was so…skilled with women, but he was acting so crudely toward her. He was her boss, signed her paychecks, but he was also her Master. She had gone into service to a Hunter, and sworn to abide by the Council law. That meant something, damn it. She not only was a Hunter in her own right, she was his First Lieutenant, his guard, his servant, the highest honor a Master vampire could afford a member of his enclave.

Kit guarded him while he slept, she ran the household and his people while he was away.

She owed fealty to him until she decided that she was going to leave, or he decided to send her away. It was still her decision—although one hundred years ago, it wouldn't have been. A hundred years ago, she would have been Byron's until he was tired of her, or until she died. The Council had changed things. She would have to appeal to them and they would allow her to leave, providing she did things appropriately. All she had to do was state her case, basically her unhappiness with the situation, and they would let her leave. The Council didn't like any of their people being unhappy.

Kit just couldn't seem to make herself do it. Yet.

But, for now, he was her Master. Although she was not subservient, if he gave her an order, she must follow. She was not a slave. She actually had a position of power in his enclave. All obeyed her as they obeyed him. Nobody could question her orders, for her orders came from Byron. She acted as his second, and if she expected others to follow his orders, then so must she.

So when he sent for her, she went, even though she knew what she was walking into. It had been Byron and Benjamin Cross, his other lieutenant—a very mysterious, unusually powerful were—who were fucking Melissa. Benjamin was buried to his balls in her pussy, and Byron—oh, hell—he was bent over her and thrusting deep inside her ass.

The blonde was screaming with delirious pleasure and Kit hated her. She stood staring at them, unable to speak, but unable to leave until Byron gave her permission. And what she wanted was to rip the bitch away and take her place.

She had strolled over to a chair and flopped into it, sliding her hand inside her panties and starting to rub her clit, meeting Byron's eyes over the bodies of the others. *Bastard,* she had mouthed at him, as she stroked and massaged.

If she closed her eyes—her mental powers were strong enough—she was almost able to imagine it was her they were fucking. But just almost. After all, Kit was still a virgin. She had never even had sex, much less the pleasure of a threesome.

Chapter Two

Byron heard Melissa crying in Kit's office, and he fought the urge to break the door down and drag the little bitch out. She had been flaunting herself in Kit's face for weeks. Had she thought he hadn't seen it? The bitch went around whispering that "the little bitch dog was in love with the Master" but that he only wanted her.

He had wanted her, for a little while.

But he craved Kit.

Kit thought he was blind as well. He knew how she thought she felt. She was still a child though, and she hadn't really experienced life outside his territory. How could she know if she was in love with him? Even when he had sent her off to college, she had done it in her own way. She had completed in less than thirty months the courses it normally takes four years to do. She had stalked back up to the house one late summer night, on a full moon, wearing that beautiful wolven form. She had thrown back her head and bayed at the moon, and she had been laughing at him.

But he had made a promise that she would have what she wanted, and he wasn't it. No matter how much he might want to be.

The tiny little dark-haired child had grown into a woman he wanted more than he wanted to see another sunrise. After more than a century of darkness, he would never have thought anything would beckon to him more than that. But if he could choose between being able to walk in daylight again without harm, or having one night with Kit?

No contest.

He forced himself to walk past Kit's door.

She would handle it. She handled everything. Every fucking thing he threw at her. And he hated himself more each fucking day. He kept waiting for her to grow tired of the orders, the commands, but she never did. She never told him to shove it, never once threatened to walk. He kept waiting to hear that she had petitioned the council to revoke her pledge to him, kept waiting to see her walk out the door. He wouldn't even be surprised to see an older Hunter come to claim her, even though he would fight to the death before he allowed it.

He kept waiting for her to leave him.

That was what he needed her to do.

He didn't have the strength to make her leave.

And she was so fucking stubborn.

Byron remembered every challenge he had thrown at her, the most recent was when she had walked in knowing full well that he was fucking Melissa. He had expected her to rage and storm out, giving him reason to rant and rave at her for not following orders. Something to anger her, maybe drive her away. Instead she had settled down and started to masturbate, staring at him all the while. He drove himself harder into Melissa's butt, imagined it was Kit's and watched the movement of her fingers in her panties, smelling her arousal in the air over that of Melissa's and Ben's.

That had been a month ago.

And it had been that episode that had pushed Melissa over the edge. Melissa hadn't realized Byron had sent for Kit just to taunt and torment her. She had rolled from the bed, furious as Kit hummed and pleasured herself. The ignorant little blonde had even tried to launch herself at Kit but Ben had caught her around the waist, while Byron flopped onto his back, still hard and aching, and watched Kit.

Melissa saw the look on his face and fumed.

Ben dragged her out of the room just as Kit erupted into her own hand with a cry. Byron slid from the bed, crossed the room and took her hand, unable to stop himself, lapping her sweet cream and burying his face between her thighs. Shoving her skirt high and ripping her panties away, he licked her folds, suckling her clit, and taking her into another orgasm before he moved to the fold between her groin and thigh and pierced her flesh to feed.

Her blood pooled in his belly, hot, potent and sweet, and he shuddered. Byron was ready to stand and take her there when she suddenly struck out, cuffing him across the head, and rolling away from him.

"Bastard," she rasped out, her voice thick and husky.

"Kit, I—"

"You think I want you to touch me after you've just been fucking her?" she snarled, her dark gray eyes swirling like thunderheads in her dusky face. He moved toward her, the heady taste of her cream and blood lingering on his tongue, and he didn't care about anything else. He couldn't keep fighting this need he had for her—he just wanted to love her, to feed from her, to touch her.

She moved away, wolf-quick.

He shifted to mist and reformed just as she tried to leave the room and he grabbed her, pinned her by the door, catching her face and trying to kiss her. She jerked her face away and snarled at him, snapping at him with sharp teeth. She caught his chin hard enough to startle, and she used his surprise to move away.

She shifted, her clothes falling to shreds around her as she changed from human to full-wolf form, not the half-wolven, half-human form she sometimes chose. She chose the wolf—the better to run with, my dear.

And Byron had to watch as she ran away from him.

He had stopped taunting her after that.

Three days later, Melissa had started with her little petty tricks. It shouldn't have angered him the way it did.

But it was one thing for him to try to drive Kit away before he lost it.

It was another for a woman he slept with to taunt her with that fact.

He ignored it for three days, thinking she would grow weary of it. She did not. Then he thought Kit would take care of it. She did not. After it had continued for a week, he stepped in and told her it would stop or she would be sorry for it.

Melissa had learned just how sorry when he had led her to her bedroom, tied her down, teased her to the point of excruciating pleasure, and then just walked away. It had been Kit who had dared to disobey him hours later by untying her. When Melissa had thrown herself at Byron, begging to know why he was angry, he had stared at her in dismay before he realized she was putting on a show, solely for Kit's benefit.

He hadn't touched her since.

Then last week she had placed her naked ass in his bed and now, a day before her time was up in his home, she was crying on Kit's shoulder because she was getting kicked out. Byron was tired of her. And as always, Kit was handling the clean-up. He paused briefly, wondering if he should just take Melissa into town and give her some money and get her on a plane back to her hometown. But that would mean walking in and seeing Kit.

Kit.

Damn it. He was losing it.

He stalked out the door.

He had a fucking job to do, and it didn't include mooning over a sweet little shifter with eyes like storm clouds.

By the time he returned that night, he had found the proof he needed to execute a feral vampire who had been running a human slavery ring. Well, slavery wasn't a good word. What was? Fast food? Byron grimaced. His morbid sense of humor was growing worse the older he got.

He heard a soft gasping cry and his cock hardened with need, his fangs dropping down in rage. That was Kit. If one of his men had dared to touch her —

His ears pricked and he vaulted up the stairs before he realized he heard only one voice, one person breathing raggedly. His people were talking, some were sleeping, the low hum of conversation buzzing...but there was just one person in that room. Just one.

He felt like a fucking pervert, but he shifted to mist anyway and moved to hover outside her window, where she couldn't see him. She lay on her bed, ass up, while she rode a thick vibrator, quick and hard. He groaned, glad he made no sound in this form unless he chose to. Then he heard her cry out his name and shove her hand between her thighs, probably to massage her clit.

Kit had never taken a lover while in his house. She most likely had in college...hell, she had been gone three years. And too many times, she had come home late from the few dates he had allowed her in high school, smelling of sweaty sex, semen, and teenage lust. The first time...he hadn't been home, although he had earlier been pacing the porch and waiting. Benjamin had taken his stead and waited for her when one of the younger Hunters was hurt.

By the look in Benjamin's eyes when Byron arrived home, Byron had known simply not to ask. It had happened that night, he suspected. Though she was washed and bathed by the time he saw her the following night, something that damn well hid the evidence, her eyes flashed and sparkled and she blushed at any mention of her date.

It had happened. She had given her virginity to some high school boy who had no idea what a precious female he held. And she had glowed with it.

It had been all he could stand not to kill the boy she had been dating then.

But there had been no lovers in his house. Not once.

He didn't know if he could have allowed it, but she had never even tried.

He wasn't being fair to her. She climaxed with a soft, muffled wail, while he stared hungrily at her sweet, exposed butt and watched as she rolled onto her back and continued to play with herself, obviously not satisfied. She took the vibrator in her hand and started to drive it deep, her eyes glassy and wild as she used her other hand to stroke her clit.

He tore himself away and reformed to his mortal self inside the hall and walked away.

He wasn't being fair.

Chapter Three

"You're what?" Kit asked, almost soundlessly. She cleared her throat and spoke again, only slightly louder. Byron was sitting at his desk, looking for all the world like an upper-class businessman. He was wearing a white silk shirt, a black vest, unbuttoned, and a pair of black, trim-fitting pants. His hair would look ridiculous on some men—like a man trying to follow the trends—the way he kept it cut brutally short on the lower sides and the back, letting it fall long on the top and upper sides. Kit loved his hair, loved how thick and soft it looked, loved the midnight blackness of it. She knew his feet were bare and she knew he couldn't do a damn thing with a computer. She did that for him, but he was a fucking genius when it came to mathematics, and he ran a small empire from this little enclave.

He was the youngest Hunter in America, and the youngest Master with his own enclave. There had been others in history, but they hadn't lasted long. So far, Byron had not only lasted, but thrived. He dismissed those facts as he dismissed his wealth, attributing it to luck.

Byron was more than a Hunter, even if he didn't acknowledge that.

Kit knew it even if he didn't. Byron was amazing. And together, they could be more so. But he didn't want that. He didn't want to share his life with her. He didn't want her.

He was sending her away.

"It's time you go to France and find out more about your mother's people," he said, forcing himself to ignore the wild pain in her eyes.

"You're sending me away."

"I'm not sending you away, Kit," he said quietly. "It's for two years."

"You are," she argued, keeping her voice level. He wasn't going to appreciate another wailing, sniveling female. She couldn't stop the pain from showing, but she'd be damned if she cried. "You're sending me away, just like the rest. But I haven't done anything."

"No," he agreed. "You haven't done anything. It's France, Katrine. Don't you want to see France? And Russia, where your father came from? Doesn't that matter?"

Not unless you are with me, she thought. She just stared at him, bleeding inside. Finally, through her tight throat, she asked, "Why?"

Byron stared at her and said nothing.

She swallowed, the sound horribly loud in the silence of the room. Her body felt terribly bruised and battered — strange. All she had done was walk in here and stand in front of the desk for a mere three minutes. And her whole life had just been irrevocably changed.

She turned and slowly walked away.

"Fuck," she heard him say quietly. "You've never been anywhere else, sweet. You have to go see other things, try other things before you commit yourself to my world."

"I've committed myself to this world already, Byron. Or have you forgotten?" she asked wearily.

He hadn't, no. How could he forget the delirious, shameful pleasure that had filled him when she had petitioned the Council to join his Enclave, to join his world? It had given him the right to keep her, for always. But Byron knew he really didn't have that right, because of the promise he had made to her father. He shouldn't have agreed to take her in. But if he hadn't, she would have been sent to another Hunter.

"Kit, you don't belong here."

She laughed—a horrible, wild sound that echoed through the room and it made them both wince. "Yes, I do," she said. And then she left.

Byron felt shaken to his soul. He had never seen her eyes look quite that empty. Damn it, it was France. For a year. Then Russia. Another year. Then she was coming back. He'd damn well see to that. She didn't truly think he'd let her leave him forever, did she?

She'd go, experience a little more of life than she could here, and then, when she returned, he'd—

Fuck, what in the hell was going on? Byron paced the room, hungry, mad, furious with himself and with her. She had looked so hurt, so unlike Kit.

He left his office for his rooms, ignoring Ben, the Inherent who lived with him, and Mathias, the vampire who served as his third in command, under Kit. All were under Kit. Kit was the only one he trusted with everything, and he had to send her away. Damn it all to hell and back, he thought furiously.

Byron tore off his fine clothes and donned tougher, darker clothes that would blend with the night as he hunted. He was a young Hunter and though he was strong, he wasn't as arrogant as some. He wasn't going to trust only his vampire abilities to save him. He knew how to fight, and he trained regularly. He made sure all his people did as well, in case anyone ever tried to bring a battle onto his territory.

He wanted a bloody fight tonight and he doubted hunting was a wise choice. He should, if he was smart, find Eli and just have a bloody brawl.

But Byron took to the woods and went searching for prey. He had set up his territory in a wooded area, buying enough land to provide himself and the wolves some privacy, but keeping them close to the city so he could hunt easily. He had known his duty was to keep his chosen prey near by.

As always, he found it in Chicago. This, of course, was why he had chosen it as his territory. Even in his former life, this had been a large city and trouble had always been brewing. A few decades had not changed that. The method of madness had changed. More guns and drugs now, instead of fistfights and alcohol, but it was there.

He found his preferred prey in a rough neighborhood. They had been stalking a pretty young girl in a nurse's uniform who was now fighting wildly against the two men who held her. There was a third, and Byron waited until the third had moved a little closer before he reformed and moved in, taking the man's neck and snapping it like a twig before catching another in a mental hold and freezing him.

The third one hadn't realized what was going on until the girl took off running. He started to go after her when Byron caught him and threw him against the wall with his inhuman strength. The blow caused the man's head to split and start to bleed while Byron stared down into the man's dazed eyes. "She doesn't want to play, my friend," he crooned, catching the man's head and jerking it to the side before he struck. He took only a little, enough to establish a mental connection while he laid a path.

The next time this bastard tried to prey on any creature, it would be his last. If he faltered in any way, it would lead Byron back to him. Drawing back, staring into his eyes, Byron promised, "I will know. And I will kill you," he promised roughly, a tiny drop of blood on his lower lip.

Then he turned to the third man. Because this one was already dead. He was the girl's brother. She had gone to the police about her brother — she suspected he had something to do with another girl's rape and murder. She'd been right — Byron saw that before he even touched the man's mind. But she'd not been careful enough and her brother had found out.

This would have been her last night on this earth.

Byron smiled seductively, even pleasantly at the younger man, stroking his face as he listened and made sure the girl was far away. "A brave girl, your sister. She'll prosper now. I'll make certain. Ah, Max, isn't it? Your sister is about to come into some money and she will find her way out of this hellhole, as you like to call it. I want you to know that, to know she will live a long and prosperous life."

"Who the fuck are you?" Max tried to snarl. Not very effectively, since he was all but whimpering with fear.

The vampire flashed his fangs. Max tried to scream, but Byron pressed his thumb against his windpipe and cut off his air supply. Max was trying to tell his body to run, but Byron had already taken control of his mind and the human couldn't move. "Why are you doing this?"

"Remember the girl you raped?" Byron murmured, pushing Max into the shadows, listening for any sign of another watching. "She was young, wasn't she? Just a child, really. All that youth and innocence, and you destroyed it. What is that saying? Oh, yes. Payback is a bitch." Byron took the memories that Max had been relishing and turned them back on him, only now, Max was in the girl's position and *he* experienced the horror. Byron's psychic skill wasn't enough to make him actually suffer as much as the girl did, but he made sure the pathetic piece of scum had some inkling before he broke the link and grabbed him up from where he had fallen on the ground.

"Now do you know why?" Byron purred menacingly. "Do you know why I am going to kill you? You stalked and killed a child and would have done the same to your own blood."

"You can't just fucking kill me," Max sobbed.

Byron laughed. "Yes, I can." He wasn't even going to feed here. He reached in with his mental hands, grabbed the man's mind and crushed it, watching pitilessly as blood started to trickle and flood from the man's eyes, ears and nose. He heard pounding footsteps and he knew company was coming.

He watched and waited until the last breath shuddered out, and then he let his mental grip go and the corpse fell at his feet.

Then he shifted and the mist drifted up and away as people started coming out to investigate the noise.

He was tired when he returned to the house, though it wasn't even midnight. It had been an easy night as far as hunting goes. Sometimes, he was given an assignment, like the feral. Other nights, he just trolled, looking for scum like those he had found tonight.

Normally, on a night such as this he would have gone for more, but he was too fucking tired, and he knew it wasn't the hunt.

It was Kit.

He could even smell her, the sweet, intoxicating scent of the soap he ordered for her directly from England. She went through bottles of it, then after she climbed from the bath, she would smooth oil onto her wet body, and her scent always lingered—

She was in his bed.

Naked.

It was not an odd thing for him to find a naked woman in his bed.

But a naked Kit, that was odd.

"Have a nice hunt?" she asked, her voice rough, soft, her eyes chilly.

"Kit—"

She pushed onto her knees and lifted a finger to her mouth. Then she trailed that finger down her body to trace over one nipple, then down her slim, golden torso before sliding through her naked folds.

"Damn it, Kit, don't." Byron stared at her hand, at the naked folds of her sex. She had waxed. The soft curls he had nuzzled the last time were gone, and the plump lips were naked and smooth. He could smell her over the distance that separated them, wet and hot, and still angry.

"Why not? You're sending me away, that's what you do with a woman, once you sleep with her. Eventually. Only I haven't had that pleasure, so why not?" she asked, moving around again, this time to lie on her back, knees bent. "Won't you give me just one night, Byron? Just one?"

His jaws ached and throbbed in time with his cock as he watched her start to stroke herself, her slim little fingers rubbing her wet, swollen clit until she was rocking her hips and moaning weakly in time with her movements. "I'm not sending you away," he rasped, haltingly taking a step closer.

"Come and play, Byron," she teased.

He moved closer, following the movement of her fingers, drawn by the scent of her body. Damn it, he loved her. He wanted her. He had for years, but this was Kit, Kris's little girl, and he had promised to take care of her, not fuck her like she was some whore.

This was *Kit.* Not any other woman. She wasn't for fucking.

"Come on," she cajoled. Her lashes fluttered closed and she whimpered when he rested one knee on the bed and brushed her hand aside, replacing it with his, lowering his head to catch one large, dark nipple in his mouth. She had large breasts, especially for a woman as tiny as she was, with big, dark nipples that always seemed to be erect. He bit down carefully, and groaned when she cried out and pressed harder against him and he started to pump two fingers in and out of her wet sheath.

Damn it, he couldn't fight this any more.

He sat up briefly, jerking his clothes off, before covering her and using his thighs to open hers. She brushed her hair aside, baring her neck, and Byron shuddered at the simplicity of the gesture as he licked her, sucking the fragile skin deep into his mouth. He started to enter her, probing the hot, wet entrance to her core, his body tensed and aching. She was tighter than he had expected. As he pushed the first two inches inside, her snug, silky little pussy convulsed around him and Byron groaned as she arched up, taking him slightly deeper.

Much tighter, but she was wet and creamy around him and her pulse beat madly against his mouth. Byron was so fucking hungry for her—for her sex and her blood. He drove deep, his fangs breaking through her skin just as his cock tunneled through her tight wet passage while she screamed in surprised pain at his rough invasion.

Kit, he reached out, touched her mind, felt her surprise — the pain, the shock, the need — as he drew one of her knees up over his hip, shuddering at the sweet, wet grip of her virgin pussy around his cock. Her blood rolled down his throat, ripe, powerful, rich. *Kit, why didn't you tell me?*

"Why? So you could turn me down?" she asked bitterly.

I don't think I could have, not any longer, he answered, a groan vibrating up from his chest. She felt the vibration of it through her neck as it shuddered down her chest, tightening her nipples, and pooling hot in her belly. He pulled his cock out, then surged back in, one big hand cupping the cheek of her ass lovingly. *So sweet, Kit. So tight.*

He pulled reluctantly away from her neck, licking away the drops of blood before leaning down, wanting to kiss her, but settling for rubbing his cheek to hers. He was surprised when she sought his mouth, surprised when the lingering taste of blood didn't bother her. He started to pump his shaft inside her, loving the way she hugged his cock — tight, wet, snug, and only his. She rocked up to meet him, eagerly, hungrily, and he slammed into her harder, control forgotten. He moved and shifted her so that he could reach her clit and play with it while he fucked her. He felt her response when she cried out, the vibrations reaching down through her body and up through his cock, spreading over him, tightening his balls, heating his blood until he was certain his entire body would go up into sweet, hot flame.

Her bud was slick and swollen and hard. Byron shuddered as he pushed back inside her, keeping one hand on her thigh, holding it high, and open, watching as he drove in, almost hypnotized by the erotic sight of his own cock invading the wet little cleft. He couldn't tear his gaze away as he pulled out — the flesh wet and gleaming from her cream — then pushed back between those plumps lips. The smooth flesh of her naked mound taunted him and he left her clit briefly to stroke the smooth lips, his gaze traveling her sweetly curved little body to meet her eyes as she moaned and reached for him.

Byron bent over her and caught her seeking hands, pinning them high over her head. "Are you mine tonight?" he asked her gutturally, driving deep inside the wet clasp of her pussy, feeling his orgasm rushing up. He had wanted her for too long and he couldn't fight this. "Are you staying with me all night?"

"I've been yours for years, you idiot. I'll be yours for always, if you'll just open your eyes," she hissed, her eyes blind and dazed as she lifted her head and tried to catch his mouth. He let her and shuddered as she sucked his tongue into her mouth greedily, biting down gently and wrapping her strong legs around his hips as he shafted her virgin body roughly. He kept her hands pinned with one of his and slid the other down, palming her tight little ass and lifting her higher against him, moving harder, more roughly into her as she started to convulse around him. The satin confines of her pussy tightened around him, growing wetter and hotter, until she started to come.

He swallowed her scream and pumped her full of his come, before he let his body fall briefly to rest on top of hers.

But only briefly.

Then he was carrying her into the bathroom, into the shower, where he started to soap her clean. He knelt in front of her, holding the hand-held nozzle, while the double wall-mounted sprays pounded them from both sides as he lifted her. Holding her weight in his hands easily, he admired the naked mound she had prepared for him. "Always teasing me, Kit," he murmured as he nuzzled the sweet little mound. He slid his tongue through her folds and then he lifted his face and looked up at her, water beading on his lashes. "Open yourself up, baby," he whispered.

He watched her swallow nervously and then her hands moved and she did it. Using both hands to spread the plump lips of her sex, she exposed the swollen bud of her clit. Byron turned the hot, massaging spray on her, grinning hotly as the sound of her wails echoed off the walls. He had dreamed of doing just this to her, for years.

Always teasing him, he had told her. She had loved to use his shower, even after he installed a similar one for her. He had walked into his bathroom once, thinking one of the human girls was in there. He had every intention of joining whoever he heard moaning so sweetly.

Kit had only just turned eighteen—he had known she had been experimenting, but how was he to know she had been masturbating in his fucking bathroom? She had been using the massaging showerhead on her clit and screamed in hoarse pleasure while Byron stood frozen, shocked, aroused, and hungry. She had opened her eyes, but instead of being embarrassed, the way an eighteen-year-old *should* have been, she had grinned at him, hot and sweet and inviting.

Now she started to rock against the pulse of the water, humming low in her throat, sobbing as the stimulation brought her to the edge hard and fast. Byron had lowered one of her small feet to the ground, still bracing her weight as he slid two fingers inside her, pumping deep as she keened and cried out. Each time she came a little closer, he backed off. And he started to work the natural lubrication of her body lower, pressing against the sweet pucker of her ass, wishing she wasn't a fucking novice.

He was finally taking Kit, but he couldn't take her the way he wanted.

Her eyes flew open at the alien caress but instead of pulling away, she pushed against him, and slid down on him, *oh, fuck,* taking his index finger completely up her snug little ass as she shuddered and screamed, flinching at the pain but riding it and rocking against the caress of the water.

Byron threw the shower nozzle away and leaned forward, catching her sensitized clit in his mouth. She screamed in startled, pained pleasure. Coming instantly, she rocked up and down, riding his mouth and riding the thick finger he had buried inside her ass. The shivers were still racking her when he stood, moving awkwardly to keep from dislodging her as he lifted her one-handed and drove inside, groaning as she continued to quake and shudder around him.

"Byron…" she sobbed, reaching up and tangling her hands in his wet hair, staring up into his face, her eyes hot and pleading.

He murmured softly, "Sweet little Kit, you feel so good. I've wanted this." He punctuated it by driving deep, pounding into her, alternately with thrusts of his cock into her pussy and thrusts of his finger into her ass. "Will you let me fuck you here? You're such a little thing, Kit. You're so tiny, so tight."

"Anything," she gasped, hot little chills racking her body as he invaded her from both front and rear. His large body covered hers completely, possessed her completely. His thick, long cock left her then burrowed back inside and she wanted to cry at the pleasure of it. Then he worked his finger back inside her ass and the hot, painful little pleasure drove her mad. Her nipples ached and burned and throbbed, his water-slicked chest rubbing against them as he fucked her.

His dark blue eyes stared into hers, full of need and something that looked like tenderness. Kit was bewildered. She tried to think past the need that fogged her brain. How could he care for her and still send her away? He lifted her mouth and kissed her roughly, one of his fangs nipping her lip. He caught the lingering drop of blood hungrily and sucked it away before he muttered, "Stop thinking and feel. Feel this, feel *me*." Driving inside, he held there, throbbing and still. Finally, he started to lift her, working her small, light body up and down his length. Reluctantly drawing his finger from her ass, Byron gripped her hips and stared into her stormy eyes.

He moved slowly at first, until she started to wriggle and squirm eagerly. Then he started to move her faster and faster until he pinned her against the wall and plundered her tight little pussy, filling her with hard, rough digs of his cock that had her screaming his name.

"I love you," she wailed as she creamed around him.

Byron shuddered against her and groaned as he came, whispering in her ear, "I love you, Kit."

Moments later, she struggled out of his arms, and away, moving out of the shower. He tried to hold her but she was nearly as strong as he, and if this wet, angry woman didn't want to be held, well, she wasn't going to be held.

"If you love me, then why are you sending me away?" she demanded, shoving her wet hair out of her face.

Byron turned off the water and moved out of the stall, staring down at the tiny, defiant woman in front of him. "Kit, your father was my best friend. I swore to him that I would see that you were happy. You've never known anything outside of this. How can you know if this makes you happy if it is all you've ever known?" he asked wearily.

Kit pounded her fist against her chest. "I know how I feel, Byron. I look at you and I feel my heart. My other half. My soul mate."

He cupped her face but she knocked his hand away. Sighing, he prayed for patience. "This is only for a while, Kit. To make sure you know this is what you want."

Nastily she said, "So I guess I'm to go out and fuck as many men as I need, live however I see fit, experience *life* to make sure this is what suits me."

Byron shoved down the insidious anger. She was trying to piss him off. He didn't have to let her know it was working.

"It's for a short while, Kit. And I've made up my mind," he said firmly.

She smiled sweetly. "And I've made up mine," she replied. She turned her back and started to walk away but Byron grabbed her and snarled, "You told me I could have tonight," as he pushed his cock against her.

"Go fuck yourself," she snapped, squirming.

"Why? You're here, and you're mine, and you're what I want," he said, reaching down and cupping her. She was wet from him still. He started to pump his fingers inside, laughing when she stiffened against him before helplessly starting to ride his hand. He pushed her down to her hands and knees and drove inside. Ignoring her furious cry, he focused instead on how she pushed back against him, and closed around his cock even though she wanted to walk away.

Byron focused on the sweet keening wails that fell from her lips as he hunkered low over her body and fucked her slowly, wetting his finger again and sliding it inside the snug fit of her ass. She rocked back against him and he laughed. "Still want me to go fuck myself?" he asked, slapping her ass.

She jumped and cried out, startled. He did it again, and she clamped down on his thick cock and came, quick and hard. She started pushing back on him hungrily, looking for another spank, another climax. "See?" he teased. "It's more fun to fuck you." He shoved her to the floor and wrapped her hair around his free hand, baring her neck before he struck. His fangs sank through the fragile skin, through the marks he had made earlier, and he fed again, groaning in rapture against her sweet skin.

She cried out and arched up, pushing her ass against him, and he gripped her hip, riding her hard until they both came.

They argued again.

They fucked again.

They showered again.

They ended up in her room, where Byron went through the sex toys she had bought and he had decided he would use them on her until she saw reason. Kit had already seen reason. And she wasn't giving in to him just because he was a big, sexy vampire who was used to getting his way.

"For crying out loud, I'm not sending you away!" he shouted. "It's just for a while. It doesn't even have to be two years. A year. Okay? One fucking year. And if you're still so fucking sure after it's over, then so be it."

She glared at him and said, "If you send me away, I won't come back." Point blank.

Byron froze. "Don't say that."

She lifted her chin and repeated herself. "I mean it. I'm sure the Council can find something for me. If I leave here, that's it. I'm gone for good."

He snarled at her and pinned her to the bed, taking her hands high over her head and tying them tight. Even an Inherent needed to be able to have leverage in order to take advantage of her strength, and he had just taken that away. He picked up one of the sex toys, the larger dildo she had bought out of curiosity but hadn't used. Spreading her legs wide, he drove it halfway inside her without even preparing her, staring at her with cool, blank eyes. "Say it again," he rasped. "Tell me you won't come back to me."

"I won't—"

He pushed it harder inside and lowered his head to suck on her clit until she was screaming and hoarse from it. Then he stopped suckling her and started to fuck her with the big dildo, watching her with those cool, almost clinical eyes. "Are you coming back to me?"

"Not if you make me leave," she gasped.

"Wrong answer," he growled, his fangs flashing in his fury. He flipped her onto her hands and knees, spread the cheeks of her ass and licked her there, listening to her embarrassed little shriek. He used his legs to pin her in place while he picked up another toy, this one a slender wand-shaped dildo with a flared base that was designed for anal use.

He lubricated it and slid it inside her, listening to her hungry cries as she tried to muffle them in the bed. He steadily slid it in even when she tried to squirm away. "Stop moving— you're making it worse, Kit," he told her impassively. Once it was lodged inside her ass, he moved her onto her back and resumed fucking her with that ridiculously long dildo and flicking her clit with his tongue. And every few minutes, he said, "Tell me that you'll come back."

Finally, she sobbed out, "Damn it, I don't want to leave! But your sending me away will kill me. If I leave, I am *not* coming back."

He moved up on her, taking the toy out and driving his cock inside. She whimpered in pain, in pleasure, in need, taking him deep inside. "Say you'll come back to me," he ordered roughly.

She sobbed out his name and screamed as the climax rolled through her before he was even halfway inside her. Byron shuddered and worked his cock completely in, pulled out and burrowed back in. She wouldn't truly stay away, not Kit, he thought as he rode her, her sweet wet pussy hugging him tightly as he slid back inside.

She belonged to him. She belonged *here.*

Then why are you sending her away?

Byron drove desperately into her, as the sunrise came ever closer. Kit's bedroom was full of windows and he could sense the lightening in the sky outside. Her silky cleft was swollen from being ridden all night, but she still lifted for him, still clung to him eagerly. Byron buried his face in her neck and groaned as his climax raged over him, building at his spine and burning through his balls and his cock.

Chapter Four

Byron gathered a slumberous Kit into his arms and carried her back to his room. A niggling little doubt was in the back of his mind as Kit nestled into his bed next to him. He clamped both arms tightly around her waist and asked, "Stay here?"

"Can't," she evaded. "Hungry. Need another bath."

A vampire's sleep wasn't one that could be fought off until he had several centuries behind him. Byron only had one and a handful of years. "I love you," he said, kissing her roughly.

"I love you," she said quietly, stroking one small hand down his arm.

Byron listened to her steady heartbeat as sleep caught and held him. He should have made the others watch her. If he ordered them to make sure she stayed—he woke up remembering that was a foolish thought. She had agreed to come back.

Then he froze as he climbed from bed.

No.

She hadn't.

Of course, he hadn't told her when she would be going. And now he was thinking he really didn't want her to go at all.

So the sensible thing to do was—

"The sensible thing? Now? When my bebè is gone he wants to do the sensible thing?" The voice that rolled through the room was one he had not heard in over two decades. Kristof was gone. Dead and gone. Of course, it was unmistakable, the odd blend of Russia and France. "Da, that is much sense you make now. The sensible thing."

And the voice that followed was also one that belonged to somebody dead. All French elegance and fancy French sex. Byron turned slowly and saw the two very solid, if somewhat, well, *ghostly*, forms hovering by the door.

"Shit."

Kris laughed, his head falling back, that familiar joyful laugh that he had passed on to his daughter. "So eloquent, my friend. Da. You have stepped into shit, you have. She say what she mean, my Kit. She will not come back to you."

"I didn't send her away!" Byron shouted.

Bella smiled sympathetically. "That is how Katrine sees it, Byron. And if you want her back, then you will have to go to her and bring her back. Now."

"She needs some time to—"

"Bah," Kris spat. "Time? For what? To be lonely and miss you? Is that what you would have my bebè do for two years? Is this how you take care? By letting her be lonely? She is your mate. Bella tells me this, long before I died. I try to tell you, when I died. And I tell you now. Go to her now, or you lose her."

It was then that Byron remembered something he had forgotten. *"My Bella is telling me...da, you had best remember that. Kit will want what she wants."*

Kit will want what she wants.

After searching quickly through the room, Byron dropped to sit on the bed, staring at his big rough hands.

Shit.

It would have been nice if Kit's parents had bothered to tell him where their daughter had gone.

She hadn't taken the tickets he had purchased for her.

She hadn't taken the car he had given her when she had come home from college, or anything else he had given her. Just her own things, her own clothes, and her anger. He could still catch her scent in the house as he prowled through it later that night. Ben eyed him warily as he continued to search for Kit via the web. She hadn't used her credit cards to purchase any tickets, which made it even harder to track her.

She wouldn't go to France, Byron suspected. She would know he'd come for her eventually and she would not be where she could easily be found or brought back. So she'd either go to ground or go someplace where she would be protected.

And then he felt like pounding the wall with his fist.

She'd already told him where she was going.

The fucking Council.

Chapter Five

Byron stared at Agnes and fought the urge to blush. She always made him feel like she was trying to imagine him naked. The fact that she was born the same year he was didn't change a damn thing. She looked like she was his great-great-grandmother. She was an amazing witch, and one of the most respected members of the council, but she was also downright mischievous.

"Don't tell me she isn't here," he warned, trying hard to keep his tone respectful. "I can hear her breathing and I can smell her. I won't leave."

Agnes smiled and took her long cloak from the peg beside the door. "I'm thinking I'll be going into town. For a day or two. The inner rooms are safe from sunlight and you are free to enter at your own will, now and forevermore, Byron Matthews of America, Hunter of the Council." With that formal final remark, she threw the cloak over her shoulders and moved away, much quicker than a woman of her age should have been able to move.

Byron crossed the threshold and moved inside. He was tired, he was fucking hungry and he was pissed. The council hadn't told him a damned thing and he had been reduced to asking individuals. Fortunately the first one he had asked had known him, vaguely, but known him all the same. Malachi had looked at him, narrowed his ancient eyes and said, "You're a friend of Eli's."

"Yes," Byron said cautiously, staring at the ancient in front of him. There was something about the red-haired vampire that commanded attention, commanded submission. Byron didn't realize what a mark it was of his will that he didn't fall and submit. He didn't realize how much it set him apart from other, lesser Masters who were already centuries older.

Malachi saw it, though—he recognized it. And wasn't surprised at all at why Eli had befriended the dark, towering American. He'd be a powerful Master, a powerful Hunter. And like all powerful Hunters, he'd need powerful friends while he was young like this. The young ones tended to be targets early on. Better to take them out quick, before they became too powerful.

Malachi's mouth quirked in a slight smile. "Fucked up, did you?" he asked. "Go ask Agnes. She has a woman at her place. A wolf, if my sense of smell serves me. And I'd say it does. I'm smelling the same woman all over you."

Byron had dashed out without even hearing Malachi's soft, "Good luck. Lucky bastard."

Now he was searching for her. Her scent filled the large house, it was everywhere. And she was nowhere.

"What are you doing here?"

He turned and saw her staring at him, wearing a big man's shirt. Narrowing his eyes, he realized it was *his* shirt. He moved and had her around the waist without even realizing it, kissing her hungrily, greedily, his hands sliding up the shirt to find her naked little body warm and soft.

"You left me," he accused, pulling away to glare at her.

"You sent me away," she snapped, her eyes hot with indignation.

"You weren't supposed to leave yet, and I'd changed my fucking mind," he snarled back, catching the hands she was shoving against his chest and pinning them behind her back. "I hadn't told you to leave *yet*, had I? Stubborn little brat. Have you forgotten yourself? Forgotten me?"

Kit refused to struggle once she realized she wasn't getting away. His big, heavy body had her effectively pinned against the wall at this point, his cock cuddled against the softness of her belly, one hand pinning her wrists behind her back. Staring at his chest, refusing to look at his face, she said, "I wasn't going to be thrown out on my ass. I've got more pride than that."

"Damn you," Byron snarled as he released her wrists and caught her face in his hands, tangling them in her short hair, kissing her roughly. "I wouldn't have thrown you out. You would have been put in a fucking limo, driven to the fucking airport, and flown to fucking France on my fucking plane. And you fucking know it! Why are you doing this?"

She tore her eyes away from his chest and made herself meet his furious eyes. They were hot, wild and gleaming. His fangs had slid down and were flashing in his anger. The air in the room felt thick with it. Her own anger had burned out on the flight here, but staring at him now was causing a different kind of heat. "Why?" she asked softly. "You want to know *why*?"

"Yes. I want to know why," he growled, lowering his face until they were mouth to mouth. "I did not want to take you into my service. You were my ward, and I did not want you to have to serve and obey any Master, even one who would indulge you. But you chose to enter our world and now you are openly and flagrantly violating our laws. You left me without my consent. You could very easily be punished by the Council, whether I will it or no, so, yes. I want to know why."

"You had already made the choice to send me away, Byron. The fact that the act wasn't yet complete doesn't mean that much. You didn't want me anymore," she stated simply. "I couldn't stay there anymore."

"After the night we spent together, you can actually think I don't want you?" he rasped, his fingers tightening in her hair to the point of pain.

She smiled sadly. "Not enough to keep me."

Byron felt his heart break as a tear rolled down her cheek. "Damn it, Kit," he rasped, bending down and catching it in his mouth. "You're coming back. You're mine." He grabbed the edges of the shirt and jerked it off of her, exposing her body.

"I won't come back if you think you can just send me away for a year. Two years. Even two fucking weeks," she swore, folding her arms over her breasts and glaring at him.

"You haven't heard a thing I've said, have you, Kit?" he muttered, taking her wrists and forcing them down to her sides. He knelt in front of her small, sweetly scented body and caught one rosy nipple in his mouth, raking the plump globe with a sharp fang and groaning when a drop of blood beaded on her flesh. He licked it away and suckled on the tiny wound until no more flowed. Then he pulled away and stared up into her eyes. "I changed my mind. You're coming back with me. You belong with me, to me. As much I belong to you."

He released her wrists, grabbed her hips and pulled her to the floor, feasting on the sweet cream from her cleft, catching her clit in his mouth and suckling it until she was moaning and crying his name. He stroked downward from her cleft, using the natural lubrication from her body to probe her rosette and he shuddered when she opened for him, when she started to rock helplessly against him as he drove his tongue inside her pussy while he screwed his finger in and out of her ass, then added a second.

He worked her close to orgasm before he turned her onto her knees and shredded his clothes. A hot musky power seemed to be filling the room, pouring from him, and Kit shuddered with it as it washed over her. She knew too much about vampires not to realize what it was. Byron was coming into more of his power, and his call was increasing. She just hadn't realized how very susceptible she would be to it.

Her body was too hot, too tight, too hungry for him and she was certain she would die if she didn't get him inside her. When she felt him probing the tiny hole of her bottom, she quivered and tried to shift, force him inside her pussy, where she needed him. He snarled at her and she felt his dominance roll over her, just like his call and she stilled, her head falling forward, her torso dropping to rest on the floor while he continued to draw the cream from her cleft to her anus.

Byron hadn't ever felt anything like what was breaking loose inside him—he couldn't fight it, couldn't question it. He had to be inside her, had to do it this way, had to do it *now*. The shuddering, creeping power inside him was almost as arousing as the sight of her slick, wet folds and the scent of her cream and sex as he prepared her ass for his invasion. It rolled from him, like waves from the ocean, and it affected Kit almost as much as it affected him.

He gripped the cheeks of her ass in his big hands and pulled her apart, stretching her a bit as he pressed his cock against her. She whimpered. Byron said roughly, "Hush, now, Kit. Give me this now. You can take it, I promise." As he spoke, the subtle power increased, and when it did, she became more aroused and forgot the burning pain as he pushed inside the tight virgin hole that he had lubricated, using only the sweet cream from her body.

He whispered to her again, and when he did, she cried out, as though his voice was touching her. "You're tight, hot, sweet. Push against me. You will like it." She bore down and he slid deeper inside.

Kit screamed softly. The more he talked, the hotter she became. It felt like his voice had developed a hand of its own and was touching her clit with every word he spoke. As he pushed deeper inside her ass, he spoke and whispered and she whimpered and cried, until he was completely seated inside her. He was too big, stretching her too tightly, too full and even his whispering roughly to her didn't help. Then he started to pump inside her, and the burning tearing pain increased. Kit screamed and said, "Byron, stop, please!"

She started to beg as the pain turned into sweet, glorious pleasure with each hot, deep thrust as he pushed her hips lower and filled her with hard, rough digs of his cock. Bending his body over her, he licked her neck before sinking his fangs into her, his weight carrying her to the floor.

Her hot blood flooded his mouth, rolled over his tongue and down his throat as his balls grew tight and tingled as the orgasm rushed closer. She felt like silk around his cock, dragging and clinging with each thrust, pushing that sweet little ass against him, moaning and crying and begging, "Harder, Byron, oh, please, again!" He lifted them back up a little so he could drive deeper inside and he shuddered as she screamed. She gripped his cock like a silk fist, tight, hot and he pushed back inside as he reached between her thighs and pinched her clit, found it tight and hard and swollen, and he drew his fangs from her neck so he could rumble at her ear, "Next time, I'm going to find somebody to fuck your sweet little pussy while I fuck your ass. Will you like that?"

She shuddered and pushed harder against him, clenching her buttocks around his cock and mewling when he started to fuck her dripping vagina with his fingers. "Tell me, Kit, will you like it?"

"Yes!" she screamed as he drove his thick cock inside just as she started to come, screaming in short, hard peals that echoed off the walls.

Byron pulled his hand from her pussy and shifted, crouching over her on his knees so he could drive inside her, hard, deep and fast, as his climax built and exploded out of his cock and he flooded the tight, hot little rosette that held him so snugly. Something inside him broke open, echoed inside her. He roared out her name and she cried out his while her convulsive climax milked the semen from his shaft.

Byron came to rest atop her body and then he rolled to the side, drawing her into the curve of his body and burying his face in her hair. He felt something inside his heart that hadn't been there before.

Her. Kit.

Kit smiled sleepily. Through the new bond, she felt his surprise. "I told you," she said, squirming against him. He still hadn't withdrawn from her and she could feel him pulse inside her.

He pushed against her and she felt his renewing arousal, then his alarm as he felt the burning pain that she was feeling. She clamped down on his arm and held tight. "I'm fine," she whispered. "Need a bath. Then you can take me to bed and put your cock to use in a little more traditional manner."

"You really did know," he whispered as he braced a hand on her hip and gently pulled out of the sweet embrace of her ass. She flinched, tried to hide it, and Byron cursed himself viciously, then he scooped her into his arms and carried her into the bathroom. "I'm sorry, sweet," he murmured against her hair. He knew now what had happened. It wasn't just the mate-bond, but his own power increasing. The call tended to get stronger with age, and usually happened gradually, not in the middle of sex. His shouldn't have increased for a good fifty years. But that was what had happened. His had just taken the mother of all leaps, and with Kit, of all people. He couldn't fight it, neither could she, but he damn well could have just found a better way to fuck her.

"No, you couldn't have," she said as she gingerly settled down on the edge of the bathtub. He glared at her.

She grinned cheekily at him. "Not very fun having somebody know your every waking thought, is it, Master Vampire?" she asked. Then she slid him a hot, smoky look from under her lashes and purred, "You know how hot it made me, dreaming of you doing just that to me some day? I *loved* it, every second. How hot you were, the way it felt when you opened me and just stared at me before starting to slide your cock inside me—"

Byron felt himself harden as she spoke and he growled, "Enough, Kit."

"Even the way it hurt at first, and how you told me I could take it," she whispered.

"Enough," he groaned, glaring at her. "Right now, *I* can't," he snapped, moving closer and jerking her hips against him. He stroked one careful finger against her bottom and she arched against him, crying out at the burning pain and he said, "See?

You can't do this again, not here. Not yet. So stop teasing me." The signs of her very obvious pain and the sympathetic backlash through their new bond were enough to cool his burning lust, and he released her slowly.

She pulled away and went for the cabinet where Agnes kept some of her more basic ointments and brews. She found the oil she needed and added it to the bath. "I'll be right as rain come morning. Between this, and my own healing—"she ended with a shrug and started to step into the bath but he lifted her and gently put her down into the slowly rising water.

She watched with lifted brows as he started to shuck his own clothes. "You're going to smell like slippery elm," she told him, admiring the long, muscular lines of his body. He had the widest damn shoulders, with a vee of hair on his chest that thinned down to a fine line over his muscled belly before widening just over his sex. His cock was long, thick, softer now, and smooth, hanging over his furred sac. As she stared, his cock started to harden and Byron snorted out a muffled half curse, half laugh.

"Damn it, Kit, how am I supposed to not fuck you again if you keep looking at me like that?"

She tossed him an arch look and said, "I expect you to fuck me again. I just said we'll use your cock in a more traditional manner." She scooted forward a little as he moved into the tub and eased down behind her, wrapping his arms around her and resting his chin on her crown.

"I'm sorry if I hurt you," he whispered.

She knew he wasn't talking about the sex. He had finally gotten it through his old-fashioned head that sending her away had damaged her pride and her heart. A smile curved her mouth. "Did it make you mad when you realized I had left?" she asked.

"Mad? No. Insanely furious? Yes." He gripped her tightly and rasped, "You won't do that again, Kit. I mean it."

"I'm your mate, now, Byron. You're no longer my Master. The Council will no longer recognize that tie," she reminded him.

Byron groaned and slammed his head back against the wall. "Are you trying to drive me crazy?" he demanded.

"No. I'm trying to get you to see you'll have to start treating me as your equal. Shouldn't be too hard. You're only a century old. You're not as antiquated as some of the other vampires. But I'm your mate, your equal. No longer your second, or your servant," she said, squirming and wriggling until she was facing him. Then she kissed him, pushing her tongue hungrily into his mouth, reaching down and massaging his cock. She blindly sought out some soap and added it to the massage and once she was certain he was clean, she straddled him and drove herself down on him, sucking his tongue into her mouth and shivering as his hands came up to cup her breasts.

He drove his thick shaft up inside her, head falling back so that he could stare up into her sweet, heart-shaped face as she rode him, her slim, muscled thighs lifting her body up and down, working her pelvis against his. He reached between them and stroked her clit and she sobbed out his name.

He felt her orgasm and he started to push harder up into her sleek wet pussy, water splashing onto the floor over the rim of the tub. Her eyes swirled and glowed in her lust, burning hot with her power and her need, her nipples stiff and hard. He groaned and leaned forward, catching one in his mouth and biting, suckling, feeling her pleasure through the bond until it mingled with his own as their combined orgasm rushed at them.

She was still gasping for breath. He had something he wanted to ask her, but he was going to wait. He'd let her rest. He'd rest. They'd go into town tonight and he would buy her dinner at some fine restaurant, where he could watch candlelight dance on her mellow-gold skin. Maybe dancing. And he needed a ring. Maybe Agnes could help —

Her slim fingers threaded through the longer hair that fell from the top and sides of his head and she tugged his face up from her breasts where he had been pondering how to propose. After more than a century of living, he wanted to make sure the one time he did it, he did it right.

"Byron, I was thinking…you want to get married?"

Her laughing eyes met his, and he started to laugh. Equals. She had beat him to it.

He kissed her and laughed into her mouth. "Why the hell not?"

JONATHAN AND LORI

Chapter One

Jonathan wasn't having a very good day.

His back was aching, his head ached, he was hungrier than hell, hornier than he had ever been, blood was seeping from a ragged gash in his side, there was a full moon coming, and he was itching to go *run*.

And Lori was staring up at him with those wide sea-green eyes and her hair was spilling down around her shoulders as she tended the deep gash in his side that he'd received while out on patrol.

As she deftly probed the injury with gentle hands, she said, "This isn't healing like it ought to. What made it?"

Curtly, he answered, "Something sharp."

Clucking her tongue, she placed her hand over it and he winced as burning, healing heat leapt from her body and into his. "No need to get nasty. What made it?"

"Silver."

Her full mouth firmed into a thin, narrow line and her eyes went flat. "Have you told Eli?"

"Not yet." He clenched his teeth as the heat intensified and spread upward from his side, and down, chasing the myriad aches and pains, seeking and finding them, soothing them away.

All but one…

His cock ached, his body hungered for hers. Sweet, sweet Lori, with her wide green eyes and that fall of red curls…too soft and sweet for him.

"You need to let him know."

Her soft, throaty voice broke into his reverie and he glanced down into her eyes. "I will. When he gets back from Paris with Sarel. They haven't taken any time alone together in years. They need this."

"I can—"

"No. I know you can speak to both of them and I don't need you to. Eli is my master and if I needed him, he would know, whether I wished it or not." He narrowed his eyes at the young witch staring up at him and said warningly, "He left me in charge, Lori. Contacting him is defying me. Defying me is defying him."

With a muffled "Hurrumph," she turned on her heel and stalked away to dispose of the rags she had used to clean his wounds. "He needs to know it's happening again."

"Damn, girl, do you think he doesn't? This is his territory. It happened here. He knew the moment it happened." Jonathan stood slowly, stretching his arms overhead, feeling the pull of newly healing skin and passing aches. Sliding Lori's rounded backside a look as she bent over her cabinet and tidied up, he muffled a groan.

"Eli knows everything that happens on his land. He is connected to it, in ways we will never understand." Jonathan felt blood start to pound slowly through his veins, in slow hot waves. A growl was building in his chest and he *ached*…

An itching was settling along his spine, in his palms, as the beast inside him tried to rouse in response to his hunger, but he pushed it down inside.

"Jonathan?"

He lifted his head and met her eyes, staring at her in silence. Her scent—soft and sweet—vanilla, lavender, and woman. Damn it.

He wanted her. He had for the past seven years, since she had first come to Eli's enclave. In the depths of her sea-green eyes, he could see his reflection as he stared hungrily at her. The pulse in her neck leapt to life as she looked up at him and licked her lips, the room filling with the scent of her body growing ripe with arousal.

She was far too aware of him, Jonathan knew that. And he wanted her far too much for his own good.

He always had, always would.

He adored the fiery little hellcat, that sweet little minx.

And she was too damned innocent for the likes of him and his damned black soul.

Without saying a word, he turned on his heel and left.

"What was that?" Lori whispered into the suddenly hot room.

Pressing her hand to her chest, she dragged a breath of air in and caught his scent again. Jonathan's scent, wild and uniquely his. The scent of pine and sandalwood, earth and male, all blended together.

She closed her fist around the drying drops of blood in her hand, his blood. "Safe," she prayed, lifting her eyes heavenward. "Keep him safe, dear God." Heat smoldered in her hand, and when she opened her eyes and her hand, the blood was gone. A smile danced on her lips as she went about setting her workroom to rights.

Keeping Jonathan safe was something that would take divine intervention, all right.

The werewolf courted disaster, it seemed.

Or it stalked him.

This was the third time he had been the target of some unseen attacker. Wolfsbane had been filtered into their water the first time. Declan had been visiting and he had fallen prey to it before Jonathan had returned from his prowling. But since Declan was only part were, he wasn't as susceptible to it and didn't fall into the painful convulsions, the coma, or any of the other nasty symptoms that were a prelude to death.

Sarel and Lori had used magick to find the source of his sudden, mysterious illness as one other shifter suddenly fell to the floor in convulsions and died only thirty minutes later. Lori had caught the telltale trace of wolfsbane only moments before Jonathan had sauntered into his snug little cottage a few hundred yards away and, using the gift so few witches had, she had gone from standing where she had been, to standing in his house in the blink of an eye, right in front of everybody, something she had never done.

No one but Sarel and Eli had known of that little gift. Alighting in his kitchen with his name on her lips had surprised him enough that he had set the glass down, all right, in fact, he had damn near attacked, until he recognized her scent and voice, but it had saved his life.

The water in his cabin had been so heavily laced with wolfsbane even a few drops would have killed him. It was untraceable to a wolf, undetectable by scent, sight or taste. He never would have known he was dying until the convulsions started.

Furious, enraged, and unable to strike, Eli had damn near torn his entire territory apart looking for the unseen attacker. There had been no trace, no sign of who had done it.

More than a year had passed since they had buried Philippe.

And three months since the last attack, one that had been directed solely at Jonathan. Jonathan had been sleeping after the night of a full moon, and spending that day in bed with Sheila, the sweet, sassy Southern vamp who had been with them for the past eight years—Lori had nearly died with envy.

That evening after Sheila had left the safety of Jonathan's little cottage to hunt—and to Hunt—he had fallen into a deep sleep, exhausted, sated, sleeping like the dead. And a witch had crept into his dreams as he'd slept and held him fast while another attacker tried a more silent approach, a death spell.

But magick couldn't be done on Eli's grounds without his witches knowing, especially when he was wed to one, and one was deeply in love with Jonathan.

Lori had felt it before Sarel and had sounded an alarm, but she wasn't sure how to protect him. She wasn't a warrior.

That was her sister.

Sarel had launched an all-out attack.

But little good it had done them.

Their enemy had stolen away into the night yet again.

But this time, Sarel had caught something, a trace of him. And she had announced that it was the same bastard that had captured Jonathan and Lori years before as bait for Eli.

"So four times, truly," she said to herself.

"Talking to yourself, now?"

Turning her head, she saw the petite blonde standing behind her. With a welcoming smile, she gestured to Sheila to come on in. "Just pondering. Jonathan was hurt again."

"So I gathered. I smell his blood all over the place. Normally, it would be an enticing smell." Wrinkling her pert nose, Sheila sauntered into the room, her rounded hips swaying from side to side beneath the long, slim denim skirt. "I smell...silver. Rosemary, earth from the grave, how very lame. Foxglove. The smells are very, very faint. But I'd bet they tried to curse the knife that cut him. Do you think it carried weight?"

"Shit."

Lori blew her bangs out of her eyes and flopped onto the lounge, staring up at the ceiling bleakly. No wonder it had seemed so easy.

They gathered around, staring up into the dimly glowing orb. The death spell hadn't been subtle enough. The warrior witch had sensed it coming from far off. But she was gone now. Now...now they could strike through the wolf. Powerful, young, but so open to their gifts...a powerful tool, he would be.

Jonathan couldn't breathe, couldn't see, and couldn't speak.

Opening his eyes, he struggled to sit up, feeling something alien inside his mind.

Something foul, evil.

Flipping onto his side, lungs aching, he reached for the knife at his bedside table—a bloodletting summons to Eli, his master—but before he could take such a drastic step, a face came into his mind. *Lori*—

He felt a rush into his mind, something clean and pure. Her power flooded his mind and the weight left his chest. Sucking air into his lungs, he opened his eyes and saw the ceiling above his bed.

Don't move, Jonnie. They aren't gone yet, Lori whispered into his mind.

The insidious creeping evil lingered inside him as Lori continued to push onward inside, forcing the blackness out, her light, easy power overtaking everything inside him until he could breathe, could move without feeling the pain, the suffocating evil that was trying to control and become him—be him.

Trying to claim the Wolf. *Let them try, little brother*, the Wolf offered, laughing. The Wolf inside him gaped his mouth in a lupine grin, but Jonathan was enraged.

Not in this life.

He changed. The wild, edgy, raw power that was werewolf exploded inside him, untamed and rampant, so close to the full moon. His long brunette hair thickened as his head fell back, a muzzle forming, teeth lengthening and exploding from his gums, blood pooling inside his mouth as they tore through. His muscles flexed as fur flowed and rippled along his skin, bones breaking and reforming. Ebony claws shot out from his nails, hooked and deadly, flashing in the light. He dropped to his knees, a ragged growl rolling from his throat as the rain of fur raced down his spine, his clothes falling in tatters to the floor.

The lean, muscled wall of his chest rippled like water as those muscles started to shift and change, becoming obscured by the flow of fur. A deep, dark brown fur flowed across the length of his body as he shuddered and slammed his hands against the floor, his legs popping and shifting as the change continued. The fur on his thighs was thicker, but shorter and silkier, continuing down his legs until it ended in slightly longer tufts around his ankles, and very short stubbly fur on the top of his feet.

Thicker, more heavily rounded muscles rippled as he rose and looked around. Nearly a head taller now, at six feet six, he searched the room, his eyes glowing gold.

The evil presence in his mind faltered as the wild power of werewolf permeated the room and forced her suffocating presence back. "What do you want?" he growled.

"You…" He felt a seductive stroke caress him, rippling through his body, around it, over it. *"What you are, what you have…your power, your soul…"*

Jonathan snarled and jerked back, away from the power, and the evil beauty it offered. "You can't have my power, or me," he rasped, forcing the words out. Speaking the words felt alien and awkward on his tongue.

"Darling, I already have you."

Jonathan would rather not admit that he was a bit afraid that she wasn't lying, or bluffing. "My power isn't mine. It's the Wolf's, and you can't lay claim to it."

The drifting music of a woman's laughter came floating to him. *"You lie. It is your power, and soon it will be mine."*

The wildness inside him exploded and he threw his head back, baying, howling, the sound rising and falling. A dozen weres answered him throughout the enclave and Jonathan snarled savagely, triumphantly, as he felt the evil falter inside him.

Jonathan banished the creeping, wild power, and the Wolf receded as it recognized that Jonathan was once again himself. As the fur melted away inside his skin and the power faded away, from his human form Jonathan looked up, smiled and said quietly, "No. The power of the werewolf belongs to the Wolf, to the Wolf and to the moon. It is not mine, though the gift is mine to call. I am powerful enough to summon the gift on my own, unlike many weres. But it is not something that *you* can control now, or ever." As he spoke, he rose to his feet, easily, in a smooth lazy motion, his naked, golden body gleaming in the dim light.

"I can control it, just like I can control you. I will control it. I will summon the wolf...NOW!" Jonathan felt it, felt the witch — whoever she was — trying to rip something from inside him. But she had no clue where to look. Where to hunt. She was looking for something magickal, something psychic or physical. But the power was intangible.

Her searching hurt.

Bellowing, his hands clutching at his head, he went back down, this time to his knees, writhing in agony as she rummaged through his soul like a box of clothes. He felt her picking up bits and pieces and tossing them aside as each one proved to be empty of what she sought. *"Damn you, where is it? I want it, give me that power. Turn, you fucking dog. Change, now!"*

Gritting his teeth, Jonathan bared a mean semblance of a smile at her and said, "Go fuck yourself," before his eyes rolled up and his back arched as a spasm of agony raced the long golden length of his nude, sleekly-muscled body.

Change, change, change!

Lori felt the angry flow of power in the small cottage from outside in the yard. She leaped the fence and narrowed her eyes at the door. It opened accordingly and she smiled slightly as she slid through. She really should learn to knock, maybe tomorrow...

That foul, evil presence permeated the air, almost choking her as she padded down the hall on bare feet. Staring through the dim light, she studied the shadow that was Jonathan and waited as darkness gathered around him.

The shadows were of people who weren't truly there, though their presence was real enough. Lori could hear their whispers to him, faintly, very faintly. *Turn you fucking dog. Change now!*

Change, change, change!

58

That high-pitched, miserable ear-piercing shriek—Lori shook her head and threw off the echoes of the voice she couldn't really hear.

"He doesn't belong to you," she said firmly, certainly. "He made his vows, his allegiances long ago. And none were made to you."

Unholy shrieks filled the air and eerie eyes pivoted and locked on her as she pushed through the heavy presence that filled the room, striding confidently to his side. Kneeling beside him, she placed one hand on his shoulder. "Be gone from here. You are no threat to him, not here." Her voice was deep, throbbing with her own power and echoing through the room.

As if her touch had strengthened him, Jonathan surged from the floor. Evil, dirty power lashed through the room and struck at Jonathan as he rose. *He is tainted. We can take what is tainted.*

Jonathan's mouth curled in a sardonic smile at whoever struck out at him. "Unworthy, perhaps. But not tainted." His voice was twisted and hoarse with pain, and it tore at her heart to hear it.

Lori felt his eyes on her as she stood ready to brace his weight, and they stood face to face against this evil that thought it could lay claim to Jonathan. *Tainted?* Evil witches didn't care if one was tainted or not if they were just seeking to steal or corrupt somebody's gifts.

"We want what is ours…we want our brothers and sisters to join us as the time nears…"

With narrowed eyes, Lori fought the terror that threatened to swell inside her. They weren't just witches. They were recruiting for the enemies of the Council. Long had the Council spoken of an unknown enemy that assassinated and murdered, poisoning the minds of young wolf packs and turning them against humanity. The Hunters would then have to wipe out entire packs because they had begun hunting humans. Enemies who sought out young witches on the streets and groomed them to suit their own purposes.

"I am no brother to you, no kin to you, nothing like you."

They laughed. "Yet, in your heart, you question your worth to your master, your worth to the pathetic Council you serve. To us, you would never doubt that worth—"

"I'd be worth kicking aside when you were done having me fetch whatever bone you threw my way," Jonathan snarled, baring his teeth. "Get out of this place. This is my home. Be gone. Be gone." He brought his wrist to his mouth and tore open a vein with sharp teeth, gathering blood on his fingers as he strode over to the door.

Painting a simple X over the door, he hissed, "Be gone, I say. Return no more. From my house, my blood bars your return ever more."

With a violent shriek, they cursed him as the simple chant of the home's owner barred them from being there in any way, shape or form.

His long, rich brown hair fell over his shoulders as he lowered his head, watching the skin already beginning to knit as he applied pressure to the gash on his wrist. Lori stared at him, wide-eyed, just now aware of how bare his rather naked butt was. The golden flesh gleamed richly over firm, muscled flesh, the columns of his thighs hard and sculpted. Her heart started to pound as heat pooled in her belly.

And all the while, her mind was reeling. Forcing the words through her dry mouth, she asked roughly, "How did you know about that?"

Over his shoulder, he slid her an amused look. "I've been living around witches for several years now. I'm gonna learn a few things, sweetheart."

As she continued to stare hungrily at the hard, muscled curve of his ass, he walked down the hall, and disappeared around the corner. Lori sighed in disappointment when she could no longer see those wide muscled shoulders, those narrow hips and that lean, naked body. She licked her lips and wiped her mouth, just in case she was drooling.

When Jonathan returned a few minutes later, she was sitting down, her hands folded around a steaming cup of tea as she stared into nothingness. "Why do they think you are tainted? Whoever they are, they seem to think this gives them a hold on you." Lifting her eyes to him as he lowered himself into a chair, she studied his rather pale, grim face as he took the mug she had prepared for him.

"I'm not gonna like what's in there, am I?"

A small, amused smile curved her mouth. Damn his talented nose. "No. The knife that stabbed you was cursed. Rosemary, sage, graveyard dirt. I'll have to rub some herbs — acacia and Angelica root and such — into your wound, but first you need to drink that. It has bergamot and Blessed thistle in it. And a whole lot of prayers."

"Did you pray to your Goddess about me? I'm touched," Jonathan said, his mouth quirking up in a smile.

A streak of hurt lanced through her and she lowered her head to keep him from seeing it in her eyes. He knew enough about witches to pick up some basic protection. But he didn't know that she didn't believe in any Goddess. "I don't worship a Goddess, Jonathan. I never have," she said softly, scooping a necklace out of her shirt, displaying the golden cross she wore around her neck. "I believe in the same God you do, and go to church on the same day, and worship the same way the average American does. I go to the church across the street from where you and Erica ago, as a matter of fact. You're much more devout than I am."

She dropped the cross back inside her shirt and nodded to the glass. "Drink your tea. The reason they work is because I believe they will, and also because they fight the toxins the other herbs put inside your body to make you susceptible to their touch. That is fifty percent of faith, and science."

"What is the other fifty?" he asked as he reluctantly lifted the mug. He took the first sip and Lori smiled, taking some small nasty pleasure as he gagged at the taste.

"Magick. God giving me the gift, and me using it wisely. And magick is my gift, plain and simple, like you have yours, Sarel has hers, and Declan and Tori each have theirs."

Jonathan arched a brow at her as he downed the rest of the contents in the mug. Suppressing a shudder, he set it aside and walked over to the fridge, fishing out a jug of juice and washing the taste of Lori's brew from his mouth. Lori studied him from under the fringe of her lashes, the lines of muscle and sinew, the lovely gold of his skin, the way his belly clenched and moved as he moved. Something hot and molten shifted inside her and she took a slow, deep breath through her nose, forcing herself to relax.

I can't do this, not here, not around him. He'll know.

Grabbing two glasses in one hand, he carried the juice to the table. "Okay. I noticed that you left Eli out." As he lowered himself back into the seat, she studied the angry, red gash in his side. It was a wound that would never fully heal.

With a forceful shake of her head, she met his eyes and said, "Did I leave out Eli, my beloved brother-in-law, out? How terrible of me."

Eli wasn't exactly the kind of soul you could overlook. But up until a few years ago, he would never have considered himself a lucky or gifted man. Now, as he rose from a long, restful slumber and stretched his body, the thoughts that drifted through his mind were those of a man contented, no, *happy* with his life.

His gift lay behind him, already sleeping. The watery rays of sunlight that slid through the drapes he threw open coming in to paint her body with an array of colors. Her name was Sarel, she was a witch, with the heart of a warrior and the only soul on the planet that would ever be a match to his.

Eli felt the spilling of blood as he walked away from the bed they shared, with the stir of power, the scent of were and the warmth of witch all building inside him.

By the Council, Eli moved into the room of Malachi's Scottish manor, his fangs unsheathed as rage and anger started to take root. Without even reaching out, just that mere touch, the briefest of connections as Lori used the tip of a kitchen blade to cut open the ugly, ragged gash on Jonathan's side and he knew—

With a light touch, he found Sheila and Rafe, both out— Sheila out shopping, having a couple of drinks, and just having fun in Charleston, as the young vamp loved. And Rafe was out doing what he did best, brooding and hunting. With a silent summons, he ordered them both back and then focused his attention on Jonathan and Lori, trying to study the wound and the scent of it, but with little luck.

He wasn't truly there, even if his people were.

"If you truly want to know what is going on, did it occur to you to ask?"

"Lori, you grow more impudent every day, sweet, did you know that?" he purred, smiling as he watched her work.

He could see her, the image of her hands on Jonathan's torso, burned on the back of his eyelids as he watched.

"What is going on?"

Sarel's voice, hot and angry, full of life and pulsating energy, echoed through the room, and the link. If ever Eli wondered of Lori's abilities and just how steady her hands would be, now he knew. Sarel's voice would have made his skin itch and crawl even if it had come booming into his mind from thousands of miles away—currently, Eli slid her a narrowed look as blood started to pound heavily in his groin and his cock stirred, lengthened, and throbbed.

But Sarel paid him little mind as she strode past him and placed her palm flat on a window. Her long hair flowed down her naked back, and started to blow back from her face as the window first glowed gold under her touch and then went opaque, reflecting first her face, then her sister's profile as she knelt over Jonathan's body. He lay on the couch in his cottage, staring up at Lori's face from under the hood of his lashes. The gash was long and ugly, puckered, an angry, bright red, and at one end, the vicious mark of a scythe was forming.

"Lori, stop, you need to make sure you've—"

"Sarel, aren't you supposed to be on vacation?" Lori asked as she continued to rub more Angelica root into the open wound on Jonathan's side, from the bottom up.

"If you haven't made him drink one of those nasty potions first, you're wasting your time," Sarel said, ignoring her.

Eli sighed, reaching up and rubbing his forehead as Lori continued to work. The younger witch never slowed, nor did she let Jonathan feel any of the pain she was inflicting on his body, Eli noticed. *He* could feel it, some of it, a distant echo, through the link he had to both of them, but the were felt none of it as he lay watching Lori with dark, dangerous eyes. The pain was nauseating, just that echo that Eli could feel. What Lori was feeling must be unreal.

"You cannot fight it forever, pup. You know that." Eli's words were soft, spoken directly into Jonathan's mind, only for him to hear.

Jonathan turned his head eastward, following the distant sound of Eli's voice as he softly said, "I'll fight it for as long she is here."

"Hush, Jonathan," Lori murmured, and with a thought, she urged him deeper into a healing trance. Eli winced as he recognized the herbs she reached for with her bloody hand, acacia, blessed thistle, and good old fashioned earth from his home, the cottage where he had lived. Fire glowed hotly in her hand as she held the earth in one and used the other to rub the herbs into it while she whispered under her breath.

"Damn it, Lori—"

Eli laughed gently. "Sarel, love. She made him drink it, the bloody bitter brew, down to the last drop before we had barely realized there was even a problem."

Eli could almost see the anger and worry that deflated her, and wasn't sure what to make of the nerves that replaced it. "All of it? Without arguing?"

With the slow, characteristic curve of his lips, Eli said, "Jonathan doesn't argue with Lori, love. He did exactly what she told him to do and then lay down for the healing like a good boy. And she's a bloody good witch. Your equal, in fact. She's just not the warrior you are. She's a Healer."

Lori studied the mark on Jonathan's side. It was closed, scarred but closed. And faded, nearly normal looking on the lean, smooth golden skin of his muscled body.

Except for the Scythe.

The Scythe.

With a deep, sighing breath, she rested a hand above it as Rafe and Sheila moved in behind her. Eli had called his people home. She wasn't exactly sure why, but it was a good thing.

That Scythe couldn't stay there on his skin. It was something evil, and draining—foul. Trying to mark him.

"Jonathan, love," she whispered absently, tracing her fingers along the rough, ridged skin of the mark, shuddering as the cold skin there tried to leech into her and grab. It was the cold of death, true death, a poison under the skin that would slowly drain the life out of him, maybe even any who touched him and tried to save him, as it pulled everything under its cold, evil spell.

And held you there.

Forever.

"They've marked you, some kind of binding spell. I have to break it," she whispered, lifting up and looking at him, her hair falling about her face as she stared down into his eyes, those dark eyes she had dreamed about for years. "I don't know what will happen if I don't."

"And exactly how do you break it?" Rafe asked, moving up out of the shadows. Inky black hair spilled into his eyes and he flicked it away with an impatient hand. "You're a young witch, *cara*. Eli will not be happy, *Sarel* will not be happy if anything happens to you."

Flicking the rakish looking Italian a flicker of a glance, Lori smiled. "Stop worrying," she said, turning her eyes back to Jonathan. Bending down, Lori opened herself to the magick and just let it fill her.

Chapter Two

Those soft golden-green eyes were glowing and fiery, with little flames licking around the irises. Jonathan felt her hands land on his sides, just above his hipbones. The palm of her right hand lying over the fresh, newly healed skin of the scar on his side, still feeling so cool, until she touched it. It was hot, very hot, under her touch—the skin quivering as she settled her hands on it.

A deep growl rumbled in his throat as her head lowered over his abdomen and her hair tickled his belly. His cock ached, swelling in the confines of his jeans as blood started to pound more heavily in his veins. The scent of woman and magick mingled in his mind until they were one, and both were Lori.

The hot satiny brush of her mouth on his side had him sucking in air through his teeth, and his eyes rolling back in dazed agony as a hot spear of magick shot through him. One hand flattened against the scarred flesh as she shifted, moving higher, until she could press her mouth against the mark that scarred him—the Scythe—touching it with both her mouth and tongue.

At her touch, Jonathan arched up in agony as burning, tearing pain ripped through him. Lori was tearing something evil from inside him and it didn't want to let go. Taking him over wasn't something she would allow this evil to do. But to take a place inside him and slowly force him aside, well, that it might accomplish.

"Hold him—"

Through the pain that racked his body, Jonathan heard that harsh barking order that came from her mind but he couldn't move to help her. *What had the little witch gotten into now? And damn it, why couldn't he move his arms? What was wrong with his head?*

His head—

"Son of a bitch!" he roared, arching his back and bellowing as agony arced through him.

Then a gentle billowing kiss of cool, soft air brushed over his skin and he gasped, sucking breath in desperately as he felt a hand reach in just under his skin, working at the small, hard little knot, like a root. But the tree was trying to grow inside.

Two pairs of hands, vamp-cool and hard, came down on him, pinning his shoulders and legs. Hair, scented with plumeria, fell across his face and her voice, soft and gently soothing, came to his ear. "Easy, Jon…easy there. Lori's nearly done, 'kay? Just…damn it…calm down."

Power trickled and rolled through him, starting to pulse in the room as a deeper voice said, "Damn it. Lori, you'd better hurry. The animal inside him is getting mad and the Wolf is getting worried. Jonathan will not be able to keep from changing for too long."

"Rafe, five seconds. Shhhh…"

"Lori, if he changes like this—" a deep, muttered grunt sounded through the room. "Unaware, in pain, he may attack."

"He won't hurt me, Rafe. The Wolf won't let him. He won't let himself," Lori murmured. Then a soft, ragged gasp and silence.

"Let him go. It is gone," Lori whispered.

Jonathan felt her mouth on his side again, hot and open as the pain faded and blew away, like ashes in the wind. Fisting his hand in her hair, he opened his eyes on a ragged sigh.

And then wished he would have caught his breath first.

Sheila and Rafe had backed away, both with eyes shuttered, but glowing under the hoods of their lashes. The scent of lust, hunger, want was heavy on the air. The taste of it, the feel of it was so powerful inside him, Jonathan thought he was about to go mad.

And there was Lori, lifting up from her knees and staring down at his side, tracing her hand over the mark on his skin. "Their mark is gone," she whispered softly, then she lifted her gaze and met his, her pale green eyes glowing, soft, sweet, but strong and confident—powerful.

He felt the punch of that look in his gut as he grabbed her and rolled, pinning her under him, pushing his tongue into her mouth and groaning hungrily at the sweet, dark taste of her. Wedging a knee between hers, he pumped his cock against the damp cleft there and skimmed his hands up her sides, palming one breast, rolling the nipple between his thumb and forefinger.

The sounds of ragged breathing, increased heart rates and the scent of aroused female came to him as he kissed his way down Lori's neck. Sheila's shuddering sigh caressed his skin, a sound that normally would be so welcome, but now was an intrusion.

Pulling his mouth from Lori's, he glanced to the side and growled to Sheila and Rafe, "Go away."

Rafe flashed his fangs and rasped, "Watch your step, pup. I'm not yours to command." His eyes slid down and rested on the soft curve of Lori's hip, where Jonathan's hand gripped it, and the vampire moved forward, his lids drooping. "I ache, hunger. She is young and sweet—"

Dropping to his knees beside them, Rafe murmured, "I think I want a taste."

Jonathan growled, rolling away and placing Lori behind him, coming up in a crouch and facing Rafe. "She is mine, vampire. Mine. Leave."

Rafe started to laugh. His fangs had slid out, protruding past his lips, and now caught the light as he rested on his heels, staring up at Jonathan. "Yours? C'mon, Jon. She's wanted just that for years, and you haven't done a damn thing about it. And now, after giving us a show like that, you wanna get possessive?"

Jonathan's lips peeled back from his teeth as they started to lengthen, a rough growl rolling from his throat. "Do not push me, Rafe." His hands, palms planted on the ground, were shifting, changing, as the nails started to darken and stretch.

"I'm not afraid of you, wolf." *Pup* was gone, though, as Rafe slowly straightened and eyed the were, who was battling the werewolf inside him. Or rather, not battling the werewolf enough. The werewolf was carefully watching the vampire through those narrowed, dark eyes. Jonathan did little to control the animal and nothing to rein it in.

"Leave," Jonathan snarled again. He ached. Lori's scent filled his head, and his blood pounded heavily in his veins, surging and throbbing in his cock as he stared into Rafe's gleaming eyes.

Sheila smiled, a bit of envy in her gaze as she ran her eyes over Lori who was still gasping and reeling from the effects of the magick coursing through her veins. Then she stepped in front of Rafe, tossing her long blonde hair over her shoulder, offering him a teasing smile as she slid her hands up his chest. "It looks like we're not welcome here, handsome. Why don't we go and find something to amuse ourselves with, sugar?" she drawled, stroking her finger over his full lower lip.

When he reached to grip her waist and move her aside, she stumbled into him and Jonathan smelled the musk of vampire blood filling the air. "Oh! How careless of me, Rafe, I'm sorry. I hope you're not hungry," Sheila murmured as she moved aside, holding up the finger she had sliced against one of his extended fangs.

Sliding it between her lips, she licked the blood away, smiling a coquette's smile at him as she drew the gleaming finger out, and cocked her head at him. More blood welled and he focused his glowing eyes on her, a deep, shuddering breath racking his large frame.

"You like to mess with fire, little Southern Belle?" Rafe murmured, moving a little closer, his eyes locked on the bead of blood that hung on the tip of her finger.

Locking his fingers around her wrist, he brought it to his mouth and slid her fingertip between his lips, sucking it as he stared into her eyes.

"Take her and go, Rafe," Jonathan growled as he turned back to Lori.

He didn't hear them leave, but he knew they had all the same. Rafe's parting words, "Too cocky, young wolf. It doesn't sit well with me," were smothered against Sheila's laughing mouth as she said, "Oh, hush." They were gone seconds later.

Sucking air into his lungs, Jonathan focused inward and sent the animal back inside. With a soft sigh it retreated, to once again slumber as Jonathan turned his head, staring over his shoulder at Lori. Her hazy eyes, still glinting with lights of gold as she blinked sleepily at him, were just now clearing of the magick.

He crawled over to her as she sat up, eying him warily. "I can feel your magick inside me, Lori, your touch, your breath, your taste. I want more." Rising onto his knees, Jonathan caught her behind the neck and pulled her up against him, sealing his mouth to hers and tasting her deeply, fully.

Sliding his tongue into her mouth, stroking it across the roof, the insides of her cheeks, across her teeth—every part he could touch, Jonathan touched. Every part of her mouth he could taste, he tasted. Moving his hands down her shoulders and arms to cup her breasts, he massaged them restlessly as he urged her back to the floor.

Gasping in her throat as he wedged his thigh between hers, she rode the muscled length with her warm, wet cleft. Sweet, soft little moans built in her chest as Jonathan kissed his way down her chin and throat, along the loose neckline of her T-shirt. Through it, he could smell her skin, her arousal, her need.

And he wanted to taste it all.

Closing his mouth over the pebbled crest of one nipple, he swirled his tongue around it, sucking it deep into his mouth. Damn...her taste, it exploded on his tongue—honeyed innocence, power, seduction, purity. Everything he had wanted and needed from her for years, but refused himself. Ever since Lori had come to Eli's enclave, Jonathan had wanted her, an innocent woman-child of nineteen—and for seven long years he had ignored that want.

With his hand flat against her torso, he slid it down over her belly, her pubis, until he cupped her, feeling her hot, molten wetness through the thin layers of the chiffon skirt. Sliding the wispy material back and forth over her, he groaned around her breast as her cream instantly soaked through the material and coated his fingers.

Lifting his head, he stared down at her, blinking slowly. Power rippled through him and rolled down his spine, shuddering off his skin as he watched her face. Her eyes opened languidly as she licked her lips, as though tasting him. Jonathan groaned, and forced himself not to take—

Not yet. Not unless she wanted it. *Her*. Not just her body.

Forcing the words through his tight throat, he slowly rubbed his sex against her, once, then again. Watching as she arched toward him, he whispered, "Look at me, Lori. Do you want this? Me?"

A slow, female smile—that Mona Lisa smile that had been driving men insane for centuries—curved her rosebud lips and she slid her hands up his chest, behind his neck, and then fisted them in his hair, bringing his face down to hers. "Would I be here if I didn't?" She rolled her hips against him, and Jonathan bit off a ragged cry as her damp heat caressed his covered cock. "Do you know how long I've wanted to be *right here*, Jonathan? Just like this? For months and months, years and years...if you don't touch me now, I just might turn you into a flying cockroach."

His control shattered. Gripping her shirt in his hands, he ripped it from her. Flexing his hand, claws emerged and he slid them under her bra, slicing it away as he stared into her eyes, looking for any sign of fear. The claws slid back into his hand like water evaporating as he reached for the skirt, taking both skirt and panties in hand and pulling them down her hips in one long smooth slide.

Kneeling at her feet, his long sable hair spilling around his shoulders, Jonathan stared at her body. Gazing along the ivory length of it, so soft, and as perfect as carved alabaster, as the scent of her filled his head and made him drunk. His mouth was watering as he reached for her ankles and slowly pushed them apart, sliding his hands up the length of her legs.

As he moved them apart, he lay forward until he was kneeling between her thighs, his face hovering just above the junction of her thighs. He stared with unconcealed hunger at the naked mound of her sex, topped with a small, neatly trimmed patch of red curls. "Soft, smooth...just how I like it...sweet," he growled, breathing in the scent of her. He slid his tongue up the gleaming wet seam, lapping the pearls of cream that glistened there, letting them linger on his tongue before parting her flesh with his thumbs and piercing her, and sliding his tongue into the deep, dark depths of her pussy.

"Jon—"

"Aww, fuck, you're sweet," he growled, lifting her higher against him, holding her ass in his hands and catching her clit between his teeth. He tugged it gently before thrusting his tongue deep inside the wet channel again.

Lori shrieked and Jonathan smiled as he did a shift, just his tongue, thrusting it deep, and groaning as he had to work even that inside her. In, out, then in again to flick it against her G-spot, as he greedily drank down the rush of cream that followed.

Pulling back, he lowered her hips to the floor and pushed two long, agile fingers inside her as he licked her cream from his lips, rasping, "You're so damn tight, so sweet. Have you been with anybody since that fool from college?"

But her eyes were still blind and her mind too muddled. Gasping for air, not hearing him, Lori reached for him, blindly, burying her fingers in his hair and pulling him back to her.

Jonathan couldn't resist the siren call of her body, even as rage ripped through him as he remembered that night. He had found them — her and her college boyfriend — on a blanket in the woods, on the new moon. Naked and sweating, smiling and laughing in each other's arms, the scent of her virgin's blood in the air, the man's come on her thighs, and Jonathan saw red.

Only months before, they had nearly died together in a trap that had been set to catch Eli, their Master. But he had wanted her with a vengeance even before that.

And then he had come upon her right after she had given her body to a man for the first time, someone other than him. Now, years later, rage still rocked him and he slanted his mouth across Lori's, kissing her punishingly, brutally, as that night echoed through the back of his mind.

Her naked body, lithe and trim, coming off the ground as she had sensed him, her head lifting, that long wild hair tumbling down her back. One hand had flashed fire, a dangerous magick. Even though she wasn't a warrior, she was ready to protect her lover as she detected the danger around them.

"Who is there?" she had demanded.

"Out rather late, aren't you, little girl?" Jonathan had asked, sliding out from behind a tree and snarling at the boy who had lain watching her with a smile — staring at her with hungry, affectionate eyes. Loving eyes. Eyes that had gone cloudy and dim even as Jonathan had watched, because Lori had turned and whispered softly under her breath some minor spell that had clouded his mind.

"Jonathan. This isn't your patrol section. Sheila runs this line."

He'd flashed her an evil grin and said, "I know. I was out...chatting with her. And I caught your scent. Don't you know better than to go getting naked with some college boy?"

She had arched a cool brow at him and said, "Then I guess I should I have gone to a bar and picked up a man I don't know instead of one I've been dating for months, one I'm halfway in love with. Would that have been wiser?"

I don't want you naked with anybody but me, Jonathan had wanted to tell her. But that wasn't possible. Not with Lori.

Instead, he had silkily told her she had better leave the college boys alone if she wanted them to remain...intact.

"And unless you want to wake up a metaphysical eunuch, you'll mind your own damned business."

Jonathan had been pretty damn certain she was bluffing. But fate had intervened before he could make good on his promise to pummel the boy into a bloody pulp. Less than two weeks later, after a lover's quarrel, he'd gotten himself killed driving home drunk. Lori, with her soft heart, still hadn't forgiven herself.

"Has there been anyone else, Lori?" he whispered. "Another man? One? Two?"

"Damn it, Jonathan," she moaned in frustration, arching her hips up, wrapping her legs around his waist and locking them just above his butt so that his cock was firm and snug in the cleft of her thighs. "Please, I want you inside me. I'm so empty."

Unhooking her ankles, he rose up onto his hands and knees, hovering over her. Staring down into her eyes, Jonathan pushed two fingers back into her silky wet depths. "Feel how tight you are, how wet and sweet?" He circled over the nub of her clit with his thumb and smiled as she whimpered, following the circle of his caress eagerly.

"Damn it, Jonathan, take your jeans off. I want you inside me, I want to feel you against me," Lori whimpered, reaching for him.

Jonathan smiled slowly, looking into her eyes, seeing the desperation there, reveling in it. His pure, innocent little witch was hungry, so hungry for him. Drawing his fingers from her snug, tight sheath, he brought them to his mouth, licking the spicy sweet tang from them as he watched her. "Not...just yet," he decided as he started to lower his head to her breasts.

He wanted her hungrier. As hungry as he had been for the past seven years of his life.

Lori could have leveled the house with her frustration. The devious, devilish glint in his dark eyes had her narrowing hers. Wind whipped through the room and she snapped her hand up and flicked her fingers, staring into his eyes with challenge written all over her face.

Jonathan's eyes widened as his jeans were rent away, much like her clothes had been. The unseen winds of magick continued to blow and Lori lay, staring at him and smiling, watching as the wind blew his hair around him, winding it about his shoulders and chest, teasing her with the sight of the small scar on his side—shaped like a phoenix.

Her mark, replacing the mark of the Scythe.

Rising from the ashes...*like I did.*

Her eyes trailed over his body—the golden, muscled length of it—so smooth and perfect, except for that shining scarred flesh of her mark. His cock rose, ruddy and perfect, denuded of any body hair. It was thick, full, and curved just slightly at the top, over toward the right. Lori felt a shudder roll through her as she imagined feeling him inside of her.

Her gaze moved down the rest of him and she licked her lips before looking back up to lock eyes with him. There was no hair on his body. Very few werewolves had any body hair in human form. Some had a little under their arms, and occasionally, a male would develop light chest hair or some hair on his legs, but it was rare.

Nothing to distract her eyes from the golden, gleaming, muscled perfection that was Jonathan.

With a smile, she trailed one finger down the center of her body and started to stroke it over the hardened nub of her clit. "Bare. Soft, and smooth, you said. Just how you like it, I know. Just for you—Sheila is my best friend. She tells me everything." With a rough gasp, she plunged a finger deep inside, feeling her own flesh, hot, slippery and wet under her strokes. She had to force her eyes to stay open as she watched his face. "So I did it, the way she says you like it. I've been watching you, waiting for you, wanting you, for years. Since I first saw you standing outside Eli's room when Tavis brought me here. I'd just left the school."

She watched his eyes as she climaxed into her hand with a sob. Jonathan growled, catching her hand and lapping at it as he stared down at her with narrowed, glittering eyes. Opening her mouth, she raggedly whispered, "I'm tired of waiting for you."

Jonathan's mouth was sealed against hers before the last word had left her lips, and she could feel the blunt, rounded tip of his cock probing at the wet opening to her core. Arching her hips up, she wound her legs around him, opening her mouth eagerly under his as he started to forge his way into her tight pussy, working his cock ever so slowly inside her, until she thought she'd scream.

Tears started to burn her eyes and she gasped as he pushed relentlessly deep, forcing his way completely in. Seating himself against the bud of her clit and holding there, rocking against her, he started to kiss her deeply, restlessly massaging one breast with his thumb and forefinger.

"Tight, sweet, hot little pussy, I can smell you," he murmured against her lips, pulling back before moving to lick away the tears. "Tasty little thing. Let me feel you move under me." Propping his weight up on his elbows, he pumped in and out of her lazily, almost absently, staring down at her expectantly. The golden muscles of his chest shifted, playing under the smooth perfection of his skin as he watched her, those dark, dark eyes so rapt on her face.

His silken hair fell across her body like a cape, sliding, caressing as he moved against her, and Lori fisted her hands in it as she lifted up against him, shuddering, quivering as spasms of pure, electric sensation raced through her. With the curved end of his cock...ah...angling against her, Jonathan was now stroking the head of his cock directly over her G-spot. Lori stiffened, throwing her head back as she tightened her legs around his hips and started to piston against him, harder and harder. Taking his hard, hot length deeper and deeper, she stared up into his eyes, feeling them engulf her.

"So soft and wild," he rasped, stroking one hand down her hip, cupping her ass. Lori wailed as he pressed his fingers against the seam there, spreading the cheeks of her ass, letting the cool kiss of air caress her rosette as he started to slow his thrusts, fucking her deep, rolling his hips so that he was caressing her G-spot thoroughly with each deep stroke. "Scream for me, Lori."

Lori shuddered as his dark head lowered to the soft mound of her breast. She sucked in a ragged breath of air as he sank his teeth into the pink crest of one dark, rosy nipple, suckling deep, nipping gently before swirling his tongue around it.

A liquid storm was building, molten and steaming, as he pushed himself inside her, angled so that he rubbed against her clit with each deep thrust. "Jonathan, please," she gasped, digging her nails into him, staring blindly into his face. His eyes were gleaming, more golden than brown now, as an animal in human skin stared down at her, long fangs pushing down past his lower lip.

Lori didn't care as she wound her hands into his hair and pulled him down to press her mouth hungrily to his, driving her tongue deep, drinking down that dark male taste—the taste of the woods, of honey and mead, and the wild. He arched his back and pumped his hips against her, his cock burying inside her, his balls slapping against the crevice of her bottom as they both started to come. Lori coming in slow, rhythmic pulses that grew in strength and duration, while Jonathan started to furiously fuck himself into her. Burying his hands in her hair and groaning against her mouth, his cock jerked and pulsed as hot, rolling waves of semen jetted free, deep inside her sheath.

Lori sobbed into his mouth, her entire body trembling, feeling his heart pounding against her, the slow darkening of his thoughts, the quivering of his powerful, lean body as he went rigid against her.

As he pumped the last of his come into her, her body went slack, and Jonathan bussed her mouth gently. Easing to one side before rolling to his back and taking her with him, he cuddled her against his side and yawned.

Lori was still lying there, cold and naked when he slid into sleep.

The magick had taken a toll on them both, but on Jonathan more than her. As she napped briefly, in the back of her mind, she was thinking. And hoping, but wondering if she dared to dream while she slept.

Her taste was on his tongue, and her scent filled his head.

Lori...

Curled against her back, his cock was cuddled against her softly rounded ass, tucked snugly between the cheeks in the sweetest way imaginable as he drifted awake. *Damnation...what in the hell have I done?*

And then he rolled and slid his hand up her side, cupping a small, firmly rounded breast in his palm. Pinching the nipple as he sank his teeth into the soft pad of muscle that topped her shoulder, he gently laved the slightly reddened love bite with his tongue. Rolling his hips, Jonathan groaned as the soft, silken skin caressed his cock before he eased away and urged her onto her back.

Leaning over her, nipping at her mouth, he stroked his hand down the center of her torso, slowly, teasingly, until he had her cupped in his hand. Sliding his hand through her wet folds, he pierced her with one finger, pushing deep and listening as a cry of rapture fell from her lips and her eyes fluttered open.

Against her ear, he said roughly, "I'm going to fuck you hard and deep, until you scream my name, Lori. I can't tell you how long I've wanted to do this to you." Rising to his knees, he brought her body with him, bowing her back over his arm and feasting on the rosy crests of her breasts as she stared up at him with sleep-dazed eyes, her face flushed, her lips parted, and the scent of her arousal perfuming the air all around them.

With quick, short motions of his hands, he moved her onto her hands and knees, bringing her soft, sweetly rounded ass back against the cradle of his hips, trailing the tips of his fingers down the line of her spine and smiling as she shuddered. Rocking against the damp cleft of her ass, he grimaced, banding his arm under her waist and bringing her back against him, raking her neck with his teeth and piercing her weeping pussy with his fingers.

A wailing cry echoed through the room and Jonathan bared his teeth in a feral, triumphant smile as she climaxed into his hand, while he stared down the length of her lovely body. Her breasts, pale and perfect, heaved with each ragged breath, as she sobbed and screamed his name, reaching behind and twining her fingers in his hair, so that she was arching her breasts up.

"Look at you," he rasped. "So damn pretty, so perfect. Pretty rose nipples, so hard and pink, and those soft white breasts, all that creamy skin. I've been dying to taste it, taste you. I can smell you, how hungry you are, how much you want, how much you need. You're wet, so damn wet...sweet, wild little witch."

Lori shuddered as the climax finished rippling through her and Jonathan grinned hotly as he painted one nipple, then her mouth, with her cream. Arching her head back and taking her mouth roughly, he lifted her up and pierced her, pushing his cock deeply inside her. Lifting her hips up and down on his aching cock, tearing his mouth away from hers and urging her to her hands and knees, he bent over her to whisper in her ear, "Are you ready?"

"Huh...what?" she whimpered, her body still shaking.

Jonathan smiled, taking her hips in his hands, drawing out slowly, staring down at the glistening wet length of his cock before driving back into her, hard. A harsh, surprised gasp fell from her lips, and her scent grew stronger in the room, filling his head—hungry, aroused woman. And magick, wild wanton magick, only the kind a witch possessed and could release when she was aroused. It prickled along his body, teased the skin of his sac and heated his blood in a way he could never have imagined.

The tight, wet glove of her sex clung to his cock as he pulled out slowly, listening to the sound of her heart and her breathing. Jonathan's hands stroked teasingly over the silken skin of her ass before anchoring her as he started another hard, relentless drive deep inside her. Shuddering as the wet, silky walls clutched at his cock, stroking over him, caressing him, hugging him, he planted himself balls deep into her.

A weak little scream fell from her and she arched up, the line of her spine curving. "Jon, I can't stand it..." she sobbed, pushing her ass back against him and trying to hold him inside her.

He pulled out and slammed in again—harder and harder—the wet, silken stroke of her pussy over his cock driving him insane. The sound of her voice moaning his name, the sight of her bending over in front of him, spread out, taking his cock as he had wanted and needed for years and years... "Fuck—" he gasped, crouching low over her, pounding into her, sweat beading on his brow as he stared down, watching his cock, wet and shining with her juices, disappear back inside her sweet cleft again.

The muscles of her pussy started to shudder and clamp down around him as he forged inside, resisting him as she started to come. Jonathan hissed, his head falling back, the veins in his neck standing out as the climax built in the base of his spine.

Lori's slim, supple body was quivering, shaking underneath the power of his thrusts. His balls drew tight against his body, fiery hot as they slapped against her clit teasingly and she started to scream. The sound of his name on her lips sent him over the edge, and he howled her name to the heavens as he raked her hips with the claws that had unwittingly emerged from his hands as he started coming. Flooding the creamy depths of her pussy with his semen, he pumped deeper and deeper, stroking the head of his cock over the buried bundle of nerves in her core.

She milked him, tightening around him, drawing the climax out until they were both sweating and gasping for air as they slid to the ground. "This isn't good, Lori." Against her nape, Jonathan nuzzled her damp salty skin and nipped her gently. "This isn't good at all."

He pulled back.

While she watched, he pulled away, drew back inside his skin, and went totally aloof on her.

With cool, impassive eyes, he watched as she gathered her clothes and walked naked to the bathroom, unsure of what to make of his sudden turnaround. After twenty minutes in the shower, she changed her mind. She knew what to make of it.

It was safer — to him, to her — at a distance.

Leaving the safety of the bathroom, her damp hair woven into a tight cable, Lori came out, watching him with blank eyes, studying his face closely.

"Last night shouldn't have happened," he said as soon as she sat down. "I know what magick can do, it affects your head, your thinking, and it can make you so damn hungry. We both lost our heads."

"Is that what it was?" Lori mused, folding her hands around the mug of tea he held out to her. *Tea*. He always kept tea on hand for her, even as rarely as she came by, the kind she liked. And it was fixed the way she liked. Yet...he was so damned blind. Didn't know she was into Wicca, didn't know what kind of movies she liked.

Or that they belonged together.

"Yes."

"Hmmm. Funny. I've used magick quite a bit. On Eli, around him, around Rafe, and Declan, damn near everybody. And I've never slept with any of them. Never paid that much attention to my body while I'm doing it. I was so aware of you though. Always so aware of you. Maybe that is it. I was so damned aware of you, and that sexy body of yours, and I was so hot for you, I couldn't help but be aware of how turned on I was. So I guess from now on, I'll pay more attention to my body, and when I'm aroused, I'll just start looking to get laid. After all, last night was sooo…pleasant.

"And Rafe was more than willing, wasn't he?" Lori murmured, smiling slyly, watching Jonathan from under her lashes. A muscle ticked in his jaw and something wild flashed through his eyes. But nothing changed on his face, in his demeanor.

If she hadn't been a witch, she would never have felt the power that trembled through the air as she spoke.

Never would have known how downright furious her words made him.

"Just because the magick makes you want to fuck, doesn't mean you have to do it," Jonathan growled.

With large innocent eyes, Lori asked, "Well, why not? It isn't like any of the people here are bad guys. Now, Eli is off limits, and so is Declan. But Rafe is quite available. And then there is Ben Cross and so many others. That's the beauty of an enclave, Jonnie. Always plenty of men."

With a smile, she put her cup back on the table and rose, strolling to the door. "Take care of your side, okay? Their mark is gone, but you did lose some blood."

Their mark was gone, but Lori's wasn't. Under his fingers, he could feel the smooth slick skin of scar tissue, and inside him, Jonathan could feel her.

He hadn't been expecting this.

No wonder he had been able to touch her so easily, no wonder her body primed so readily. As she walked away, he could feel her smug satisfaction. Damn it.

This couldn't be permanent.

Could it?

Maybe distance would help.

But the distance to the house didn't help, and neither did the walls between them, because he was aware of her through damn nearly everything she did. Not enough to distract him from what he was doing, but all he had to do was stop, and think of her, and he was aware of her.

Stalking into the bathroom, he stripped his shirt off and stared into the mirror at the odd, birdlike shape.

A phoenix.

Rising from the ashes.

Lori had learned of her origins, how Eli had rescued her from her father's house only moments before the man would have raped her, and most likely then have killed her. Sarel hadn't wanted her to be told, but Eli had known the witch would find a way to learn.

So they had told her.

"A brave Phoenix, you are, my sweet," the Master Vampire had told her. "You and your sister rose from the ashes of a bitter life and look at what you have become."

Jonathan rubbed his finger over the mark and closed his eyes, shuddering as the touch of it brought back ultra intense memories of the night before. Her mouth on his, her body moving under his, over his, the tight, wet, slick muscles in her pussy as he rode her hard.

It was just the magick.

But he knew better.

"Sarel, do you know anything about a Scythe mark?" The mirror glowed softly as they spoke back and forth through it, a faint humming echo following their voices.

The reflection of her sister wrinkled her nose and the taller woman shrugged. "The scythe can have a lot of meanings, sis. Why?"

"I'm looking for one in particular," Lori murmured, flipping through her ancient book. Kelsey had left several with her, but so far, none of them had yielded anything. She just might have to contact Kelsey or Agnes. "It was what the witches left on Jonathan, it wasn't on him at first, but the curse the knife held had carved it into him later, as they tried to take him. It did something to him, tried to take hold of his Wolf, of him. Something about...*soaked in blood*..."

"They call themselves the Scythe. And they hunt us," Lori whispered, lifting her eyes to the reflection and meeting Sarel's eyes. "They seek to kill us all and end the Council. They want us all dead."

Sarel's eyes flashed with fire as she stared at her sister. "I'll talk to Agnes. Kelsey is in the States. Find her. And for God's sakes, keep that damned wolf out of trouble. He courts it, for crying out loud."

Sarel's image flickered from sight as Lori breathed out a sigh. *Indeed he does. But how am I supposed to keep him out of trouble?*

Then she settled herself and started the time-consuming task of searching for Kelsey.

It wasn't exactly as easy as calling the woman on a cell phone.

If only...

Kelsey didn't like them. Moreover, they didn't like her. High-tech gadgets didn't like the magickally gifted. They tended to...malfunction. In earnest. And the more gifted one happened to be, the more they malfunctioned. And the older the witch got, the worse the problem got.

With Lori, Kelsey and Sarel, well, cell phones, pagers, and computers, were pretty much out of the question.

Fortunately, they had other means of communication. They just weren't quite as fast.

But they were untraceable.

Wind filled the room and Lori's face was lit from within as she fell into a light trance, searching for a path inside her that would lead her to Kelsey. Kelsey, once a teacher, now a friend.

A wise woman, quick-witted, with a dry humor and vast knowledge that belied her youthful looks. You'd never guess by looking at her that she was nearly fifty years old. Witches were a long-lived species, and the more powerful the witch, the longer they lived.

Kelsey was going to live long indeed, even if she never bonded to another paranormal creature.

Soft, musical laughter filled Lori's mind as she heard Kelsey say, "Tsk, tsk...such odd thoughts you are thinking. What's going on, little sister, why are you looking for me?"

Lori's eyes opened and when they did, she could see Kelsey's form standing in front of her, nearly solid, wearing her standard flannel shirt, unbuttoned over a T-shirt and jeans, her hair in her characteristic pigtails. Like Pippy Longstocking.

"The Scythe...who are they? They mean something. Something dangerous, and I need to know what." Lori wasted no time on pleasantries, didn't smile and tell Kelsey how much she had missed her. The burning in her gut wouldn't let her rest until she knew more.

Kelsey's eyes darkened, her head inclining imperially. "Why do you ask?"

"They've paid us a visit."

Kelsey's form wavered in and out of view, her jaw clenching, light shooting around her form. "That cannot be possible. They were eradicated more than a thousand years ago. Malachi destroyed them."

"They were here. They marked Jonathan, tried to take him over. I took their mark, and replaced it with my own, but they were *here*. They've been haunting our steps for months, Kelsey. I think this is who has been preying on the Hunter enclaves."

"Lori, sweetie. Malachi destroyed the Scythe. It just isn't possible—" Kelsey broke off mid-sentence. "I'm being foolish. Of course it's possible. Just because he destroyed the first band, doesn't mean that they won't arise again. Evil has always existed, and will until the world spins no more. I'll find Malachi and bring him to you. He'll know better than I if this is truly the Scythe."

Kelsey took damn near a week tracking Malachi down. The bastard knew she was looking for him. He just didn't bloody care. As she lit upon his home in Nome, Alaska, she shook her head. "Why in the world is a vampire living in Nome in July?"

The sun rarely set here. And the population was scarce. Little prey, very little in the way of animals to hunt.

Pounding a fist on his door, she waited until he opened the ramshackle thing before she finally released her pent-up exasperation and spat out, "You have got to be one of the strangest creatures known to man. You have next to no prey here. The sun hardly ever sets, and there's nothing to do."

Malachi lifted a bronzed brow at her. "Is that what you've been tracking me over half the bloody continent for? To tell me that, little witch?"

"How can you possibly *Hunt* here? I've seen a handful of people. What is there to Hunt? Deadbeat dads? Jaywalkers?"

"I'm on vacation," Malachi drawled, leaning against the doorjamb, folding his arms across his bare chest as the sun shone down, painting half of him a cool gold. His face was in shadow, but Kelsey saw no pain, no fear.

Sweet heaven, it's all true.

"Vacation? You're here on vacation? In the middle of nowhere?"

"Yes, the middle of nowhere, where I'm not bothered by a bunch of thugs, murderers…mouthy little witches who won't mind their own business." His eyes dropped to her mouth and his lips curled up mockingly. "Though, of course, there is something t' be said for havin' people 'round. I do miss havin' a woman in m' bed, pretty little Kelsey. D' ya care t' be joinin' me?"

Kelsey snorted. "Not hardly. I need to talk to you."

Malachi shrugged, not looking the least bit put out. "Either way, darlin'. Talk away."

"Inside?" Kelsey asked, arching a brow.

"Weelll, I don' know 'bout lettin' you come inside. Unless I kin be comin' inside o' you," Malachi murmured wickedly, trailing his eyes over her, heat flashing through his dark, midnight eyes.

And for the first time in decades, Kelsey felt it, the sexual pull of a vampire. And his was like no other she had ever felt, running over her skin like a hand covered in raw silk, tweaking her nipples, dipping between her thighs to pluck at her clit and thrust inside her cleft. A ragged sigh left her lips and she blinked, once, twice, slowly.

"Don't," she whispered. He'd done it on purpose, dropping the shields he always kept up, those he had to keep up, otherwise, women would flock around him in droves. As a witch, Kelsey was more immune. As a powerful witch, even more so.

No vampire, not Eli, none had done this to her for more than three decades.

Malachi's eyes remained on her face as he reached out and stroked his thumb across her lip. Kelsey shuddered, her entire body going liquid and soft as moisture gathered in her pussy. Gathering her focus, she reached up and flattened her hand in front of her, just an inch in front of the rather magnificent chest he displayed as he moved closer, lowering his head, his mouth hovering just above hers.

"I said don't," she said, more harshly.

An unreadable smile curved his lips. What drove him, she didn't know. But Kelsey wasn't about to fall into bed with this vampire. She wasn't getting addicted to him. She had too much going on, too much and too many depending on her.

Heat flooded from her, through her. Sunlight may not affect him, but fire would.

Malachi disappeared.

Reforming on the other side of the room, his eyes wide and furious, his fangs down as he glared at her. Fire still hovered over her palm. "I said don't. I don't say things I don't mean, Malachi."

"I've killed for less than that, witch." The menace rolling off of him had the blood in her running cold.

"I don't believe you're willing to kill a fellow Council member," she said softly, tossing the ball of flame back and forth in her hands, eying him warily.

"I'll kill any damn soul who tries t' touch me w' fire. I don' bloody care who he or she is." He studied her as she tossed the flame in her hands, as though trying to figure out if she was going to lob it at his face. "Council member o' not. Woman or not. I've done it before, and dealt with the consequences later."

Kelsey had no doubt he meant it. None at all. But showing her fear would only further arouse the creature in him that craved blood and battle. No matter how good his soul, he was a predator. "Perhaps you should keep your hands to yourself, then. A woman wouldn't be forced to defend herself."

His face went blank. It was almost comical.

"Are ya tellin' me that I was forcin' my advances on you?" he snapped, stalking closer. Like a door was slammed, the menace he exuded was sucked back inside him, along with the sexual call. All he exuded now was pure and simple anger and righteous indignation.

"Damn right."

"And you would burn me, even though fire is death to a vampire, for darin' to touch that pretty mouth o' yours?" Malachi asked, his eyes narrowed.

His accent could go from being untraceable to pure Scots in seconds. And it was pure Scots when he was angered, she mused, shaking her head. "Get over it, Malachi. I knew you'd get away. I didn't believe for a second you'd burn. And you were doing more than touching my mouth. With the call you have, you were all but stripping my clothes off of me. And I already told you to stop. I don't want to sleep with you. I don't want to have sex with you. But with you touching me, how much choice would I end up having? It's about the same as date-rape."

Malachi snarled at her.

Smiling angelically, Kelsey said, "I'm not wrong. Am I? Wanting to have sex with you, would be me coming to you with you still shielding, and me asking you. Which, of course, is not why I'm here. I don't even know you."

He eyed her narrowly. "I believe you are quite the biggest bitch I've met in a very long time." After a moment of silence, a slow smile curved his mouth and he decided, "I think I rather like you."

Kelsey arched an eyebrow and said, "Well, I'm still not sleeping with you."

Heat rushed into Malachi's gaze and he studied her with hot intense eyes. "You will." Then he settled down on the chair behind him, watching her as she slowly pulled the flame back into her hand. "So, Kelsey Cassidy, Witch of The Council, why have you come?"

"I'm seeking information on the Scythe."

Chapter Three
The Underground

"You let him get away."

"Mistress, dere was a witch, young, pure, full of a clean and shining power, like none ya have ever seen. She hails from de Council and she shielded him, sliding in like a gossamer thing, but standin' between us like solid iron. It was her, just her. Otherwise, we would have had him."

She did not give voice to the doubt in her mind. The one of the man's power, of his innate goodness. The Mistress was so certain of this man, of the wolf, certain she could command him, and control the power of the wolf. But Leandra was not so certain. Not at all.

"I do not care if there were a thousand witches. You let my prey get away from me." She paced away from the three witches gathered in front of her, her hips swaying under the beaded belt she wore over her naked hips. Her long hair, blonde, lush and thick, fell in loose waves to her ass. Over her shoulder, she said coldly, "You shall have to find a way to compensate me for this loss. If not with his body, then with your blood. I shall give you time to think of a way to deliver him. If you fail this time, prepare to offer up your blood in payment."

Her voice was the pure, clear bell of a young girl's, sweet, innocent, charming. Gazing around the room, she beckoned to one man and then curled against his chest after he came and pulled her to him, cuddling her. She rolled her hips against him, pouting a bit. She had been anticipating the coming of the Wolf. *The Scythe* had long awaited the coming of the Wolf.

She had been craving his coming, craving the wild wicked power she sensed burning under his skin, had longed to feel his tall golden body under her, at her command. Her core wept and ached and she wanted to scream in frustration. She'd not be fucking him tonight.

Possibly not any night soon.

Her ladies-in-waiting had failed her. Leandra had never failed her before, so she'd give her another chance, but damn it. She *wanted* Jonathan.

Directing them a chilly look from her icy blue eyes, she said, "Go now. And prepare to fetch me my wolf. Do not fail me again."

The oldest of the three ladies bent low, her long black braids caressing the leader's feet before she turned, her trim, naked bottom swaying as she led her two sisters away.

Turning her eyes to the man who held her, she licked her lips and smiled, a sweet, pleasant smile that belied the evil in her eyes. "I ache."

He smiled in return as she pushed him to his knees in front of her. "I'll soothe all your aches, Mistress. All those, and more."

Jonathan stalked out of the house. The effects of the mark on his side weren't lessening.

All he had to do was think of her and he could feel her, almost see through her eyes what she was doing.

He had thought of her just now, and what she had been doing had shaken him to his core. She had been in the shower, but her mind hadn't been on hygiene. Unless she was very concerned about washing her sweet little cleft extremely well, since she was holding the handheld spray full-force against her pussy. The pulsing and pounding of the water on her clit had her sighing raggedly as she trembled through her climax.

Hunger, lust, and power shuddered and slid through him, a dangerous mix with the full moon not far away. Flexing his hands, Jonathan waited until he was sure he could control it before he opened his eyes. The werewolf, the animal inside him, hadn't controlled him since he had been young, not since his teens. Eli had seen to that, had saved him from becoming one of the ferals.

With the power of the Wolf being as strong in him as it was, the wildness could have overpowered Jonathan at some point, if he hadn't learned the precious gift of control.

In the dream paths, he had learned control—from the Wolf, and to control the werewolf. They were not one and the same, not completely. The werewolf's power was what gave him the shifting abilities, it was the beast inside him, and it stemmed from the Wolf, that lupine creature that lived inside his soul. The werewolf though, it was more basic. The urge to hunt, to run, to *mate*.

From Eli, he had learned control of himself and the demons that haunted him.

He wouldn't lose it now.

Lori studied the vampire in front of her with wary eyes. He had been here before. She'd had little contact with him then. He'd avoided her. Right now, he was studying her with dark, ancient eyes. Yeah, she had heard stories about him, but the actual vampire was something she couldn't have prepared for.

Intimidating wasn't quite the word.

His eyes were wise, deep and ancient like nothing Lori had ever experienced.

And sad. Sadder than anything Lori had ever known. Shaking that feeling off, she turned and looked back at Kelsey—the safer of the two—and tried to throw off the odd discomfiture that being around Malachi caused. Kelsey smiled easily. "Don't worry, honey. He has that effect on a lot of people. You actually are handling it better than most," Kelsey said, tossing Malachi a bland look.

Lori arched her brows. She would have said something but an odd ripple raced down her spine. Jonathan. He was coming.

Turning her head, she eyed the door. "Jonathan's coming. They're looking for him, for some reason. They want a wolf, but not just any were. Him in particular."

Malachi eyed her appraisingly. "How do you know he is coming?"

"I can feel him. I took their mark away, but it wouldn't completely heal. I had to leave something else in its place. My mark."

Kelsey nibbled her lip. "We can't be sure this is the same sort of people that Malachi wiped out before."

"Either way," Malachi said slowly, his deep voice throbbing with anger. "They pose a threat."

Something flickered in Mal's eyes and he glanced at Lori. "I hear your wolf now. Odd, he is just now approaching the house. I can smell him. He is disturbed, hungry, frustrated. Yet, you knew he was coming before I did. Remarkable."

"I can feel him. I've been able to feel him since the mark. I don't know if it will last, but all I have to do is think of him." She wondered what would happen if they thought of each other at the same time, and then she decided it would be wise if they didn't find out as Jonathan came into the room and his gaze moved to hers, slid over her face, down her neck and roamed over every visible inch of her body, tightening her skin, making her breathing ragged.

Her nipples tightened and cream flooded her pussy. A sharp, sudden intake of breath let her know that Malachi was well aware of the situation. Blood rushed to her cheeks. *Hell.*

But she couldn't take her eyes from Jonathan as he stalked over to a chair and curled his long, lean body into it. His eyes never leaving her face until he had settled into the chair. Once he had claimed his spot, he flicked his eyes briefly to Malachi before looking at Kelsey.

"Milady," he murmured, inclining his head to her gallantly and smiling warmly. "You look lovely as always. I hate that my sorry tail is what had to bring you for another visit."

"I'm not," Kelsey replied cheekily. "You've got such a fine one. I never regret having a chance to check it out." She wagged her brows at him teasingly before leaving her perch on the window seat and walking over to him. Kneeling in front of him, her jeans stretching tight over her thighs, Kelsey grinned up at him. "Jonathan, I swear, you're about the sexiest thing I've laid eyes on in ages. I've just got this thing about being a cradle robber."

He flashed her a wicked grin. "Doll, nobody needs to know you're in your fifties. I wouldn't know if you hadn't told me." As they flirted back and forth, she intertwined hands with him, her eyes going cloudy as she read him, searching inside him.

He had a darkness inside him, but it was his own darkness, his own demons, nothing evil. Nothing treacherous. There was no sign of anything evil taking root in him, like Lori had described.

But there had been. As Kelsey searched inside him, she found it, the empty, hollow core where something had been forced into him the night he had gone patrolling. Kelsey relived it, forcing him through it with her, the Hunt, the kill, the trap, the fight. A woman all in black launching herself at him, a grim, blank look in her exotic amber eyes as she lashed at him with a knife, not to kill but to cut.

And a tattoo on the outer corner of her left eye.

A Scythe.

Opening her eyes, she smiled into Jonathan's and murmured, "So, when are you going to talk me into it?"

"Baby, I've been talking my best talk for years. And you keep turning me down flat. I just can't handle that kind of rejection anymore." Both of them were breathing slightly harder, and smiling raggedly at each other.

Tossing Lori a look, Kelsey said, "You did a good job, hon. No trace, no sign of them anywhere. They won't be able to take him, mark him, call him at all. I'm sure that is going to infuriate them. They'll try something else, and soon."

"I want to know who they are."

Malachi asked quietly, "Isn't that why Kelsey dragged me here? I thought you had some questions for me, young witch. If not, then, I want to leave."

Lori slid Malachi a look and asked, "Who are the Scythe?"

Malachi's entire face went cold and blank. He gave Kelsey an odd look. "The Scythe?"

"She asked me. I know the laws. I told her nothing of them. She asked, so I would think it would be wise for you to tell her."

"The Scythe were destroyed a millennia ago. Their knowledge and how they were formed, their history and all they knew were eradicated with them. I saw to it. Now, how did you even hear of them?"

"They marked Jonathan," Lori said in a hushed voice. "They have been haunting his steps, and our enclave for months. They were the ones who marked him. And I have a terrible feeling they are the ones behind the dead Vampire Masters."

Malachi looked at Kelsey. Slowly, he rose from his seat and moved over to where she still knelt by Jonathan. Going to one knee beside her, he laid his palm on her face and stared into her eyes, his own eyes glowing with an eerie, pulsing blue light as he looked into hers.

Kelsey opened her mind to him and shared what she had seen in Jonathan's mind.

And by the look in Malachi's eyes, she knew he was not happy.

Chapter Four

Malachi sat on the roof of Eli's house, staring at the moon, his mouth grim. The wind tugged at his hair, blowing his clothes around his large frame as he listened to the night. He could see Jonathan as he left his cottage. The were could sense him out, something that rather surprised Mal. Very very few should have been able to feel his presence, besides the land's Master. How very surprising.

There had to be something extraordinary about that were for these dark bastards to want him.

He was a powerful were. Eli had rescued him from what would have been a certain death, Mal knew. When the changes came upon Jonathan, they had been powerful enough to drive him mad. Eli had saved him. He had brought the half-mad adolescent home after a night of killing and locked him in the cage in his house, calling Europe to find whoever could help control somebody with such a powerful Call of the Wolf.

Malachi had come, bringing with him Tavis, the most powerful were the Council had.

But even Tavis was overshadowed by the power he saw lurking in Jonathan's eyes. Jonathan had power that rivaled that of an inherent. He would change at will, once he gained control, and might even learn to ignore the call of the moon.

The Call of the Wolf was so strong in the beginning that it had nearly driven him insane. And the werewolf's call, the animal inside him, was madness itself.

"You can give in to the madness now, and become a killer, which means we will hunt you down and kill you, or you can become something more, something better." Eli had stood at the iron bars staring at Jonathan's blood-covered form, his skinny, nude body crouching on the floor like the animal he was about to become.

His dark eyes were rabbiting around the room, furious and half-wild. He remembered the night before. Remembered the blood, the killing. None of those he had killed had been innocents though. His father had lost too much money, but wanted to keep gambling. So he had offered Jonathan in payment.

Jonathan's fear had been what induced the change. As two men had laughingly taken him struggling to the ground, he had shifted for the first time. In a house out on the lake in West Virginia, secluded, away from anything and everything, he had feasted on the flesh and blood of men.

When, instead of a boy's terrified, pain-filled screams, the men upstairs had heard an animal's ferocious roars and blood-curdling screams, the other five men rushed downstairs. Not one of them ever saw the light of day again.

"The men you killed deserved death, well and truly. But if I let you leave here, without you knowing how to calm the beast that has roused within you, you will fall upon an innocent, and that will scar your soul," Eli murmured, kneeling down and watching the boy with sad eyes.

"Wouldn't you rather prey upon monsters such as you destroyed last night, those who would destroy the innocent? Or do you want to become a monster?"

Malachi's heart, so jaded and cool, had broken a little, as Jonathan had looked up through a tangle of filthy hair and hissed, "I already am a monster."

"No, boy," Mal said softly. "You're a gift. You *have* a gift. To defeat those who prey on the innocent. If that's what you choose."

Eli waited until the boy stopped rocking and looked up at them again before he said quietly, "Those men you killed last night will never rape another child. Can you tell me that you regret that?"

"*No*. I want to do it again. And again."

Malachi looked over at Eli and said quietly, "You have another Hunter in your enclave. And what a young one, he is."

Malachi jerked himself out of his reverie and watched as Jonathan disappeared into the woods. That had been more than ten years ago. Not a long time, no, but the boy had certainly changed. He had fully achieved his potential and then some.

His body had the witch's scent through and through. And he watched her with the eyes of a wolf guarding his mate.

The part of Mal that just liked to pull a tiger's tail, or in this case—a wolf's, made him want to find the pretty little witch and see just how easy it was to make her purr. And he imagined she purred rather nicely when stroked the right way. A gleam made his eyes glow brightly in the night for a moment as he pondered it, watching the spot where he had last seen Jonathan.

You are up to absolutely no good, mate.

A smile crooked his mouth. "Hello, Eli," he said into the darkness. "I didn't know you knew I was here."

This is my land, my home. I am Master here. Of course, I knew. The dry sarcasm in his friend's voice made him want to laugh, but Malachi just smiled. "You have trouble brewing here, lad. Ye'd best be comin' home. If ye knew what is good for ye."

It cannot be that bad, Eli replied. There was the impression of a shrug and a dismissal. *Nothing feels wrong. If things were wrong, I would know.*

"An old evil has returned, lad. I canna tell ya how, because I don't know th' answer to tha' meself," Malachi said with a sigh. "But it is here, all th' same. And they want Jonathan, with a dark passion."

There was a stillness from Eli as the younger vampire realized how serious Malachi was. *Jonathan is no easy target. He may court trouble, but he doles it out just as well.*

"Aye, I believe that, I do. But he canna fight an army of evil. Weel, it may not be th' whole army. There is jes' one woman who will want him. If we kill her, her ladies-in-waitin' will die with her. She will have blood-bonded with them, and her death is theirs. But an army of darkness is rising, and they have already made th' first strike, lad. Th' Masters we have lost dinna die o' pure chance, nor freak accident. They have been assassinated."

Eli's rage started to surface and Malachi stood. "Ye need to be comin' home. I'll no' be going anywhere soon. But you are Master here. Come home, Eli."

I am already leaving.

Lori lifted her eyes as a presence disturbed her.

There was no sound, no change in the air, no scent. Nothing. But she wasn't alone in her chambers anymore.

Running her eyes over the room, she sighed and said softly, "Malachi, these rooms are spelled against everybody but Eli. I don't know how you managed to slide under them, but show yourself."

Her brows rose as the mist pooled in a slow spiral, forming so that he was settling at her feet, with his arm draped across her lap. A long, deep-red braid, shades darker than her own, even darker than Sarel's, spilled over his shoulder as he stared up into her face. "Caught me, didn't you?" he murmured.

His accent was so impossible to place. Earlier, he had sounded like he was from Scotland, but now…vaguely European, but nothing more. "What do you want?"

A rakish grin crooked his lips as his eyes trailed over her face, settling on her mouth. Lori felt blood rush to her cheeks and cursed herself as his nostrils flared. "Hmmm, well. What do you have to offer?" he asked teasingly, sliding his midnight gaze to her neck, settling on her pulse. In response, it flared and beat faster.

"Coffee, tea or brandy," she said tartly, pushing his arm off her lap and sliding away from him. His scent was stronger, had filled the room, and it was intoxicating, like something from the woods and fields of Ireland, the lochs of Scotland and Welsh moors. Lori had spent one long, wonderful summer there, and it had called to her, every bone in her body, just like his body was calling to her now.

Deep in her belly, heat pooled and she felt his call, banked and shielded, but she could feel it.

Sliding him a narrow look, she slammed shields of her own in place. Not all witches would be able to do it, and have a chance in hell of it working, but since she was a Healer, empathy ran strong in her. Blocking him out was something she *was* able to do. She saw the knowledge in his eyes as her shields clicked into place, firm and solid as a steel wall.

It wouldn't keep his sexual call out if he decided he wanted her, but at least she wouldn't have to feel that low level tug from him. "Hmmm, well, a wise little witch we have 'ere, don't we?" he mused, settling down like a big mountain cat, watching her with patient, amused eyes. "In all my years, only a handful have figured out that little trick."

With a smile, she replied, "I'll send out a memo."

"A memo?" he repeated, narrowing his eyes thoughtfully. "Ah, yes. A note. You're going to take all the fun out of my life."

Lori smiled a little sadly. "You have no fun in your life, Malachi. You're one of the saddest creatures I've ever seen. When was the last time you ever felt true joy, your own true joy, not something you experienced through another?"

His eyes flashed. The rage she felt explode through him had her blood running cold as he slithered up from the floor, leaning closer as his eyes started to glow and gleam, his fangs dropping down. "Watch your words, witch. I'll no' be havin' you analyzing *me*. Donna be forgettin' who I am…"

His hands closed around her waist and he pinned her against the chair, leaning up against her as he growled into her ear, "I smell fear, and woman. And witch…young hot witch…"

Lori's pulse rabbited in her throat as the menace filling the room grew to mammoth proportions. Bad mistake. Do not allow the big, ancient vampire to know you could feel his torment. Never, never, never…her eyes widened as he bent low over her face, his hands bringing her hips into contact with his pelvis as he rocked his cock, hard and swollen, against her belly.

Jonathan felt the menace flood his brain as he patrolled the perimeters of town. There was a drug deal going down. He needed to stop that.

A gang fight...

But Lori...

His fangs dropped, ripping through his gums as he turned and raced through the streets. Anger, rage, possessiveness gave his feet wings as he raced to the edge of town and shifted in mid-lope, from man to wolf-man to wolf in three long strides, tearing through the woods in moves faster than the human eye could track.

He had scented Malachi's torment even as he left home, just a few miles from town. Too far away. Springing into the trees, he shifted, and was half-wolven again as he caught the tree limb, climbing the trees that led up the cliff face.

Do not touch what is mine, Malachi.

Malachi's mouth hovered over hers, his hands lifting up the edges of her shirt as his body forced her back along the overstuffed top of the chair. Lori turned her head aside and snarled, "Damn it, Malachi, get off of me."

He laughed. "But I am lonely...needy. You are a Healer. Don't you wish to end my pain?" he mocked lightly, his voice belying the half-mad light in his eyes.

She had gotten too close, hit a little too close to home, and he didn't like being stripped bare, not by one so young, Lori realized. In all his years, it hadn't happened. None had ever realized his torment, and now he was all but naked with it. And he didn't like it.

"Loneliness is the curse of the vampire, Malachi. There is no shame in it," she said quietly, lifting her eyes to his.

"No. No shame. But in more than two thousand years, I canna find a heart mate. There is no love for me in this world. I am cursed to walk it alone," he purred roughly, moving away from her gaze, kissing the pounding pulse in her neck, raking it with his teeth but not breaking the skin. "So many, many women...yet not one who is *the* one for me. My shame...my shame is in fucking as many and as often as I can to take some respite from this aching loneliness. And now, I wish to add you to that list."

Lori's incredulous response ended in a gasp as his mouth closed around the tip of one breast, taking it deep. He had her arms locked behind her back, wrists held easily in one hand. Forcing the hot surge of need to clear from her mind, her loins, she said, "Stop it, Malachi. This isn't right. Not for me. And not for you."

"I canna care less," he murmured, lifting his head and studying his work. Her nipple was red through the sheer white cotton of her camisole. "'Tis right for me. For now...that is enough. And you are wanting, and needy. Isn't that enough for you? Besides, if ya truly didna want me touching you, why not scream for help?"

Lori's head fell back as a sound caught between a laugh and sob fell from her lips. His cock settled between her thighs, thick, hard, perfect. As he cupped and massaged her breast, working the nipple with his fingers, she forced the words out of her mouth. "If I scream, Eli's people—loyal people—will come rushing. Werewolves don't always think. They act. And how do I know you will not kill first? Those are my friends. And Rafe, Sheila, the other vamps in this enclave, they can't possibly fight you."

Malachi's lips quirked. "There is that." Of course, if she'd just scream...he'd stop. Though he didn't tell her that, she was *sooooo* sweet.

"I love Jonathan. *He* is right for me," she rasped, jerking against his hold.

Malachi lifted his head, meeting her eyes. "A noble thought, that."

Jonathan eyed the edge of the cliff, his lips peeling back in a snarl. Hot waves of lust, confusion and fear were flowing from Lori. He could feel them. And Malachi's hands, all over her. He lunged forward and raced over the grounds, covering the half mile that lay between him and Lori in a moment that flew by so fast he never noticed it, yet it dragged out forever.

He could hear them now…soft whispers of movement. Malachi's voice, then Lori hissing, "I love Jonathan." Jonathan leaped toward the windowsill and hauled himself up as Malachi replied, "A noble thought, that. Though the wolf doesn't see himself as worthy. He doesn't think himself worthy to serve the Council, so why would he see himself as worthy of your love?"

Jonathan gripped the windowsill and gathered himself, then lunged, flipping up and through her window, landing on his haunches, snarling at Malachi. Mal's eyes lifted from Lori's, though he didn't rise from his position, bent low over her firm, supple body where he held her over the back of a chair.

"Take your hands from her, Malachi, Hunter of the Council," Jonathan growled. His hands flexed, the glistening ebony claws catching and reflecting the light as he fought the urge to attack. "She doesn't want or welcome your touch. No man with honor trespasses so."

"Wolf, you are truly a brave soul to involve yourself where you cannot possibly win," Malachi mused, rising slowly, still keeping Lori hugged tightly against him. "She is a sweet thing, your mate. I canna help but crave a taste."

"I've no mate, vampire. But Lori doesn't want you, I feel it. And I wouldn't bet that I can't win. Every man must fall. Even the very ancient."

Malachi's eyes slid to Lori's face, suddenly so pale. His lips crooked gently. "He's a young fool, love. Give him time." Lowering his lips, he kissed her forehead gently. "I beg your forgiveness. My pride is bruised, such a young thing seeing so clearly through me. Those eyes can see much."

Jonathan snarled as the vampire's mouth touched that ivory skin, but Malachi turned glimmering midnight-blue eyes his way and said obliquely, "Young fools, old fools. We're both fools here tonight."

And then, he was gone.

Lori met Jonathan's eyes, her soft green ones, troubled and bruised. Her mouth was swollen from Malachi's, her nipples still erect, a damp spot on her shirt where he had been suckling on her.

"He touched you," Jonathan rasped, as he banished the wolf. He was kneeling naked on the floor, a ragged gasp hissing through his teeth as the change receded.

Rising, he stalked over to her, his nostrils flaring. He could smell another man's touch all over her, and rage twisted sharply through him. "His touch, his scent is all over you."

Lori said quietly, "What do you care?"

His lips peeled back from his teeth and he reached out, catching her against him, one arm at her waist, his other hand buried in her hair. "Do you want him to come back and finish what he started?"

"No. But you obviously do not want the scent on me to be yours, so why do you care whose scent is on me?" Lori asked, lifting her hands and pushing at his shoulders.

Jonathan stared down at her, breath heaving in and out of his lungs. Her hands, those slim, warm hands, so exquisitely soft, pushed against his shoulders, and her eyes glared angrily at him, and under the anger, was pain. Groaning, Jonathan leaned down, catching her face in his hands, pushing his tongue inside her mouth.

When she tried to turn her head aside, he stopped her. When she bit him, he bit her back, sinking his teeth into her lower lip and suckling at it until she whimpered and yielded to him. Her hands curled into his shoulders, her body softening against his in welcome. Pulling back, Jonathan rasped, "Take my hair, rub it against you," before bending low over her, kissing her neck, rubbing his cheek against her shoulder as he reached for the waist of her shirt, stripping it away.

Eli wasn't happy.

After settling down on the plane, he tapped his fingers on his thigh as Sarel told him what she had learned while he had slept. Her eyes, those golden green eyes, were weary, bruised, but snapping with the fiery light of battle.

The Scythe.

"They are the ones who attacked you seven years ago," Sarel finished, running her hand over the smooth skin where the bullets had ripped through him. "They nearly took you from me. They kidnapped my sister, and tried to kill Jonathan. And they've been exterminating the Masters, brainwashing the younger packs. We've been out battling our own people and waging war on them, because of these people. I know it."

"Aye," Eli murmured, taking her hand and lifting it to his lips. "We've a score to settle there, don't we, love?"

Drawing one leg up, he stared into the distance, focusing on his land. There was a strain there. New ones, old ones. But a weakening in the links that bound it to him.

"They are hunting Jonathan with a vengeance now, Eli," Sarel said quietly. "Agnes said something like it had happened once before. A young, powerful were with a dark past was converted. He led them on a bloodbath. They want him—his soul, his body."

"They cannot possibly hope to have him," Eli said smoothly, confidently. "Jonathan's heart is the purest I've seen, next to your sister's, perhaps."

Sarel laughed. "You're joking. That brooder? He's a warrior, yeah. But he has such a darkness in him sometimes, I'm amazed it hasn't overwhelmed him. I was surprised he was accepted into the Council." Her mouth firmed and she shook her head. "He is nothing like Lori. We will have to be on our guard with him. He could easily be swayed, if he was broken."

"Jonathan will die before he breaks," Eli said flatly, rising. He moved away from Sarel. "I know him, love. His soul has darkness in it, but he was tormented in his youth, even more than you. He battles that darkness daily. Of all in my enclave, I can see any of them breaking before Jonathan. He will not yield."

Sarel's eyes narrowed as Eli spoke. "Even me?"

Eli sighed, running a hand through his golden hair. Under his shirt, his muscles shifted and moved. "Love, you do not know Jonathan. The...power of magick is more easily corrupted. The power of the wolf, once bonded to the person's heart, it...it isn't. Jonathan's path is set."

"Then explain why we have had to kill entire packs of weres," she snapped.

"Because they were simply weres," Eli replied. "Jonathan is not simply were. He's been touched, and heavily, by the power of the Wolf. If you bothered to speak with him, or look at him, you would see. The Wolf only lays his touch where he sees fit, but once he lays his touch, he is bonded to that person. The Wolf and Jonathan are bonded. Jonathan is as likely to be corrupted as your sister, or as any true empath."

Sarel's eyes went flat and she folded her arms across her chest. Eli met her eyes squarely. "I'm sorry, love. Touch the wolf, let it touch you. Or talk with your sister, though you still insist on seeing her as a child."

Eli felt the ice settle in the cabin and he sighed, draping himself in a chair across from his wife, watching her with opaque gold eyes. But his trust in Jonathan was unshakeable.

And the were deserved to know that.

* * * * *

Leandra studied the pretty young child, her head bent low over her schoolwork as she flipped a page back and forth, lips pursed.

She had the wolf's scent in her room.

Though she lived in the main house, it was strong here. A picture of him hugging her, pictures of them riding horses together. That was where Leandra had first seen the child. She was watched closely, escorted to and from the private school she attended twenty miles away by guarded limo. Licking her lips, she decided this was it.

The way to draw him out.

The guarded limo would be a task. The weres who traveled with it weren't fools, or weaklings by any means. Which was why the Scythe had made sure to convert weres of their own.

But this was a task for their inherent.

Turning on her heel, she strode away. She caught the scent of sex on the air and smiled. With pleasure. She couldn't help it. She liked the wolf, his arrogance, his handsome face and form, his confidence.

Sometimes, the Mistress didn't deserve to have everything handed to her on a silver platter.

Tonight, the wolf was fucking all right. And Leandra was damned glad it wasn't Mistress.

Then she scrubbed those thoughts from her mind before they got her in trouble.

Erika glanced up, frowning. A cold feeling ran down her spine and she slid from her seat. Most would have gone to glance out the window. But she moved away. She resisted the urge though, to call out to Sheila.

There were monsters in the dark, she knew. In her twelve years of life, this was something she knew as fact. Monsters that ran on two legs as well as four, monsters that could grab you and pinch you and whisper terrible things, and then smile at your teachers the next day. Monsters that could be human or not, that could be a creature of magick or of human blood.

But the most revolting creatures were sometimes those standing right in front of her.

Like her own monster had been.

Jonathan had saved her from that, years ago. Uncle Jon, her best friend, her buddy.

This was her home now, and Jonathan was her adopted dad, though they had decided he was more like a brother, or an uncle. He was, simply put, her guardian angel, Erika thought. But she had stopped screaming out to him every time something spooked her years ago.

Squaring her shoulders, Erika settled down at her desk and went back to her calculus homework. She needed to finish this. She wanted to finish up early again this year. Jon and Eli had promised a surprise if she did well.

* * * * *

Lori gasped as Jonathan slid his hands down and cupped her ass, lifting her up against him, rocking his naked cock against her through the thin cotton of her pajama bottoms. She was wet, and felt him sliding against her, over and over her clit as heat pooled in her belly, tightening and tightening until she thought she'd go mad with it.

His mouth fastened on her nipple, where Malachi's had been only moments ago. "I want his taste gone from you, his scent. I do not share," he rasped, pumping his hips more forcefully against her. "If he had fucked you, I would have torn his head off."

Lori shuddered, even though her heart felt broken. *I've no mate...* Tears welled in her eyes against her will, and she turned her head as they burned hot, wet tracks down her cheeks.

His head raised, scenting her distress, and Jonathan lifted up. Gathering her in his arms, cuddling her against him and taking her to the floor, he held her in his lap. Cupping her cleft in his hand, he slid one finger back and forth over the erect little bud of her clit, murmuring against her face as he licked the tears away, "Why are you crying, sweet thing?"

"Because you don't *care*," she gasped, unable to still the hungry movement of her hips, even though she wanted nothing more than to tear away from him and lock herself in her room.

The slow, almost lazy movement of his finger circling her clit was driving her to distraction and Lori sobbed, her head falling back against his shoulder.

Her breath left her in a rush, as he savaged her lips. Her pajamas fell in shreds around her as he tore them off, tumbling her to her back and looming over her. Snarling into her face, he demanded, "Don't care? What in the hell are you talking about?"

"You don't want Malachi touching me. You may enjoy fucking me, but that's about all you feel for me," she sobbed. Between her thighs, his erection throbbed, and she sobbed as he settled between them, his chest crushing her breasts.

"That's all?" he repeated, his face going blank. Then his eyes narrowed as he caught her hands and pinned them above her head, the corded muscles in his arms bulging as he leaned over her. "I left patrol because I felt your fear, your confusion, and your lust...yes, your lust. You wanted him even though you didn't want to. I left patrol and ran here to keep him away from you. *Malachi*. Most people would think that's enough to have me certified simply for squaring off against him. But I would fight to the death to keep him from burying himself in your sweet body, and you think I don't care?"

With one savage thrust, he buried himself in her pussy, growling with pleasure as she enveloped him eagerly, a hungry cry falling from her lips, her body arching up as he burrowed in to the balls. "Little fool," he rasped, capturing her head and forcing her eyes to meet his. "Open your mouth, I want your taste."

Glaring up at him, Lori stubbornly closed her lips and lifted her chin.

He bared his teeth in a grin, and whispered, "A wolf loves a dare, baby. You ought to know that by now."

Lori quivered deep inside her belly as he started to pump in and out of her cleft with slow, deep thrusts. His hand still held her wrists pinned high over her head, as he rubbed his chest, his hair, his entire body against hers, replacing Malachi's scent with his own, he lowered his mouth to hers, nibbling away, licking at the seam of her lips. One hand slid down the long line of her side, cupping her ass for a moment before clasping her knee and lifting it up, opening her wide for his thrusts.

The long silken skeins of his hair slithered over her body, teasing her nipples, her torso, all the bared inches of skin as he released her wrists and settled back on his heels, gripping her hips and staring down at her with hooded eyes. The play of muscle under skin as he moved deep inside her had her eyes fluttering wide. Drawing her forward, he draped her thighs over his, and with a roll of his hips, Jonathan had her shuddering as he surged upward into her, his cock caressing the bundled nerve bed of her G-spot. His teeth raked the cord in her neck and he crooned, "Sexy little witch. I love the feeling of being buried in your wet little pussy. You're so tight, so hot, like a silk glove, all wet and covered with honey. I'm gonna lick that honey dry in a bit…but first…I'm gonna make you scream."

A sigh escaped her lips and Jonathan's mouth swooped down on hers, plundering the depths triumphantly, rampantly as he started to fuck her with deep, hard strokes. Her spine arched as his fingers breeched the seam of her ass, separating her, exposing the pucker of her rosette. Cream from her pussy was sliding lower, coating her, and Jonathan gathered it, sliding it around and around, until he could probe that tender hole easily, a caress that had her shaking, quivering, while heat and chills racked her body.

The broad, rounded head of his cock left her sheath, stroking over her clit teasingly, and Lori threw her head back, screaming. Jonathan pushed his finger into the tight little pucker of her anus and surged back into her pussy, sinking his teeth into her lower lip as she came.

Growling in savage triumph, Jonathan bore her back down onto her back, pumping into her, he rode her hard, grinding his pelvis against her clit as she came, and Lori saw hot little flashes of light as her vision went dark. Hot splashes of come scalded her as Jonathan ejaculated and Lori whimpered, shaking in his arms. His balls slapped against her in a rough, quick caress as he reared up, planting his hands beside her head and thrusting with a series of hard, deep drives into her sheath, his head falling back as his mouth opened and a long, eerie howl filled the room.

To Lori's ears, it was the most beautiful song she'd ever heard.

He collapsed against her with his head between her breasts, sliding his arms under her and holding her against him. "Don't ever cry because you think I don't care," he panted out. "Hate me because I won't make promises, if you have to. But I do care. More than I want to."

Lori wanted to know why he wouldn't make promises. She really wanted to ask him that.

But she let it go, snuggling against him as he carried her to the bed, laying her down and spreading her thighs. Pressing his face against her and sliding his tongue between her folds, he shocked her speechless as he cleaned the seed from her pussy, her thighs, before returning to suckle gently on her clit, working two gentle fingers inside her slippery, swollen sheath.

Lori's eyes fluttered closed in heavenly bliss as he took her to a slow, lovely orgasm that welled inside and lingered, melting through her veins like candy. He moved up and lay on his back, growling against her neck as he draped her body over his, "You are so damn sweet, so pretty and soft. I think of you, yearn for you, all the time."

Tears burned her eyes as he steadied his cock and whispered roughly, "Ride me, sweet. I want to watch you."

Catching her lower lip between her teeth, she worked herself down on his swollen, engorged length, staring into his dark, deep eyes, her hands planted on his chest, nails digging into the sleek, golden skin there. Rolling her hips slowly, she shuddered as she felt him throbbing inside her, the thick blunt head of his cock caressing the nerve bed by the mouth of her womb. Her lashes fluttered and she moaned weakly. "Oh..." licking her lips, she stared down at him and lifted her hips slightly before sliding back down on him.

It sent a lightning streak of hot pleasure through her, and she shuddered before repeating it, arching her back and leaning forward to deepen the caress on the upstroke.

"Sweet thing," Jonathan purred gruffly, reaching up to cup her breasts in his hands, rolling her nipples, plucking at them, as he stared up at her face. His eyes had started to glow, gleaming and swirling with colors of gold and brown as his hunger grew. His hands flexed against her breasts, his nails scoring her lightly as he arched his back, driving his cock deeply inside her.

"Hmmm," Lori hummed in her throat, her head falling back. "I like that." The air in the room grew thicker, and Lori stared into his eyes, watching as the glowing increased and his eyes continued to brighten. "Jonathan?" she whispered, shakily.

"Shhh..." he murmured, reaching up and burying his hand in her hair, pulling her face to him. "It's all right. I feel your magick, your heart—it's intoxicating."

Magick was breaking free, rising from her skin like faerie dust and evaporating into the air, lighting up the dim room with occasional puffs of light. The magick from her, the power from him, tightened the air in the room, and the bond between them—tighter and tighter—as Jonathan thrust deeper and deeper, while Lori rocked against him. Sealing her lips eagerly to his, she pushed her tongue into his mouth, greedy for that unique, wild taste that was his alone.

His cock pulsed and throbbed—hot, burning—and her nipples stabbed into his chest...so much sensation...too many focus points of pleasure. Jonathan reached down and stroked the small puckered rosette of her bottom, and Lori arched her back and screamed as he pressed against it, her belly and loins tightening.

The muscles in her pussy clenched around his cock, milking it greedily as she came, shuddering in his arms and thrashing when he sank his teeth into the fleshy part of her breast and growled. Gripping her hip with one hand and holding her still, he ground his pelvis against her, arching up and jetting off inside her—hot, molten seed flooding her womb.

As she collapsed against his chest, she closed her burning, tearing eyes. No. She couldn't keep doing this.

Something this beautiful and he wouldn't let them have it for always. Wouldn't let them claim it as *theirs*. She wouldn't hate him for not making her promises.

But she might start to hate herself for not demanding it.

Chapter Five

Jonathan sat across from Erika, grinning at her as she chattered away. His adopted daughter was the one person in life he made promises to, the one person he allowed himself to love.

His eyes wandered briefly to the ceiling. The other female he loved was upstairs, silent and still. His sharp ears knew she hadn't left the bed yet.

Yeah, he loved her. But he would never tell her. Especially not now. And he couldn't ever touch her again. The wolf wanted to claim her as his mate, his one and only.

Dragging his attention back to Erika, he shrugged when she asked about a shopping trip. "Don't see why we can't. You've been doing great in school, and you always help out and do your chores. Shelby says you're wonderful out in the stables." He couldn't understand that particular fascination himself, but Erika adored the horses. "We'll go this weekend."

"I kinda wanted to go with some friends," Erika stalled. "Just friends."

"No can do." Rising from the chair, he carried his bowl and plate to the sink and dumped them before turning around and facing her across the gleaming expanse of the kitchen. Folding his arms across his chest, he met her eyes. "We've talked about this, honey. You're twelve years old. A brilliant twelve, but still twelve. Walking around a mall alone is not wise. Especially not now. We've got some new trouble brewing and it isn't gonna happen."

"Jonathan, I can't go shopping with friends with my big brother around! It just isn't cool," Erika sulked, poking out her lower lip and aiming her baby-blues his way as she sat back in her chair, suddenly completely forlorn.

"Then we'll have one of the ladies go with you. Hell, it is winter. Wait until five and Sheila can take you."

Erika's brows lifted and she perked up a bit at that. None of her friends knew a darned thing about her life, or any of her odd...housemates. Just the thought of taking a vampire with her to go shopping would be totally...*bitchin'*.

Jonathan shook his head as the thoughts rolled through her eyes. Those pretty eyes were always so open, so easy to read. "Think about it. Sheila would love it. Or I can ask one of the ladies. And Sarel is going to be back sooner than expected. Maybe she could do it."

Hell, if things were as bad as Malachi was suggesting, it wouldn't surprise him if Tori and Declan came strolling up the walk.

His lips curved at the thought of Tori.

Okay, there was one other female he let himself love.

But she was safe. Not only did she belong to somebody, the Huntress was more than capable of taking care of herself.

Tori held down the struggling, snarling *were* and flashed fang at him. "That's not very nice. You're as good as dead and you know it," she said when he attempted to gouge out her eyes before she managed to get his hands pinned. Whipping out the reinforced cuffs, she cuffed him and sat on his chest, drawing a long, nasty looking silver blade from behind her neck and flashing it at him.

"You know, Cooper, I've been Hunting you for a month now. You led me and Declan on a merry, merry chase," she said quietly, shaking her head. "So many deaths, so many shattered lives, battered bodies. You like them young and pretty, don't you, Coop?"

He spat at her.

Declan moved up from behind and knelt by the man, offering Tori a handkerchief as he said, "Now that was just plain not nice. Don't go doin' something so rude again. You knew the risk you were takin', and you knew the consequences when you left your pack and went rogue. Cuss and fight all ya want. But ya had best watch how ya carry yourself with my wife."

"With your bitch, you mean," Cooper Manning panted, his blond curls spilling into his face as he bucked and struggled uselessly. The one hundred thirty pound woman on top of him wouldn't be budged. And her scent...damn it, her scent was intoxicating. Scared as he was, frightened as he was, furious as he was...he was also damn near drunk with hunger for her. "Is she a good piece of ass? When I get outta these damn cuffs, I'm gonna gut you, and find out for myself, fucker."

Declan's face went blank and he bent to pull Tori away but she batted at his hands laughingly. "Now, now, Declan. He's just pissed because he got caught by a girl." Leaning down, she asked, "Is that it? Do you have a superiority complex?"

He lifted up as though to bite her, and she drew back quickly. A mark on his cheek, no...by his eye, right at the corner, caught her eye. Something curved, like a crescent. "Nice tattoo," she mused. "I didn't think the were could take tattoos very well."

Declan's eyes caught it too. "We don't. Unless it's helped out by magick. We heal too fast, and our bodies reject the ink. What's this for, Cooper?"

Tossing his head back, laughing, Cooper said, "Oh, wait. You're gonna see, very soon."

"You like stars and moons, puppy dog?" Tori jeered, leaning down in his face as menace started to flow from her, a frightening menace that rolled from her body in waves.

His eyes widened and a cold sweat broke out on his body as those pretty blue eyes started to look like what they really were. His death.

"It's not a moon, love. A scythe, it is, for harvesting." Cocking his head and staring at the suddenly frightened man, Declan smiled charmingly. "You look like you've seen a ghost, mate. Tell me, what have you been harvesting? Or were you harvested?"

His eyes rolled back wildly in his head as he moved his gaze from the woman on his chest to the man standing behind her. He had thought the inherent was the one to fear, not the woman. What was she anyway? Human? Inherent? Not vampire...couldn't be. She had tracked him during the day, too many times.

Tori smiled, gently, sweetly, leaning into his face as she caught his thoughts. Her gifts had grown over the years, expanding and developing to dimensions she had never dreamed. His jumbled, skewed thoughts weren't easy to keep track of, but she did it well enough. Smiling, nose-to-nose with him, she whispered, "I am what I am, Cooper. And you should have stopped when I gave you the first warning, darling." Stroking his face, rubbing her finger over the mark by his eye, she purred, "Now tell me, what is this?"

"It's your downfall. The end of the Council," he snapped. "The Scythe has gathered, and rejoined. We're amassing before the coming of the Huntress. We band together and form our own army, we will infiltrate the Council and swallow it whole. We will annihilate it and feast on the blood of the newborn Huntress before she takes her first kill."

"Oh, really?" Tori laughed, sitting up. Her hair tumbled down her back in a fall of silken black as she started to laugh. "Darling, hasn't it dawned on you yet what I am?"

"*No,*" he rasped. "You cannot be. She foresaw it."

Tori smiled gently. Flashing fang at him, she softly whispered, "She was wrong."

And then she lunged for his throat, as Declan turned away, refusing to watch.

He hated to see the arousal it gave her to feed off a man other than himself. Even if it was to dole out a death sentence ordered by the Council.

Tori spat out the first mouthful of blood, rising slowly, her face pale. There was none of the normal rush that came from giving out righteous death. Declan heard her movements as the man scrambled away, staring up at her with shocked eyes. "Don't you have the guts to finish it?" he hissed, his voice garbled as blood pumped from the ragged hole in his throat.

Turning, Declan stared at her, frowning.

"Your blood is tainted," she said flatly, reaching up and wiping her mouth with the back of her hand.

"Then I will heal…and live. No matter where…ahhhh…you put me, they will find me and…free me…"

Tori laughed harshly. "Idiot. You cannot heal from my bite. The bite I give in death never heals. You are already dead. You are just too damn stupid to realize it," she said, running her tongue over her teeth and gathering spit in her mouth. Turning her head, she spat again, shuddering at the corroded, foul taste in her mouth.

"Weres can heal…anything…short of silver."

Declan knelt by the man's head and gave a thoughtful, "Hmm." Glancing up at Tori, he said, "Odd, then. You'd think this silly little vampire bite would be closing by now. That he could be standin' up o' his own free power instead of pumpin' more and more o' his lifeblood onto the ground. You look a bit pale, girl. Some water, that's what you need."

A brief smile curved her lips. Ever the lighthearted one, her lover. Sliding the dying were a look, she shrugged. "I can wait. Let's finish this first."

Cooper was starting to realize his body wasn't healing, wasn't getting stronger. Struggling weakly, he rolled his eyes to Declan. "What…what did she do to me?"

Declan smiled, slashes appearing in his lean cheeks, his hair tumbling into his dark green eyes. "She is the Huntress, creature of legend, a woman like none ya have ever seen before. Her bite is deadly t' those o' your like, Cooper. You'll never see another sunrise, mate."

"*No*." Even in death, he refused to believe it.

"Why do you refuse t' believe? And how do ya even know of the legends?"

"The Scythe amass…before the Huntress. That is how…we will…prevail…" blood bubbled up from his lips and he started to cough. Declan settled back on his heels, watching as death took him.

"Go to the devil, you evil bastard," he said quietly when the man's breathing stopped.

"Who is the Scythe?" Tori asked, a frown on her face as she watched Declan remove the cuffs from the body. Catching them, she slid them back into her waistband, watching with blank eyes as he moved things away from the body.

Burning this one. *Well, it's better than watching him cut the heart out.* Too much of Tori was still far too mortal.

Declan tossed her a glance and lifted strong, broad shoulders as he stalked around the body, making sure nothing could be traced to them. Of course, Tori McAdams and Declan Reilly had died a few years ago. He had, regretfully, seen to that, once he realized how badly they were needed by the Council. Completely by the Council.

It had just taken some fancy computer work, and some money—rather a lot of money—to erase certain details from the computer files. Nothing was foolproof, no matter what the FBI thought, no matter what anybody thought. Declan O'Reilly's fingerprints had been replaced with somebody else's, as had Tori's. They had new identities, new passports, new everything.

And each other. Always each other. "Never heard of them, darlin'. I'll be calling Eli. I'm not sure if he's home from Scotland though. Maybe he's heard of the Scythe, whatever or whoever they are."

"Agnes may know. Or Sarel."

"They may," Declan said with a nod. "Can you fetch me the petrol?"

"Gas, Dec. It's gas. And I don't care to be a help to—oh, all right." She yielded as that flinty green gaze skimmed over and settled on her face. She really needed to get over this part of the job. They couldn't go leaving paranormal corpses intact, really.

And if they left too many of the predators they hunted, untouched except for her bite, sooner or later, people would start hunting *them*. Damn it, though, sometimes she felt like she was…well, Tori couldn't even explain it to herself.

She didn't like committing a crime to cover her Hunting. She didn't see the Hunting as a crime. It was justice. Vigilantism, yeah. But still, it was justice. And the police would have been slaughtered if they had gone after Cooper. And Declan wouldn't burn the whole building, just the body.

"Well, well, well, what have we got here, boys?"

In her thoughts, Tori hadn't paid that much attention to what lay outside the warehouse where they had cornered Cooper. The stink of his blood on her clothes, and in her mouth had tricked her nose a little, though not that much. She had simply not been paying much attention and now…she was smiling angelically into the eyes of three very big, very brawny men, dressed in worn biker-style jeans, one in a leather jacket.

He had spoken, eying her with hot, hungry eyes, not noticing the dark stain on her mouth, perhaps thinking it was lipstick. The rag on his head held back oily hair from his face, and he stank from a body not washed in several days. How she hadn't smelled it, well, Tori would now have her own ass to beat. And Declan would enjoy yelling at her thoroughly over this one.

"Looks like a little lady, all alone. Are you lonesome, sweet thing?" the second asked, laughing a little as he jabbed one of his friends in the ribs. His eyes had fastened on the breasts showing under her tank, the smooth expanse of naked skin, and as she met his eyes, he licked his lips and winked at her, reaching down to cup his crotch.

"No. Not at all. Why don't y'all go on about whatever you were doing and I'll finish up my business as well?"

"Business, huh?" Tall, Oily and Ugly asked, grinning nastily. "We're here on business, too. Meeting a friend right in there. You oughta come with us. We can have a…get together."

Oh, shit.

They had been meeting up with Cooper.

The third one still hadn't spoken. Meeting his glittering brown eyes, Tori felt a shiver run down her spine.

Not human…and as she watched, one lid dropped in an easy, friendly wink, as his mouth curved up in a smile. His body, tall and rangy, powerful, was clean under the rather ragged, filthy clothes, and as she took a deep breath, she scented it on him. Magick…and…*inherent*…narrowing her eyes at him, he mouthed the words, *Hello, Huntress.*

Well, either they had a new friend, or more formidable foe than they had been expecting. Smiling in challenge, she lifted her chin before looking back to Tall, Oily and Ugly before saying in a falsely coy voice, "I'm sorry but I've already got a date. I'm afraid I'll have to decline that *charming* offer."

Turning on her heel, she swayed back into the warehouse, ears pricked. She heard two sets of footsteps. The third, she did not. Of course, she really didn't expect to.

Declan didn't like the glitter in his wife's eyes. So he wasn't surprised to see there was no petrol in her hands.

She hadn't even moved five steps into the warehouse when he heard the others. Oh, he had heard them outside, and kept a good ear on the conversation, but, bloody hell, Tori could handle it. He was busy stripping the signs of Tori's fight away from Cooper. The skin under his nails, hair, all of that had to go.

But when two men rushed his wife…well, that was just more than a man could tolerate. Even when she did pivot, delivering a swift sidekick into the solar plexus of the first before squaring off with the second. A third hung back in shadow, not even glancing at the one who lay semiconscious on the ground.

"I'm not interested, Tall, Oily and Ugly," Tori chirped with that signature charm of hers, slowly raising her fists and squaring her shoulders as the second one slowed his rush, eyeing her narrowly.

Since his partner lay eight feet away, Declan didn't rightly blame him. Of course, Tori had also pulled her kick. She could have killed him.

"Mouthy little bitch, ain't ya?" he asked, laughing as he eyed her. In her tank and form-fitting pants, Declan knew she was a very delectable looking mouthful. But, well, the fucker had just called his wife a bitch.

Moving away from Cooper's corpse, Declan rolled his shoulders and suggested, "I'd be watching my tone if I were you, mate. That's my wife you're talking to."

Tori's lashes fluttered and she pressed her hand to her half-naked breast. "Oh, be still my heart. He always gets me weak when he gets protective."

As the six foot ex-cop moved into the light, the shaggy looking biker's face tightened, moving away from the lone woman. She wasn't looking like such a fun target anymore, but he still had four guys here, didn't he?

"No, you have three. And one of those three is just about unconscious, with broken bones," Tori supplied, smiling.

"Stop showing off, sweet," Declan said, shaking his head.

Now, confusion was starting to enter the man's eyes as he looked at Tori, and then looked beyond Declan and saw the corpse of Cooper. His eyes narrowed. "Was that your business partner for the night?" Declan asked. "I heard you talking. Sorry. We had a meeting with him before you did. It didn't end well for him."

Tall, Oily and Ugly was now getting pretty pissed, Declan decided. He slid his eyes to the man still in shadow. Nostrils flared as he studied him. There was something almost…familiar about that scent, the slant of those shoulders, the build. Friend or foe?

"C'mon out, Ben," Tall, Oily and Ugly shouted over his shoulder as he reached behind his back. But his hand never touched his gun. Of course, Declan never got close enough to stop him either.

He was at his shoulder, but Tori was behind him, with his arm shoved high between his shoulder blades, as she purred in his ear, "Don't. That would be such a bad, bad idea. I missed my dinner tonight, and even as filthy as you are, I'm hungry enough that I just plain don't care."

Menace was rolling from her now, and the man's eyes were wide with fear and confusion as he rolled his head over his shoulder, trying to see her face. But she was so small, he couldn't. Turning, he faced Declan.

Obligingly, Declan grinned, flashing a toothy display of his canines, much, much longer than they had been only a second earlier.

"Ben!"

"Oh, shut up," a deep, almost growling voice said from the shadows. Moving away from the door, and into the light, the third man said, "I've really no desire to help you get yourself out of this mess. Especially since the entire reason I was following you was to find Cooper. And he's dead as a doornail now."

Declan cocked his head, studying the man before him and feeling like he had been flung through time. Michael Cross...but no...his father, second lieutenant to Connor Reilly, had been one of the men who had been killed protecting him. Narrowing his eyes, he studied the powerful, rangy form, trying to remember. There had been a boy, just a babe, really, that William had secreted away to another pack. Where he'd be safe, both the boy and his mother, a pretty fae-looking witch who used to tell Declan stories.

"Benjamin Cross," Declan said quietly, shaking his head. "What a small, small world we live in. I'd heard you had joined the Council."

Lowering his head, the inherent nodded in acknowledgment to Declan as he moved around Tori, aware of how nervous he was making her by being at her back. "Yeah, a few years back, a big eerie vamp tracked me down. Malachi. Don't suppose you've heard of him, have ya?" he asked drolly.

"Bastard," Declan replied affably.

Ben chuckled. "Yeah. Well, I told him to go fuck himself. Then they sent this pretty little witch, Kelsey…well, her…I had a harder time saying no to. That, and duty called." With a sigh, he rubbed his hand over his chin and studied the sweating, swearing man as Tori forced him to the ground so she could glare at them without Tall, Oily and Ugly blocking her view.

"He looks a little petrified," Ben decided.

Declan laughed. "Why don't you put him out of his misery? You probably know his crimes better than we do, and my Tori still has a soft stomach."

"I do *not* have a soft stomach," Tori said as Ben and Declan later put out the flames.

"Of course, you do. That's one of the things I love about you," Declan whispered against her neck. Then he turned his eyes back to Benjamin and said, "We have to get out of here. We need to make some calls — but I would like to have you come. It's been a while…since I've talked with people who knew of my father."

Benjamin nodded as he scuffed the ashes with his shoes. "I was hoping…" he smiled rather sadly. "I don't remember Dad. I was too young to remember much more than how big he was, how full of life."

"He was an honorable man, big and funny. He loved ya, lad, and took me for rides on his back," Declan said as his eyes grew distant. Tori lay a hand on his arm, rubbing it gently.

Ben closed his eyes and sighed, shuddering faintly as he scrubbed his hands up and down his face. "The bastards that stole our fathers from us, all of them are dead, I know. But it isn't enough."

"It can never be enough. But we do what we can to keep people from poisoning other packs and robbing more children of their fathers, Ben. That's what we do."

Ben nodded slowly. "Duty, that's what called me here." He met Tori's eyes over the distance and studied her. "The Scythe— they thought they would gather before you came."

Tori eyed him narrowly. "What are you?"

He smiled, a rather, grim disturbing smile. "Something that the Scythe really didn't want running around. Any more than they wanted you." Lifting one hand, he stared into her eyes as a gleaming ball of fire formed, spinning rapidly in his hand. "For some reason, when a witch mates with an inherent, it seems to cancel out one gift or the other. But not always."

Tori stared, mesmerized, into the gleaming ball, as the fire seemed to thin out and become transparent, until she was staring into a golden orb, filled with faces of children, of women with lost, broken eyes, of young boys who wandered the streets, homeless, and then a place she knew. Excelsior.

Where the young and gifted went to be trained.

Then the Hall of the Hunters and Malachi, and another Hunter, vaguely familiar, Byron. Eli, so many faces. Agnes, Kelsey.

Then she and Miguel, the bloody bastard who had sired her, as he stalked the streets, taking down his prey and laughing at their terror. Swallowing, she tore her eyes away from the gleaming orb that had grown and grown until it was nearly half the size of a VW bug. "A witch. How can you be both a witch and a wolf?"

Through the gleaming golden-orange glow, she could barely make out his outline, though his voice, that deep growling voice, was powerful, almost palpable. "How can a woman be human and vampire? And smell of wolf as well?" he asked as the orb started to melt away.

"I am what I am. What the Council needs me to be. God has a habit of sending down what is most needed, when it's needed," he said, lifting one broad, heavily muscled shoulder as he studied her face, which Tori was certain was even paler than normal.

"God?" Tori repeated. "How quaint," she mocked lightly as she tried to steady herself. Hell, she was being a bitch.

"Yes, God. You believed in Him a few years ago," Benjamin said softly as he moved a little closer, studying her face with penetrating eyes. "Has a few years of Hunting changed that?"

Sliding his eyes to her husband, Benjamin said, "I think I'm disconcerting your wife."

"I'm thinking that you have a habit of doin' that to many folk," Declan said, moving up behind Tori and stroking his hands up and down her arms. "Tori doesn't...care for expediency. Tonight has been a night for it, and we've more yet to do."

"Hmmm. Indeed." Benjamin smiled slowly, almost sadly. "I lost that innocence a long time ago."

Chapter Six

Erika cuddled up in the limo for the drive, nibbling at the cinnamon roll Sheila had cooked during the night. Though she no longer ate, she still loved to cook, and Erika was a big fan of her cooking.

A crumb fell onto the romance novel she had sneaked out of Sarel's room and Erika flicked it away, glancing to make sure Mike wasn't paying attention. Her eyes caught something and her breath lodged in her throat. Mike glanced up, ever alert. "Okay, brat?"

Just before the silver bullet ripped through his shoulder. If he hadn't shifted position, it could have been his head. As they slowed at the intersection, Erika had seen somebody in the car next to theirs lower the window and aim...and now, they were rushing the limo.

Mike bellowed with rage, leaping for her and tucking her body protectively under his as he shouted to Brad, "Take off!"

But the bullet aimed at him hadn't missed, and he lay slumped over the steering wheel as his heart's blood pumped out of his chest.

Drawing from his boot the gun Eli had ordered all to carry, Mike rolled, working them back against the seat, waiting and calling out to Eli. But it appeared there wouldn't be enough time.

And Erika had no bond with any of them. No blood bond, no soul bond. She was just a sweet, innocent kid.

As the exotically beautiful face swam into his vision, he raised the gun.

"Put da gun down, wolf. I'll let ya live, so ya can tell Jonathan where to be findin' da girl. It's him we want."

"Fuck you," Mike rasped as he pulled the trigger.

Leandra swore into the darkness of the alcove as one of the clumsy idiots pressed too hard on the bullet wound in her side, tearing it and causing more blood to flow.

"You should have let me kill him."

"No. He is a warrior, protectin' his charge even in da face of death. No warrior should be killed like a sick dog. He deserves t' die in battle," Leandra said, lifting her gaze back to Vincent and staring him down. "And he will tell da tale t' Jonathan. Dat is our prey, not de girl."

"The girl is a pain in the ass, too much trouble. When can we dump her?"

Leandra narrowed her dark eyes. "She goes back to her home when Jonathan turns himself over. I fight honorable battles."

"You cling too much to honor. We are the Scythe, not the Hunters."

"I am a warrior," Leandra said, rising slowly, her leanly muscled body unfurling like a sleek cat's as she stalked over to glare up into Vincent's pale, angry face. "I fight with honor. I know whom I serve. Ya do not tell *me* how I fight me battles."

Slowly drawing the long wicked blade from the sheath at her back, she cocked her head, studying him, her amber eyes flashing in the flickering light. "Do ya understand me now, Vincent? I wouldn't want for there to be misunderstandin's between us over dis," she said. "I don't want dat."

"Don't threaten me, Leandra. I don't care what kind of Voodoo shit you know—"

A slow, cool smile curved her mouth up and she flexed her free hand, before curling the fingers in a slow, easy fist. "I am no Voodoo priestess, Vincent. Being from Jamaica doesn't make me a Voodoo priestess. I am a witch, born in de blood of it." As she spoke, she watched with clinical eyes as his face grew paler and paler as his air supply was cut off by the slow flexing of her hand.

Finally, as he started to get first red, and then blue, she opened her hand and he fell, gasping, to the ground. "Make no mistake, Vincent. I am a warrior, a witch. And I don't make threats. I do not need dem. And ya will not touch de girl. If ya do, or if any of de men do, I'll kill ya, nice...and slow," she purred.

Turning on her heel, she stalked away, catching the eyes of two of her ladies and nodding to the girl.

"Poor ting," she murmured, stroking her forehead as they brought the terrified little hellcat over. "It will be over for ya soon. Jonathan will come and I'll send ya home."

"Liar. Why would you?" Erika spat, struggling even though it was useless, jerking her arms, kicking at the knees of her captors and damn near catching one of them.

Leandra eyed Constantine narrowly when the woman went to jerk on the girl's hair for insulting Leandra. "I do not blame ya for not trustin' me. I wouldn't trust, either." Inclining her head regally, Leandra walked a slow circle around them, careful not to let them see how much the wound in her side bothered her. "But I do not lie. Ya will go home, little Erika. I am no child killer. I serve my Mistress. I seek only to destroy dat pathetic Council for de many lives dey ended, for tinking dey are so above sin, so above reproach. Dey are no better den da rest of us, yet dey hold our deaths in their hands."

Erika shook her head forcefully. "The Hunters are brave, and strong, and proud, you stupid...stupid...*bitch*." The word popped out and seemed to surprise the child as much as it surprised the women holding her, but Leandra just laughed. But she didn't stop her tirade. "They protect us, the people, from the monsters. If Jonathan hadn't saved me, my dad would have raped me. That's what the Hunters are there for. And you call him pathetic?"

And Leandra could only stare at her in shock when the girl had the nerve to spit at her.

Jonathan's hands were flexing, the nails darkening to black as the claws slid out from under his skin.

Mike lay pale on the bed, in pain, suffering, but not dead.

The silver was slowly working out of his system, and he would recover.

Brad was dead.

And Erika was missing.

Lifting his head, he met Malachi's gaze for one brief second before he rose, leaving the room.

Lori took a deep breath before turning and meeting Kelsey's eyes. "I'm going with him. If he does this alone, he won't come back alive. Erika will, but he won't. My gut is rather insistent on that," she said quietly as the other witch mixed up yet another poultice to press to the wound on Mike's shoulder to leech out the poison.

It had taken them far too long to get Mike out of the hospital. Far too long to convince them that he would recover better at home. Even the inherent Doctor who had taken over the case had had trouble convincing the emergency room physician who'd admitted Mike that he was an old family friend. Their network of people was vast, but sometimes…hell, the verbal acrobatics they had to perform to get one of their people out of a place was nothing short of mind-boggling. Now, during the night, Eli would slink in and stare into the person's eyes, and simply hold their mind sway, pull them under with a vampire's abilities.

Somebody would die for this.

Lori dug her nails into her palms as she stalked into her room, away from the workroom that smelled of the were's blood, and the poison the silver had infected him with. When silver entered the body, it changed chemically, slowly melting away as it filtered into the were's bloodstream. Since the bullet hadn't stayed in his body, it wasn't likely to kill him, but he had lost a hell of a lot of blood waiting for the medics to arrive. The wound wouldn't close on its own, and the poison was still there. A weaker, younger were, Mike would just have to heal slowly.

And Erika…where was their baby?

A snarl twisted her face as she took down a knapsack and filled it with a few supplies, some herbs, and a small vial of water that would have quite a few people laughing at her. No. It wasn't holy water. It was pure and simple spring water that came from a spring in Ireland, a place that had more earth magick than any she had ever seen.

Full of potent magick. Something to bind the herbs together when the time came, if she needed them.

Strapping a long fighting knife to her hip, she flipped her braid back over her shoulder and tossed some energy bars into her bag on her way through the door. And timed it just right. Colliding with Jonathan, she smiled innocently, fluttering her lashes at him.

"Where do you think you are going?"

Glancing down at her clothes—the dark sturdy clothes she wore when she occasionally took a patrol with a partner, something Eli required to make sure she stayed in shape and able to fight—she lifted her eyes and cocked her head. "Hmmm, out to a soiree?"

"No, Lori," Jonathan said, striding past her and shaking his head. He had woven the long brown fall of his hair into a tight cable that nearly reached his firm, excellent ass and Lori hummed under her breath in appreciation.

"My, my, my…now, Jonathan. You can't tell me no. Eli doesn't allow one-man rescue missions. You know that."

"My daughter, Lori. My baby they took." Jonathan's voice was a deep, rough growl as he leaped the stairs and strode out of the house.

Lori jogged out after him, tossing the rest of the household an expressive look. She caught him by the truck and snagged him by the arm, whirling him around. When he moved to brush her aside, she simply pressed herself against him, crowding him against the truck. His eyes slid to the low-fitting scoop-neck of her tank before moving his eyes back up to hers. "Move, Lori. They have Erika. I've raised her for seven years, I've taken care of her. Promised nothing bad would ever happen and I let her down. I have to find her."

"How?" she asked simply. "By scent? They took her in a car, in town. You can find her, and will. But I can do it and faster. And if they've hurt her, you'll need me. Jonathan, I'm a Hunter as well, just not as strong as you. And I'm a fighter. You trained me yourself. Take me with you. You need me—*Erika* needs me. My gut tells me this."

"Tell me where she is."

Stepping back, her eyes never left his. "I'm going to where she is. Even if I have to go by myself. And if I go alone, I'm likely not going to make it out alive. Even though I'll make damn certain Erika does. I'll send her home in one piece, but I'll pull the place down on top of me in the process. You know I can do it." Her voice rippled with the power and passion of her words, and her throat felt tight as she stared into his dark eyes.

Because if she didn't go, he'd die. So she'd get there before him, and make damn sure the one who was sacrificed would be her instead.

"Damn you," Jonathan rasped, shaking his head, his eyes gleaming red with his rage. His fangs slid down and, as she watched, his skin made a slight ripple, like water moving on a lake.

Turning away, he stalked around the truck. "Get in. Fuck."

Now he had two females to save, to protect. Because Lori could damn well find Erika. All she needed was to focus on Erika's face and she could find her anywhere on the planet. And the witch didn't even need a car to get there.

Hell, not even Kelsey could do some of the tricks that Lori could do.

The teleporting was an unusual gift, Jonathan had been told. A rare knack among witches, and it only showed up, as most rare witch gifts did, when it was going to be needed the most.

Lori could slide into a place where someone was that she knew, just by focusing on that person's face. Whoever had taken Erika hadn't been counting on Lori. Too bad Jonathan couldn't count on Lori being able to stand in a fight—

"I damn well can stand in a fight, you brainless moron," Lori interrupted, her voice cold.

"You're a Healer. You may be a member of the Hunter's Council, but that doesn't make you a true Hunter." Jonathan jerked, startled as he realized she was fully aware of his thoughts. "Fuck, the mark has affected you, too, hasn't it?"

"Jackass. How many vamps do I have to take down in front of you? How many rapists, thugs?" she demanded, ignoring him.

Jonathan sped into town, following some distant feeling from Lori. If he went the wrong way, she'd tell him. "It touches you just like it touches me, doesn't it?" he asked gruffly, thinking of the night before when he had thought of her again, as she was dreaming, sweet, hot dreams of him. The dreams had sent him prowling into the night, stalking and then shifting and running, higher and higher into the cliffs until he could howl his frustrations to the sky and she wouldn't hear.

"Fuck off." Her voice was cold and clipped, harsh. Crossing her arms over her chest, she glared out the window and ignored him. Totally, completely pissed.

Sighing, he rubbed one hand down his face. "Lori, you're a woman, a powerful witch, but you're not a shifter. You are in incredible shape, more than any human, but you're not as strong as we are. You can't run as fast as we can and you can't hide, you don't have as powerful a sense of smell, and—"

"You were smoking in here about three days ago," she said coldly. "And sometime in the past week, Sheila was driving your truck. I can smell her shampoo. I also, very vaguely, smell Rafe. I bet they are fucking. But not sleeping together. He probably won't let it happen. He doesn't want attachments." Lori smiled sadly. "Poor Sheila. I hope she dumps his vampire ass."

Jonathan reminded himself that sitting there with his mouth hanging open didn't look particularly intelligent. Closing it with a snap, he drew a breath. He had smelled all the scents the moment he opened the truck door and filed them all away, the way he always did.

No mortal should have been able to smell any of them, not even the bleeding cigarette he had smoked out of desperation a few days ago. It had been one damn cigarette and he'd opened the window for crying out loud, and left it open that night while he slept.

Sheila's scent had faded, and Rafe's scent had been so faint, just barely clinging to her clothes.

No way in hell Lori should have scented it.

"You don't know much about witches, do you, Jonnie?" she asked, sadly, curling up against the door. "And hardly anything at all about me."

Suddenly, he felt his chest tighten.

Lori would leave. He felt it in his gut. Once Erika was home, was safe, and this danger, whatever this new danger was had been eliminated, Lori was leaving Eli's home.

"A witch has refined hearing and a refined sense of smell. My eyesight is that of a normal woman's, but my hearing is almost equal to a vampire's, though not as good as yours. But my sense of smell, well, it's damn near close. Most people who know anything about the witches of the Council know that, I thought. You need to turn up here. They've gone into Virginia. We need to get on the turnpike," she said quietly, pressing her brow to the cool glass of the window.

"I know what I need to know about you," Jonathan said softly, frowning at the slim line of her back, her lowered head.

"And what is that? That I can heal your body when you break it? Close up the cuts you get when patrolling? That I can help Erika when she gets a pimple right before picture day?" She laughed, a dry, brittle sound. "You know you like fucking me, and you know your baby, the little girl who calls you Uncle loves my cooking, but you don't know what kind of movies I like, or what kind of books I read. At my birthday, you bought a gift certificate to the mall, so you wouldn't have to pick out anything."

Because I won't let myself get close to you...

"You don't know me. You don't want to," Lori said softly. A long, shuddering sigh racked her body as they climbed higher and higher into the mountains that would lead them out of West Virginia. "And that's fine. I won't keep waiting for you to see me, Jonathan. Malachi will help me find a new Master to serve. I'll have him see me to the Council when this is all said and done."

Blind, pulsing fury started to build. Claws ripped through his nail beds and a growl echoed up from his throat.

Leashing the animal, he continued to drive. Now wasn't the time to confront this.

But he would see the ancient bastard dead before he'd let him see Lori to the Council.

No fucking way.

No fucking way was she staying.

She was a Hunter, damn it. So what if I chose to devote my gifts to healing the Hunters rather than working alongside them? I'm more gifted, more suited for that. But I've taken my share of killers off the street. I've taken down ferals before.

Damn him.

She felt a subtle touch on her mind. Over the past week, she had learned to sense him when he was reaching for her through the mark, thinking of her. And she had learned how to block it. Solidly, she blocked it, refusing to let him touch her mind, think of her and possibly interlace his thoughts with hers right now.

So what if she was acting like a brat?

Even Healers were entitled to it every now and then.

Lori was tired of being the sainted one all the time. Tired of being the sweet and quiet one that nobody expected to be upset or quiet, or disturbed. Well, she was not upset.

She was so fucking mad. And hurt.

She hurt so much, her entire body ached with it.

Forcing a deep, slow breath into her lungs, she forced herself not to breathe shakily, not to sob. But she couldn't stop the few tears that trickled out, seeping from beneath her eyelashes in slow, hot trails.

He had no faith in her.

She could have lived with that alone. Hell, even Sarel doubted she could stand in a true fight, though Eli insisted she could. Sheila believed she could.

Lori *knew* she could.

But Jonathan wouldn't ever love her.

Jonathan had all but closed his heart to everybody. Everybody but Tori and Erika.

Erika...she pulled the face into her mind and focused. "She's sleeping, her belly is full and somebody is being kind at least. They wait underground for you.

"The cave is by a lake in the mountains," she murmured as her voice trailed off and she pressed her fingers to her brow. "A big, big lake. Stretches out farther than the eye can see."

Lifting her head, she met his eyes. "They think the cave will make you nervous, intimidate you. No animal likes to go underground. And they are so certain you will come alone. The bypass into the Blue Ridge Mountains. That's where you need to go. She's there, somewhere."

Shaking her head, she jerked herself out of that deep reverie and forced her eyes to open, staring at the cars and trees that sped by as they climbed ever further into the mountains. Over, let this be over and soon. She wanted to be alone and away from this.

Chapter Seven

"Stop it," he growled.

His voice slithered down her spine, wrapped around her body like a caress and she stiffened, shoving out the hot, shaky feelings it inspired in her. "Leave me alone." Her voice was soft, nearly soundless in the quiet of the truck, but she knew he heard her.

"Don't, Lori. Your anger, I can handle. Even though you are wrong. You are not the warrior your sister is. You've never had to be. You don't know the warrior magicks. Even Sarel doubts you...I'm sorry. I know it hurts to hear that. But you are a powerful Healer, that is where your talents lie, in the witch healing.

"It's your pain that tears at me. You're hurting, I feel it, I know I caused it...I can't take it. Stop," he repeated, his voice softening. Heat, a soft, silken heat started to fill the truck and Lori's breath caught in her throat.

Curling into herself, she turned her shoulder away and stared out the window, refusing to even acknowledge him as he whispered softly to her. She was half in a daze, focused totally on herself and soothing her pain. A meditative state that was so complete, Lori didn't even realize when Jonathan pulled off the road, away from the traffic, as the road started to wind down the mountain. Taking one of the roads for runaway trucks, he followed it to the end, to a small fork that wound back.

She was still staring blankly—not seeing the green of the trees, not hearing the birds call or smelling the forest—only aware of the gnawing pain in her soul that just grew bigger and bigger every time he turned away.

Big, warm hands came to rest on her shoulders. "Where is Erika now?"

Her lids lowered. "Sleeping. Safe. Somebody there is watching over her. Protecting her. Somebody with true honor who can keep her safe. She will see that Erika makes it back to her home," Lori whispered roughly. Her lids lifted back to half-mast and she stared into nothingness.

She had to see this through. See Erika safe. See Jonathan safe.

Then she could leave and find someplace where she was needed, where it didn't hurt just to live there.

"Lori."

Her lids lowered again and her head slumped, her body shuddering as she sighed. A gasp tore from her lips as he pressed his hot open mouth to her neck and slid his arms around her waist, pulling her back against him, into his lap. The warm, strong, flat of his hand pressed hard against her belly. "Look at me," he rasped. "I don't want to see such stillness from you."

She pushed and tugged at his hands. "Stop it, Jonathan," she said softly. "Stop it, now. I won't do this again, sleep with you and then let you walk away until you feel the need to touch me again. If I can't have you for always, I don't want you at all."

"Liar," he said easily, sliding his hand down the center of her chest, her torso, until he could cup her crotch. And when he did, he ground the heel of his hand against her clit until she arched hungrily and lifted herself weakly against his hand.

"Sex is easy, damn it," Lori hissed, and whimpered. "I could have slept with anybody. Hell, I could have slept with Malachi and then you would have been nothing more than a memory as he led me away from you forever, with me in his thrall. But I am not—"

Lori's words died in her throat as Jonathan pressed his mouth angrily against hers, driving his tongue into her mouth, down her throat, arching his head around and growling when she tried to push him away.

One hand captured her wrists, while the other cupped one plump firm breast, massaging the nipple, rolling it between his fingers, milking it until it throbbed and ached as he ate at her mouth greedily.

Lori's head spun, her pussy growing wetter. One slow, aching throb moved through it as she arched back against him, her eyes fluttering closed as she whimpered deep in her throat.

Finally, he tore his mouth away from hers, "One thing is saving you now," he said raggedly, leaning down and whispering gruffly into her ear. "And that's Erika. If she wasn't alone and in trouble, I'd throw you down onto your hands and knees, and mount you, fuck you, until you screamed my name and swore you'd never let another man touch you. Sex is easy, yes…" His voice was a rough purr against her flesh as he caressed her throbbing, yearning body with skilled hands. Dipping his fingers between her thighs, he stroked her clit back and forth until she was keening in her throat. Her face flushed as his other hand pinched her nipple roughly, milking the hard, pebbled flesh. "What I feel for you is not *easy*."

"Breaking my heart certainly is," she cried, tearing herself away and hurling her body against the truck door, cowering there, pressing her face against the window as her body trembled.

Her voice rough and shaky, she said, "Don't touch me again, Jonathan. I mean it, don't do it."

"I'll touch you, and stroke that sweet body of yours to a fever pitch and have you begging for more," he said, reaching for the gearshift and throwing the truck into reverse.

"Even when I tell you no?"

"Your body says yes."

"My heart begs no."

"I'll make your entire body — your heart and soul — scream for more," Jonathan swore heatedly, sliding a hand toward her.

"Then you would rape me. Because my mind will never say yes. My mind knows this is not good for me," Lori said, wrapping her arms around her knees. "No matter what my body asks for, or begs for, my mind is smarter. And so far, when it comes to you, my heart has led me astray, but if I had listened to my head…" a harsh laugh left her lips. "If I had listened to my head, I would have left Eli and this place a long time ago. And you would have never hurt me this badly."

Jonathan slammed on the brakes and Lori went flying forward, only to have a long steely arm shoot forward, bracing her, then whipping her in front of him. His eyes were gleaming red with his fury and his canines had lengthened as he stared at her. "I'd never hurt you like that. Have I ever taken you against your will?"

"You just threatened to," Lori said simply, lifting her lashes and staring into his eyes, those bottomless, soft eyes of chocolate silk. "And every time you've touched me without really caring for me, without loving me, without wanting me the way I want you, you've broken my heart. I don't want empty sex, Jonathan."

His face went wooden, impassive. Moving her away from him, he eyed her with cold, blank eyes. "Then so be it. I won't touch you again until you beg me. But the day will come that you will beg me. But I won't make you the promises you want, Lori. I'm not the man for them," he said flatly. "I told you years ago. You want a fairy tale prince. I'm the monster from the fairy tale."

Lori suspected Jonathan had believed it for so long, he was starting to become it.

His words echoed in her ears.

"But the day will come that you will beg me…"

His precious Lori really believed he could hurt her, take her by force—no—against her will. A difference, slight, but still a difference. Jonathan's hands flexed as he followed the road down the mountains to the bypass in Virginia. And his rage only grew.

Her resolve to leave was firm.

It was for the best, wasn't it?

A deep throbbing growl built in his chest as his hands tightened and his nails darkened, the claws showing and lengthening as his rage called to the soul of the Wolf within. He heard the ancient, wise creature rouse and felt a questioning from him.

So very few were could communicate with the Wolf on such a level, and the creature was amused at Jonathan's frustration. And simply thought the one word that would shatter what was left of Jonathan's composure.

Mate…

Jonathan adamantly thought, *No.* Even though the word resounded through his soul, his heart, his gut. And the Wolf was ancient, wise…

Mate…lose your mate, lose yourself, brother.

Jonathan sent images of himself to the creature, his dark, shattered soul, while glancing at Lori out of the corner of his eye. *I have no right to take a mate with all this darkness in me. I may not be tainted, but I have too much darkness, too much unrest. She is too pure, too…decent for me to risk bruising her with my personal demons.*

He felt a chuffing in his head, the Wolf's laughter. Personal demons? Brother, you have none but those inside your head. Your heart is pure, or you would not feel my touch so strongly.

The were can be tainted. How many feel the call of the werewolf and go feral? Jonathan said.

The Wolf's touch is always within a pure babe from birth. My touch is pure. And I speak of my touch, not of the werewolf, and you've been gifted with both. My touch is that of my wisdom, my control, my love. I was one with the were, once, before they stopped listening to my voice, and more to their own, to their greed.

What a person does with the soul is his choice. Know that, if nothing else.

Jonathan stiffened as the wolf's words, so easily understood, sank home. Tavis could bespeak the wolf. A handful of others…Declan, on very, very rare occasion mentioned feeling his touch. But he was inherent, only part *were*, so the touch wasn't as strong.

Tell me this, young brother…can you see yourself without the witch in years to come? Can you see her with another?

Bleakness filled his soul at the thought of a life without her—years stretching on into forever—year after empty year without the sight of that lovely face, her enchanting laughter, never sinking into her tight, wet little sheath. And fury twisted through him as an image of another man, faceless, nameless, appeared in his mind.

Another Hunter…she would go to the Council. Her sense of loyalty ran deep, and she would continue to help those who had saved her. Rage—hot, deep and pulsating—worked through him, pumping in his veins as his mind's eye saw them together, laughing, working…fucking…

And then, years down the road, her lovely face finally starting to show slight signs of age, she was walking. Alone, and lonely, down a cold and empty road on a blustery day, her long hair whipping around her as she looked back, and Jonathan could have sworn he was actually seeing her, and she him, through the span of time.

Their eyes met—hers older, wiser, sadder.

A scar marred her face now, thin, from the corner of her eye down to her mouth as she stared at him. And her voice, when she spoke, was substantial, but only inside his head… *"I wish it had been you, Jonathan. I really wanted it to be you."*

"What?"

She laughed sadly, wrapping her arms about her and looking around the cold wintry plain that surrounded her. *"This."*

Frowning, he shook his head and said, *"I don't get it."*

She smiled, sadly, an echo of what it used to be as she stared into his eyes. *"I know."* She stared around her, turning in a slow circle, her gaze moving over the landscape, leaves rushing around them, pausing as her eyes rested briefly on a trio of stone markers. Her face flinched with pain and she turned away too fast for Jonathan to see the names. He couldn't take his gaze too far from that face…he couldn't.

Moving her gaze back to his face, she smiled as a tear trickled down her cheek before she dashed it away. *"This was my life."*

The word *"NO"* was working its way past his tight throat even as her body started to fade away. Jonathan lunged for her, but she was already gone and he fell, shaken, to his knees.

Grimly, he rose and walked to the stone markers and found her there, resting. With two babes, twins. Dropping to his knees, Jonathan rasped, *"No."*

"She didn't choose her life, or her death."

Turning his head, he watched as the Wolf padded into the dreamscape he had woven. "It chose her after she walked away. It was the only thing she could do. There were other paths, true. Other paths she could have walked. And paths she may walk still. But none hold any true joy for her. Except with her heart mate."

The sound of baying wolves, their cries full of sorrow started in the distance. Jonathan's throat tightened and trembled with the need to release his own howl, but his teeth clenched shut as he refused to give voice to it. *"A woman's heart can only take so much bruising, brother."* The Wolf spoke softly yet again, and though his mouth didn't move, the words were spoken aloud.

"What happened?"

The Wolf stared sadly at the stones. "She married a Hunter from the enclave she joined, a rather formidable psychic. They were together nearly twenty years before they decided to have children. He never…quite felt he had her heart. Knew he did not. And he fell prey to a witch like the one who struck you, only his heart was full of anger, and doubt."

Jonathan felt the anger, and the horror rising. A Hunter turning on his wife and children... *"This isn't real. This is the dreamscape, one of the ways you taught me control."* Shaking his head, he rose and stalked away, the howl building inside his throat, seeking release.

"It may come to be true, unless she stays. It is one of her paths. But regardless of her path," the Wolf sighed, gazing around him at the bleak, empty desolation. "This is what is in her heart for her future. There is no changing that."

The howl erupted from his throat and Jonathan fell to his knees, his fingers sinking into the earth. *"He killed them."*

"Yes. First the babes, one night while she was out Hunting with a partner, training to stay in shape. He had gone insane, through the curse's touch upon his mind and heart. It was easy for the witch to break him, his heart was so full of self-doubt. He was a powerful man, big and strong, more powerful than any human the Hunters there had ever seen, and his rage infused him with a strength that was unreal. When she came rushing home, feeling their loss...she found him. She was the only witch there other than him, otherwise, somebody else would have felt it, stopped it.

"Dirke had insisted they have their own home away from the main house, so by the time he had torn her body to shreds as she tried to bring her babies back, it was too late to help her."

Jonathan's howls rose and fell in the dreamscape, eerie, forlorn, that of a wolf seeking a mate who was lost to him.

"She was a WITCH!" His words came through a thick throat and the tears that all but blinded him refused to fall, as though the release was refused him.

The Wolf nuzzled his arm gently. "The dreamscape, brother. Not reality, not yet. Yes, she was a witch. Did she fight back, you want to know? She flung up spells to hold him. But...once she saw her babies couldn't be saved, that they were indeed gone, smothered by the hands of their father...she let them fall. And she did not fight. She knew he would not leave the enclave alive. And she wanted to be with the two souls who had given her joy, her children."

"So he just fucking killed her," Jonathan rasped. "And she just let it happen?"

"She wanted it. She waited for it and welcomed it and in the end, screamed for help loudly, blocking off his retreat so that he couldn't possibly run, spells that bound him even through her death. The Master slaughtered him, but it was too late for her."

Jonathan's entire body shuddered, and the Wolf curled his great body—three times that of a normal wolf—around him, nuzzling his neck. *"The choice, always, my brother, is yours. But your heart is pure. And you have no personal demons beyond those you see in yourself. For I see none. I laid my mark heavily upon a boy I knew would become a remarkable man. I see beside him a most remarkable mate. But first, you must claim her..."*

And then the ancient creature sighed, and as the dreamscape started to fade, Jonathan realized the Wolf had guided him to pull over and wait, and he was half in a daze, his eyes slitted, hands relaxed on his thighs.

Lori's scent filled his head, and he whipped his head around as hunger clenched his body.

A brief, lingering laugh from the Wolf echoed through his mind as he reached for Lori. Her cold voice filled the truck. "Don't touch me, you bastard," she hissed.

"But you had best wait to stake that claim...until she is more willing to hear it."

Jonathan wasn't so certain such a brief talk with the Wolf could change what he had always felt. But...the lingering memories of what he had seen, his rage, and even the pain he had felt before he had walked to the stones. How desolate her eyes had been when she had looked around the dreamscape at the emptiness and said, *"This is my life."*

They had to stop at the base of the mountain. Lori insisted. Refueling the truck, eating, and then she just wandered around, staring up into the air, her eyes slitted and thoughtful. "I'm so confused by this woman who holds her. She is the one who took her, who planned this. They defer to her. Yet, as I touch her mind through Erika...I feel nothing but honor. Not even true evil."

"She organized an attack on the Hunters, has killed Hunters, and kidnapped a child. That is the epitome of evil," Jonathan snarled, pacing in a tight circle, his hands clenching and unclenching. He could smell her. Faintly. Erika hadn't been outside, but somebody who had touched her, and recently. And Lori...damn it, he needed to touch her, hold her, assure himself she was real. And *safe*...that she would stay that way.

Damn it all to hell. What in the name of heaven was he supposed to do?

"A man came into the cavern where she is being held while the woman was out. Touched her, scared her badly. Might have done worse, but the other woman...this warrior came in and she went ballistic. Not because her orders were disobeyed, and not because merchandise was soiled."

In an eerie voice that sounded like somebody else's, Lori said, "De girl is a *child*, mon. How dare ya touch a child dat way...and I warned ya all, didn't I? Da girl is not t' be harmed."

The passion in that voice was that of anybody who was repulsed at a child being hurt. "Erika was...pulled under magick after that so I don't know what happened, but the woman came back and whispered that the bad man was taken away forever and wouldn't hurt her, and wouldn't ever be able to touch her again. And she feels remorse for the...necessary casualties in a just war, is how she thinks of this."

Shaking her head, Lori glanced at him, meeting his eyes for the first time. "I don't think she understands the Hunters." Brief, very brief amusement lit her eyes for the first time in hours as she showed him something beside blankness. "Something the warrior witches of the world might have in common."

Erika felt the hand on her head, urging to eat and drink. She accepted the milky drink, knowing the witch had put extra stuff in it to keep her healthy, but she didn't want to eat. "Why are you being so nice? Kidnappers aren't nice."

"We need Jonathan...he is necessary for our war to be won," Leandra said.

Erika shoved the cup away, curling into a ball. "I need him more. He's my dad, damn it."

"Wars are important, child," Leandra said, sighing and shaking her head, her exotic eyes showing too much pain, too much sympathy. Erika didn't want to feel sorry for her. Didn't want to like her. "My mistress needs him. We are preparing for a battle, against da Council before da Huntress comes."

Turning away, Leandra paced, her long, loose clothes flowing around her lean body. Erika bit her lip and hid her face in her arms, hoping the woman wasn't what Lori was. "Da Council wants all witches, all weres, all vampires who are not wit' dem to be *dead*. And we cannot allow dat to happen."

Erika sat up, outraged. "That is not true!" she shouted furiously. "If you didn't go around eating people and killing people and drinking blood till they died, they'd leave you *alone*!"

"I had never killed a soul," Leandra said, amused, glancing at Erika with indulgence an adult shows a wayward child. "And dey came, looking for me when I was just your age. An old witch and a big red-haired vampire, down in Jamaica. And why...if not t' kill me? They had already killed me father. Not dat he didn't deserve it...but I saw dat redheaded vamp kill him meself, just a few days earlier as I hid on de roof of de house across the street, glad I had been out picking pockets. Me father liked to bring home...friends who sometimes felt I should be part of deir parties so I was never dere. But he smelled my magick. And he came Hunting me."

Erika started giggling. And she giggled until tears came out of her eyes. "You're silly. They weren't Hunting you. You weren't dangerous, especially not to Malachi. He could have eaten you for breakfast—shoot, he probably knew where you were hiding but brought the old witch there to make you feel better." Wiping the tears away, she snorted and giggled again, staring into the dark eyes that just glared at her with anger. "I bet that old woman was Agnes. They weren't Hunting you. They were probably trying to get you into Excelsior."

"A breeding ground for *killers*." Leandra hissed.

Erika cocked her head, and smiled sadly. "Somebody really did a number on your head, didn't they?" Shaking her head, she added, "You are a killer. Call yourself a soldier all you want, but you're a killer all the same. Because you don't really know about the people you're killing. You know what *those* people told you."

"Dey are killers. Dey only hunt down those who don't join them."

"They hunt down those who won't stop killing or hurting others," Erika said quietly. "They are heroes." Reaching up, she lifted her shirt, pulling it out of her waistband, showing what she never showed anyone. The brand her daddy had put on her shortly after birth—shiny, smooth, and flat. His initials. M.B. "My dad did that to me. And my mama. He killed her a few years after I was born. I don't know for certain, I didn't see it. But Eli searched the records and he knows. Jonathan saved me. My daddy would have raped me. Jonathan didn't tell me that—I just know it. I remember it, all of it. And Jonathan saved me. That is what the Hunters do. They save us. Protect us. From whatever we need protecting from."

Leandra's mouth snapped shut at the sight of the scar on Erika's belly. "Your father did dat? Your real father?" Moving closer, she brushed her fingers over it, and as she did it, Erika could feel her touch on her mind.

"He did. And worse. But I'm okay now. Jonathan made sure of it. Eli made sure of it," she said, smiling. "I don't even have nightmares. Lori and me talk a lot. She worries, but I'm fine."

"Lori...de Healer."

Erika nodded, keeping her mind and eyes blank even though Leandra's hand had fallen away. "Dey are killers, girl."

"Yes, they are." Erika sighed, letting her shirt fall. "Maybe they are. But some people, don't they deserve to die?"

Leandra didn't like it when people made her rethink her way of life.

Particularly a young, guileless child with big innocent eyes. A child who talked like an adult, with a sure, certain way of looking at her, a way that said, *I'm right. And somewhere inside, I think you know it.*

Calling her ladies, she assigned them guard over the girl, and stalked to the men, harshly reminding them, "I warned ya, what would happen to de man who was fool enough to hurt or scare dat sweet girl. Do not mess with me."

Once she was safe within her chambers, she closed the manmade door, locked it...and left...smiling and laughing as the freeness of it moved around her. It was almost like flying without wings. For the few brief seconds that it lasted.

None knew she could do this. She kept few secrets...but this was one. She kept it, holding it fierce and close. None she knew could do it. None she'd ever heard of could come and go with a thought, simply by concentrating on that person's face.

Leandra focused on the mistress and as her hair whipped around her face, her body weightless, she was suddenly there, back in the commune where she had landed more than fifteen years earlier. She pressed against a wall, making sure none had seen her rather unusual arrival.

And then she turned and strolled confidently down the corridor to the Mistress's hall and her quarters. It was when she heard Marick's voice that she stopped. Halting, she slowly and cautiously moved against the wall.

Marick. She didn't trust him...especially since he had left her command last night without her permission. He was supposed to be out patrolling back where Leandra had set up camp. And he hadn't returned just yet. She had sent others out looking for him, but she hadn't notified the mistress…

Hadn't thought he would be here.

The bastard.

"She's kidnapped a child, which surprises me. You know how Leandra is about what she considers innocent bystanders," Marick's deep voice echoed through the chamber.

"Yes…we call them fodder. But she is a very capable witch, and warrior. Plus, she came to us already fearing the Hunters." Mistress, the only name Leandra knew her by, gasped and the woman in the hall shook her head in disgust as a long slow moan filled the room.

"But she intends to free the girl once the dog comes to her. And she killed Joseph over touching her."

"Leandra is beginning to cross too many lines with her talk of righteous war. I have lost too many good soldiers to her hands. And the little brat will make a tasty treat for a good soldier."

Leandra heard the sound of a hand hitting flesh and Marick's gasp. "As to the *wolf*…do not call him a dog. He is a pure wolf," Mistress said, her voice level and cool. "Do not insult him so. We have enough mongrels around here that you should see the difference," she purred.

Leandra shuddered as she heard the sounds of leather striking flesh. Mistress so loved to beat. Her body recalled that.

"We shall have to either cull Leandra from the Scythe or pull her teeth," Mistress mused as the leather thwacked him again.

Leandra moved up to the door, her eyes dark and angry. Cull. They meant *break* or *kill*.

"Perhaps, once we've turned the wolf, he shall want her," Mistress mused. "After we've banished that wretched Hunter's heart. That soul of his."

Leandra stepped into the doorway, her eyes narrowed and watchful. Surely enough, Marick lay face down, nude and stripped. Lines marred the sweet golden perfection of his body, some still oozing fat, lazily flowing drops of blood. And he was loving every painful second of it as Mistress flogged him.

Sick bastard. "Well now...I'm not so easily broken, Mistress. Nor so easily killed," Leandra purred. "Marick, is dis why ya abandon your post? Shame on ya, mon."

They both whipped their heads around to look at her, with looks of incredulity on their faces that were nothing short of ridiculous. It might have been wiser for Leandra to flee in silence.

But when had she ever taken the easy road?

"Lady, how dare you," Mistress rasped, tossing the whip down as Marick rose, his eyes flashing and gleaming red. His skin rippled like water and Leandra could all but hear the growl rumbling in the inherent's throat.

"How dare I?" Leandra scoffed. "How dare I wish to speak with de Mistress I have served loyally for fifteen years? Am I not permitted to ask you questions? Am I not permitted t' tink for meself? No, I am not, I see. Ya wish t' cull me like I am one o' de brainless fools ya like to keep underfoot."

Tossing her long braids over her shoulder and lifting her chin, her amber eyes flashed with pure fire. "Ya are a fool if ya tink I will be so easy t' subdue, *Mistress*," she hissed in a low, mean voice. Behind her, she heard creeping footsteps and caught a familiar scent. With a slow curl of her lips, she whispered, "*Inferno.*"

A gleaming ring of fire surrounded her, just barely there but as two hands tried to seize her from behind, the fire raged and the *were* bellowed as it singed his skin, solidified and blocked his grab at her.

"You fool," Mistress whispered. "You think you can get away from us?"

"I tink more dan dat…I know I can," Leandra challenged. Laughing, she angled her chin at them and said, "Besides, I have the da best bargaining chip in da world. Da girl. I can have da wolf…all mine. And ya cannot stop me, either."

With that, she drew the long wicked knife from her side and lunged through the people gathered at her back, the flames singeing the people who tried to grab and hold her. She thrust the knife into somebody's gut, and pivoted, delivering a sidekick into Marick's belly. Smiling viciously at him, she slashed her knife across his exposed throat as more people barreled into the ring of flames, screams and growls filling the corridor.

"Damn it, she's one fucking witch," Mistress shrieked.

One of the ladies hissed, "But it's Leandra, Mistress."

And Leandra dove through a narrow opening in the wall of people, tucking and rolling, running for all she was worth, her knife clutched in her hand. The moment she hit the door, she focused…the girl's face and she was gone. The vicious screaming and furious curses were still echoing in her ears.

"Damn it, did she tunnel into the ground?"

"Witches can't run that fast."

"D' ya think she has a bleedin' broom, mate?"

Leandra materialized in Erika's room with her breath coming in ragged pants. Eying the girl, she ran her tongue around her teeth.

Choices…she had several. The question was, which was the right one?

Erika stared, frightened, into Leandra's eyes. They were glowing, the way Eli's did when he was furious. Or when he stared at Sarel too long. And sometimes Jonathan and the other wolves would come in after a night, and she'd be up getting a drink and their eyes would be hot and gleaming red…full of stress, rage, anger…

But Leandra's were glowing gold, almost like a cat's.

A panther's.

Blood splattered her face, and a long, thin cut marked her chin. Her chest was heaving with ragged, panting breaths as she studied Erika. "Someting tells me dat we have trouble comin', girl," Leandra said. "In da form of da Mistress in all her glory and de ladies and men who serve her."

"Doesn't that mean you?" Erika asked, frowning.

Leandra laughed. "No. Not anymore, it don't. Dey tink to cull me, do dey now? We'll be seeing 'bout dat. We'll see. Dey tink I've been showing my teeth? Well, I haven't even taken a nibble."

Erika felt those eyes, full of anger, full of power, land on her and an odd, eerie feeling rushed down her spine. It wasn't fear, not exactly—more like, she had let a panther out of its cage, thinking to turn that panther free. But the panther had decided she wanted to adopt Erika.

And Erika really didn't know how to handle a small cat.

Much less a big one.

Leandra tossed her long black braids out of her face and smiled—a small, almost gentle smile—at Erika. "Don' be afraid, Erika. You are de last person on de planet I plan on hurting. In any way. Dis…Agnes you tell me about. I want to see her. Come. We have no time left."

Erika jumped when Leandra strode forward and wrapped her arms around her. But she screamed when the room around them just *vanished*.

Agnes had dealt with a lot of odd happenings in her life.

But that phone call, placed in the middle of the night from America, well, she was quite certain it would never be topped.

"Erika, I cannot just come and meet you without telling Eli and Jonathan."

"You have to. If you tell them, they'll come. She has to talk to somebody alone, and they'll kill her—or try to. I don't think she's bad."

"*Who*, child?"

155

"The woman that kidnapped me," Erika said on the other end of the line.

A kidnapper, not evil, but she had helped kill other Hunters. But Erika wasn't a fool. She was actually very insightful. So Agnes was flying across the Atlantic at 2 a.m., her old bones weary and wanting her bed. She didn't usually fly to the States, hadn't in years. Her last flight across the ocean had been for Malachi, to Jamaica, for a young witch-child. And what a waste that had been. The girl, a wild, powerful young thing had gotten away.

Away from them.

It haunted Agnes…what could have happened to her, what awful things could have become of her, or what awful things she could have been pulled into.

There had been such a flux of residual magick lingering in that house from that girl. Agnes couldn't comprehend what the woman must have grown into. For a twelve year old child to dodge and dart and evade a witch like Agnes. *And* Malachi. Not one, but two Hunters and members of the Council.

It should have been laughable.

But it had filled Agnes with a sense of foreboding.

Shifting, she sighed and tried to make herself rest.

But she was too edgy.

None of it sat right.

None of it at all.

Chapter Eight

"Call for help," Lori said quietly at the mouth of the cave.

There was too much life underneath the surface of the earth.

"There are too many people here for us to hope we can counter them all," she said, turning to face Jonathan. "Two against what feels like eighty. It is madness."

"Is Erika there?"

"Jonathan…"

"*Is Erika there?*" he demanded, crouching low to the ground as though he'd be able to see her through the dirt. His eyes were swirling, glowing red around the edges, and his skin rippled with power.

"No. She's not. Both she and the woman who took her are gone. There is some sort of…illusion that the woman placed that makes them think they are still there, barring themselves in the room. She is very good. The less powerful witches there don't realize it is illusion. I don't believe anybody who isn't a Master of the craft would see through it." Lori ground her teeth and thrust her hands through her hair. "*Damn it all!* This woman is a bloody mess—she is a member of a fucking lunatic horde of monsters. Yet…there is something pure within her. And Erika is safer with her than she'd be with, well, anybody, except for you and Sarel and Eli. Even I couldn't protect her as well as this woman."

"Lori, you're making me very angry—when I find this woman, I'm going to kill her," Jonathan rasped as he rose and paced in a tight circle, his hands clenching into fists. He tossed her a harsh, angry glare, one that let her know all he wanted to do was to fall upon something and rip its throat out. To feed and bathe in the blood of whatever had taken the child he loved so.

Lori smiled gently. "No. You won't. Erika is falling in love with her—you'll see it. You'll see her. She's a warrior, just like you, she understands you far better than you think, and she respects you more than you believe. And even if she didn't, she cares for children and she's protecting Erika. You owe her for that alone—"

Never piss off an angry werewolf.

A very important rule.

Lori's bemusement over this woman had her letting that rule slide to the back of her mind and she didn't even feel or see him coming. Which would explain how she ended up with her back against a tree and Jonathan pressed against her. His eyes were more gold than brown as he struggled to remain human, a red rim surrounding the irises. His fangs dropped down as his body trembled with suppressed rage.

"This bitch killed Brad. This bitch shot Mike. This bitch took Erika. I owe her pain. I owe her death. Whether she is a misguided soul or not, I don't give a flying fuck," Jonathan snarled against her ear.

"As you say, Erika is being treated well, and is not hurt. That alone is keeping the bitch from being turned into a hide I'd like to stretch out on that blasted cave wall, over there. That alone is keeping me from showing that little cunt what happens when you piss off an Alpha. Nobody takes what belongs to me," he growled.

Lori jerked her head away as he scraped his teeth along the cord in her neck and turned her mouth aside when he pressed his lips roughly to hers. "Mine," he snarled.

"Not fucking likely," she snapped, pressing her hands to his chest and using the leverage to work her way back. "The only time you want to pretend interest is if you're pissed, or too fucking horny to ignore me."

"*Mine*," he growled, and power shuddered through the air so loudly it was amazing none below the ground noticed.

Lori narrowed her eyes and rasped, "Not until you face some cold hard facts, Jonnie." She started to whisper under her breath, focusing her mind, herself, her magick, as she lifted one hand. Jonathan was running his hand down the middle of her torso, and as she cupped her hand in front of her mouth, he cupped *her*, rubbing his thumb over the covered bud of her clit. Taking all of her strength, she breathed in through her nose and blew air into his face.

Jonathan went flying back, losing his grip on her as though he had no strength. Head over heels, he tumbled back, landing on his ass, and then his head flew back and hit the sandy earth behind him, the water from the lake coming up to soak his hair.

Lori tossed her hair back and smoothed her shirt down, watching as he slowly sat up. Running a hand over her hair, she quirked an eyebrow at him and said, "Still under the illusion that I can't handle myself, wolf-boy?"

"You are no warrior."

"I just laid one out easily enough," she purred sweetly. In challenge, she turned her back on him and eyed the entrance to the cave. There was a labyrinth below ground, a veritable catacomb of caves. A near perfect stronghold. Only one way in, so none could spring a sneak attack upon them. But only one way out as well. Which meant if the way out was collapsed…smoothing her hand over the tree, she listened, thinking what a fool he was if he thought he could sneak up on a witch.

No. She may not hear as well as he did. But why did she need to? The land spoke to her. The cave, the lakes, the air, the trees…

She ducked and rolled just as he lunged for her. She came up smiling as he landed empty-handed, scowling.

"You've always wondered why Sarel was such a good student to Eli. It's not just because she's a natural born fighter,"

Lori said, dusting her hands off. "Witches have a connection to the earth, love. We're so difficult to spring anything on. Well, one that hasn't wronged the earth at least. It whispers to me…"

Her eyes closed and she spread her hands out, absorbing. "There's several deer feeding not too far away…they were going to run when they scented you. But I told them they need not fear you. You hunt other prey. Coyotes in the woods are heading south, they don't like your scent. The cave…ancient, used to be a habitat for passing Indian tribes. I can still feel their shaman magick. And you…don't try that again."

Jonathan lowered back into his crouch, his eyes narrowing as he studied her still, peaceful face.

"If it's that easy, then why not tell me where Erika is?"

"Because she isn't around here."

Jonathan snarled and slammed his fist into the ground. Lori felt the impact reverberate through her feet and her heart ached for him. How could she convince him that Erika was safe?

"Follow the blood path, damn it. She's a fucking blood witch, has to be, falling into that pack of killers. Are they blood killers?" he asked, skimming his eyes to the cave below.

Lori's entire body shuddered and she nodded. "Yes, they are. But she is not like…them. She hasn't spilt another's blood for her magick. And though the land was suffering for the past few years, it has been recovering, through her."

"There has to be something, some kind of path you can follow. No witch like her can travel like that and leave nothing."

Lori smiled sardonically. "She has no blood path to follow. The woman has never used the blood of another to complete her magick, or to start it. What little blood she has needed, has come from her own veins," Lori said, turning east, studying the vague direction her heart pulled her toward. "There is no blood on her soul, on her heart, save for those she has killed in what she felt was a righteous battle. And those souls torment her."

The worst thing about an empath, they could see clear into a person's soul. Jonathan knew she had already caught a glimpse of this woman's soul, and he didn't like knowing it wasn't somebody twisted and evil. He wanted blood on his hands. A woman's blood was something that twisted his stomach anyway. In order for him to kill her, she would have to be an evil, foul woman.

And Lori was insisting she was anything but.

As they stood in the woods, arguing in hushed, quiet tones, he had to deal not only with that, but with his wounded pride as well.

She had knocked him flat onto his ass.

Quickly, easily, and without laying a finger on him.

A gleam had lit her eyes, and for a brief moment, he had seen more of her sister in her than he had ever realized.

But Lori was a Healer, she wasn't a warrior.

She wouldn't be able to stand in battle. Of course, now he was carefully shielding his thoughts, the way he did when he was thinking around Eli and wanted his thoughts kept private.

Lori's eyes were cool and blank as she studied the cave. Her lashes lowered, her lovely face going quiet, thoughtful. Jonathan didn't like the look on her face. It was too…eerie.

"I can collapse the cave," she said quietly.

"Excuse me?"

"I can collapse it. Totally. If I get inside to the middle, I can collapse it. The structure that holds it up. If I crumble that support, the cave will go."

"No." He narrowed his eyes as he studied her face, looking for any sign that she wasn't serious. "Too dangerous. You aren't sliding in there and relying on yourself to slide out. If you get caught, get hit in the head or something, you're trapped. You don't go anywhere without me."

Turning his back on her, he studied the mouth of the cave. Collapsing it though, had possibilities.

"You still haven't figured it out, have you?"

Her voice was a ghost of a whisper behind him, but a hot, angry woman was whispering it. He could feel it, could feel the heat, the hot wash of her anger. "I may not bloody be Sarel—Eli took me out of hell before I had to run from it. But I was placed in Excelsior, and I was trained by fighters from childhood. I am *not* the soft, weak little flower you think. I do not have to be protected from all the evil in the world."

"How lovely…"

The low, laughing, purring voice that slithered around them was the only warning they had before he launched himself out of the woods at them. Jonathan shifted and lashed out at the man who seemed to explode in a burst of fire from the woods.

"Oh, it's the dog the Mistress wants so badly," the newcomer snarled, his blond hair blowing around his face from some unseen wind. With a sulk, he flung his hand toward Jonathan. Jonathan swore furiously, the words falling from his muzzle in low growls as a series of gashes appeared across his furred belly, leaking blood down his groin, across his naked sex, before trickling down his thighs.

Paying it no heed, he reached for this new witch, only to have his hand frozen, just bare inches from its target. "I'd best no' be 'urtin' ya t' badly, ey?"

Lori moved into the line of fire as Jonathan went stock-still, unable to move, his mind all but frozen with fear. Her lips were curved with a small, pleased smile. "Well, well. What have we here?" she mused.

"Pretty lil' piece you are," the witch smirked, running one hand down his flat, naked belly, the ring in his navel winking at her. Casting Jonathan a dismissing glare, he said, "You're in the way, mate." Jonathan grunted as air whooshed from his lungs and he slammed into a tree. Limber, rubbery branches came around to entrap him, like something out of a poorly written horror film. Blood was oozing down his belly and legs, matting in his fur, trickling down the bark of the tree, and pooling in the grass, although he could feel the flesh already starting to knit together.

Cupping his groin, the witch flashed a wolfish grin at Lori and said, "Be good now, an' maybe this could be fun, huh?"

"Oh, I'll be nice. I'll leave your skin attached, which is more than you've done, isn't it?" she responded, lifting one hand, palm out.

He narrowed his eyes, cocking his head as he studied her. His long, narrow face darkened and he licked his lips. "Hmmm…a witch. What a pretty lil witch you are, too, luv. But you kin't fight the Scythe, gil. You jist kin't. We're too strong fir the likes o' you."

Curling her fingers, she beckoned to him, and said, "Prove it."

A volley of fire flew toward her and struck something only inches in front of her face, melting into it like water, fading into it and flickering out to the edge before dying away. As it faded, Lori looked up from under her lashes, a cat's smile curving her mouth.

"Lovely fireworks," she smirked.

A snarl curved the man's lips and the ground shook, wind snapping through the trees. Lori's eyes took on an unfocused look, and Jonathan swore roughly as his gut ran cold when her eyes started to glow, hot, green and fiery with anger. "You've done enough damage here," she rasped.

"Foolish gil," he spat, hissing under his breath as the winds started to converge upon them. "Think you kin stop me? Us? We are the army. The Scythe."

"You are fools," Lori declared, falling to her knees.

Lori's hands were steady as she reached into the bag at her waist. Oh, she had no qualms in shedding blood for magick. She had shed her own enough times. And today, she had every intention of shedding his. This land, these trees, they reviled him, rejected him, but were inexplicably bound to him.

He had sacrificed women here, slaughtered men here.

Her eyes met his as she sliced her palm open and pressed it to the earth, whispering softly, "Blood of the pure believer cleanses you. Blood of the righteous warrior frees you. Both have already been shed. You are free."

And with a cool, icy smile, she rose, her feet braced as the earth started to tremble and shake. "The pure believer." Cocking her head, she brought her hands together in front of her face and let the still flowing blood pool there, breathing magick into it as she stared into his eyes.

"I am the pure believer. I am the righteous warrior. I will mete out punishment for your wrongs against the earth and your wrongs against mankind." A hot, glimmering, golden ball had risen and formed out of her blood as the witch stood, staring at her, still smirking, although his eyes were starting to flicker as she breathed into the blood.

It was when the trembling started at his feet that he tried to back away. Launching the golden ball at him, Lori watched it strike him square in the chest, propelling him into the nearest tree. Expanding, flattening into a thin shield that bound him to the tree as it slowly and inexorably pulled him, screaming, within it. Then it held him silently within that golden shield.

"*What the fuck…*" the words were low, guttural, forced from a throat not human.

"The land takes back what it has lost. Always." Lori didn't need to turn to know that Jonathan was back on his feet. "Come on. We can't stay here now. I don't know if they know we are here, but we can't risk it now. His loss will be noticed soon."

With a rapid touch, she swept the area clean of the signs of battle, releasing more bursts of magick than Jonathan had ever seen. When she turned, he was in human form once more. Long, lean, naked, his sable hair falling around his body like a cloak, he gathered up the shreds of his clothes before turning and striding toward her, his eyes grim. The healing gashes on his belly still bore traces of blood, and his sex hung thick and heavy between his thighs, thickening and lengthening as he stared at her.

Lori turned away. Before she could fall to her knees and beg.

"No damn hotels," Jonathan growled as Lori drove toward one. He shifted, arching his back to relieve some of the pressure on his stomach. *Damn it.* Getting a slice from a fucking witch was never a good thing. But this one wasn't healing right.

Shit.

It had pulled together inside, but then it had stopped.

And that meant only one thing.

"I still smell blood," Lori said quietly, as though she could read his mind. "You're not healing. You heal fast, faster than any were I've ever seen. He didn't do anything other than an elemental trick. No poison, no curse." Her breath slid out between her teeth in an angry hiss. "It's his touch. His magick is fouled. I can't think of any other way to explain it."

"I know." Arching a brow at her, he said, "I can feel it inside my veins. It's cool, murky, oily."

Lori poked out her lip, a thoughtful little pout before she blew her bangs out of her eyes as she headed back down the lane, her look dark and brooding. It wasn't a look he normally associated with Lori. Lori was light and laughter, wasn't she? Lori wasn't a warrior—yet, she had battled like one.

"You're going to need a Healing," she said grimly.

"What of it?" Tension raced up his spine as a sulky snarl formed against his will. She didn't have to sound so damned unwilling. So what if he hadn't been too thrilled a moment ago that she was going to have to lay those slim, wonderful hands on him? It was okay if *he* wasn't real thrilled about having to fight down the need to touch *her*, especially after she had made it clear that she didn't want him touching her anymore.

And he had said he wouldn't...not until she begged. Damn it, why had he gone and said that? Gnashing his teeth together as his cock started to throb and swell, Jonathan wondered exactly when he was going to start listening to something other than his dick and his pride, and his fool excuse of a brain.

A soft, growling chuckle echoed through him. The Wolf was awake. Something had roused him, most likely the lingering pain in the wound that hadn't healed.

'Tis high time you started thinking with your heart, brother. High time. Didn't think the day would come. A warm soothing presence settled around him, like the Wolf had wrapped his great body around Jonathan, and he felt the pain and the aching cold recede some, his mind clearing as he focused on Lori.

She is a warrior, the Wolf whispered. Perhaps not as fully as you. But a warrior nonetheless. Do not continue to doubt her. You cut her deeply each time you do, a blow to her heart, to her soul. Listen to your heart, see with more than your eyes. Look at your mate. Your heart chose her, a lady fit for a warrior. It wouldn't have chosen poorly.

Blood started to pound thickly in Jonathan's veins. The knowledge had been brewing dimly within him for some time. He hadn't accepted it, for reasons he couldn't face, but it had been there. *My soul is too dark for her.*

No. The Wolf shook him mentally. Your fears are too dark. But they are groundless. There is nothing of the evil that spawned you inside of you. Lori and Sarel came from evil—do you see the dark inside of them?

Nothing dark lived inside Lori.

And though Sarel battled her demons, her soul was not dark.

And neither of these women could love a man of darkness, not after what they had lived with, been through.

With eyes that glowed, Jonathan turned his head, studying Lori. *Leave us, Wolf. I think I understand what you are saying now.*

The Wolf laughed, deep and heartily, his presence stroking over Jonathan's body like the warm brush of faerie wings as he slid away. *Yes, I see you do.*

Lori swung off down a path, her eyes vague and unfocused. She didn't even seem aware that he was there, watching her, his eyes moving over her face, down the line of her neck before following it to the neckline of her shirt. Her rounded breasts were full and smooth, the nipples soft. He could smell her, the scent of vanilla and jasmine, delicately scented skin, sweet on the air.

And the scent of sweat, the smell of the earth and adrenaline still pulsing under her skin. The scents of battle. She had fought, and she had done well. He hadn't stood a bloody chance against the witch—witches had something against the other paranormal creatures that many of them couldn't fight. Sarel could only be in so many places at once.

Lori had done more than prove her worth as a fighter.

Hell, she had been trying to get out of the safehold of the Enclave for months, and Jonathan had refused it. Not soft, pretty Lori.

The firm lines of her face right now looked anything but soft. She looked strong, serious, and capable—and damn it, that was just as arousing and intriguing as the soft Lori.

"We'll be safe here."

Her voice broke into his intense study of her face. Looking up, he glanced around the small clearing. "Where is here?"

"Shenandoah National Park," she said shortly. "Nothing's wrong in here. I can feel it. If one of them comes, it will disrupt the flow of things and I'll feel that. It will give us enough warning to prepare."

"What do you mean, nothing is wrong?" he asked, reaching over and catching her arm before she could slide out of the truck.

"They haven't tried tapping into the land here, or committed any evil that stains the earth. If they move in around us, the earth will feel their evil—and I will know. We'll have plenty of warning," she said, tugging her wrist free. "Come on...let's make some sort of camp."

Jonathan slowly loosened his grasp on her wrist, a smile curling his lips as he met her eyes. He'd have her whole body under his hands soon enough. Whether she begged or not.

Lori met his eyes, and her cheeks flushed, her gaze dropping to his mouth. He heard her heart rate kick up, saw the stiffening of her nipples under the shirt she wore and scented the sudden sharp rise in the unique smell that was *her*. Meeting her gaze, he saw that she knew it.

Smiling, he lowered his gaze to her lips, a touch as gentle and light as a kiss. He climbed out of the truck, reaching behind the seat for the camp gear. Every Hunter who owned a car had a similar pack. He made damn sure of it. Never knew when it would come in handy. There was water, basic food and other stuff back there as well. He might not have been a Boy Scout, but he sure as hell studied a similar handbook.

Lori eyed him nervously when he didn't argue with her about helping with the camp set-up. Jonathan could scent her anxiety, hear her heart rate as she moved into the tent to unroll the two separate bedrolls. His lids lowered and his mouth started to water, his ears tracking her movements.

"I'm done. Get in here so I can deal with your stomach," she said shortly.

A slow, heated smile curled his lips at the sound of her voice. Jerky, short sentences, when she usually sounded so calm, so confident. Ducking his head under the flap of the tent, he met her eyes and dropped to his knees, crawling over to her, pausing a long moment to stare into her eyes.

She met his gaze, her lips parted, their noses nearly touching, the light kiss of her breath touching his mouth as they watched each other. Jonathan could all but taste her now, wanted to taste her, wanted to grab her to him and rip the clothes from her body as he sank his cock deep inside her sweet, wet pussy.

But that lingering, cold ache in his side was getting worse, and he could feel it spreading to his bones. "Such a pretty little witch," he murmured, lowering his head and stroking his tongue across her lower lip in one slow pass. "So sweet."

Her breath left her lungs in one slow, shuddering rush as he shifted and lay down, rolling onto his back. Staring up at her through the fringe of his lashes, he gripped the bottom of his shirt and slowly pulled it up as he watched her face. She was staring at his hands, watching as he bared his belly and chest, a flush spreading up her neck, her cheeks going rosy, her eyes clouding.

Jonathan could smell it as her arousal grew. Shifting onto the elbow of his uninjured side, he pulled his shirt off and tossed it away before he lay back down, still watching her.

Carefully, she probed the cold skin around his wound. "It must be his signature. Some witches can leave one in their wake. Some leave a poisonous, almost gangrenous stench. Others, an acid-looking burn. His is cold. Icy. And it spreads." Flattening her hand against his belly, she hummed with sympathy, deep and low in her throat. "Very cold. This would have killed a mortal. Could kill lesser weres. Weres are so hot-natured, this cold would be a big danger."

Heat started to chase the cold away as her hand pressed harder and harder against his flesh. Sliding her eyes to meet his, she said, "I don't use cold. I've always used heat."

The powerful heat arced through him and his breath hissed through his teeth as it punched him in the gut. Hot, fiery licks of magick sought out every icy-cold corner of his soul where the malignant magick had taken up hiding. The pain swelled, intensifying, and Jonathan swore raggedly and bellowed, feeling something putrid and evil flee his soul as her Healing flowed through him.

Darkness washed over him from above as her hands, and her soft, soothing whisper guided him into a restful slumber.

Chapter Nine

Jonathan could feel her eyes on him as she finished the task of closing the wound as he drifted up from the healing slumber, feeling revived, refreshed, hungry. The major healing had been removing the ice of the other witch's magick from his body.

Closing the wound was child's play to her.

Opening his eyes, he met her gaze and felt his mouth curl into a hungry smile.

"I like the way your eyes feel on me—I like knowing you watch me," he murmured. Taking her hand, he pressed it flat to his belly and held it there.

"Stop it." She swallowed thickly as she slowly moved her eyes up the line of his body, tugging her hand out from under his, trailing the tips of her fingers over his side before folding her hand into a fist that she held in her lap. "I've been watching you for years. You've never given a damn before. And on the rare occasion you did, it only pissed you off."

"Because I wanted you too much," he said hotly, reaching out and sliding his hand up the side of her thigh where she knelt beside him. "And those sweet, innocent eyes that followed me everywhere."

Her eyes sliced across to meet his, narrowed and angry. "I am *tired* of being called *sweet* and *innocent*." The air between them was all but vibrating with her anger, Jonathan could feel it. "I lost my innocence years ago, once I realized what I would be expected to do when I joined an enclave. And I'm only sweet in *your* eyes. Eli knows I can be a veritable shrew. Sarel thinks I'm a bitch and a half. To everybody else, I am just *me*. Only you label me as *sweet* and *innocent* and then bother to call me by name.

Bloody hell, I spent several years wondering if you even knew it. All I ever heard was she is too sweet, too soft for this life."

"I always knew your name. I've been whispering it in my sleep from the time I met you," Jonathan rasped, rolling to his knees and catching her face in his hands, tilting her chin up. Her lips parted and she tried to jerk her head away, but he covered her mouth with his and plunged his tongue inside, sliding his hands down the line of her back and rocking the hard ridge of his cock against her belly.

With a furious, muffled curse, she tore her mouth from his, and wedged her hands between them. "Whispering it, and probably cursing it," she laughed bitterly, her eyes sharp as glass as she stared up at him. "I've lost count how many times you tried to send me back to Excelsior, how many times you tried to convince Eli and Sarel that I wasn't fit for this life."

"Because you were too damn tempting, and I didn't want to give in. I didn't want to have to fight myself every time I saw that pretty face or smelled your sweet body," he growled, lowering his face and burying it in the curve of her neck, raking his teeth along the curve. Against his chest, he could feel the hot burning stab of her nipples and hear the pounding of her heart, feel her pulse against his mouth as he sucked a patch of delicate skin.

"I'm not begging you, not now, not ever," Lori rasped, trying to arch back out of his grasp. All she succeeded in doing, though, was pressing her pelvis against his cock and making him groan as she wiggled and undulated against him.

Moving his lips up to her ear, he murmured, "What about if I am willing to beg you? What if I say I was a fool, a blind dumb fool?" Sliding his hand up her side, he cupped her breast and massaged the soft, malleable flesh there, pinching the nipple, milking it as he told her, "I've always wanted you, needed you, loved you. I never opened my eyes to see how much, though. Never opened my eyes to see just how much you are the other half of me."

Her body tensed, as though folding in on itself, a rabbit going still and silent as a predator started to stalk the woods. "Don't. Don't do this to me," she said quietly.

Shaking her head, she slowly started to work herself out of his arms and Jonathan let her. "I've been waiting for you for weeks, months, years. Only hours ago you told me that it would never happen. That there would be nothing but sex. I will not let myself start to hope only to have my heart broken," she said, moving away from him in the tight confines of the tent. Sinking down on her pallet and drawing her knees to her chest, she rested her chin on them and stared blankly at her feet.

"I didn't think you were strong enough—I was a fool. My eyes were opened in a very harsh way, admittedly. But even before that, I knew I was wrong," Jonathan said gruffly, drawing in a deep breath, taking the scent of her body into his lungs and shuddering as it flooded him. Crawling across the tent to loom over her kneeling form, he murmured, "I will have you, Lori. Make no mistake of that. You're mine, forever."

A tiny smirk crossed her lips. "It's odd...up until just now, you didn't even really want me for more than thirty minutes."

A wolfish smile curved his mouth, and his eyes flashed. "Don't push me, Lori. I've wanted you for years and you're the only one who's been too blind to see it. Push me, and I'll push back."

He pulled away, moving faster than her eyes could track, leaving the tent before he gave in to what they both wanted.

Lori felt the strength drain from her body.

Damn it.

Sagging back on the blanket, she pressed a fist to her breast, feeling her heart pound there as she sucked air into her lungs. Had she really just passed up a chance to feel Jonathan's warm, naked body against hers?

Yeah, and damn him to hell.

He was the one to blame.

If he hadn't been so difficult lately, she wouldn't have been so on edge and felt so guarded, so desperately needing to watch her every move with him. Otherwise, maybe, just maybe, she could have given in.

With a sulk, she settled down to rest.

Leandra eyed the rocky shoreline.

"Why here?" she asked, shaking her head. "'Dis place, it is cold, and dark, and dreary. I don' like it."

"You just don't like it because you have less chance to take off running. Agnes will blunt your powers, I'm betting. She did it before, just by being around you. She'll do that and more," Erika said, smiling with satisfaction.

She loved this beach. Here, on this rocky shoreline in Maine, she could feel the wind on her face, taste the salt in the air, and she felt free. She didn't feel quite so…normal here. She didn't feel quite so human when she stood here. Something in the ocean had always called to her. Jonathan had brought her here for the first time after he had saved her.

They used to come here all the time. Lately, he hardly brought her at all, but Erika remembered this place. And so did Agnes.

The wind started to calm.

Erika smiled as Leandra's topaz eyes narrowed. The Jamaican had expected the wind to pick up around Agnes. But the earth loved Agnes. It didn't go into turmoil at her arrival. It calmed. Except for the ocean. Nothing and no one of this earth could calm the ocean. So as the water crashed onto the rocky beach, the wind died down around Agnes Milcher as she made her way down the beach toward them, eying Erika with faded blue eyes, shaking her head mildly. "You're a naughty girl, calling me when you've your whole family worrying themselves mad about you."

Though she was still more than a hundred yards away, her voice sounded all around them, as though she was above them, next to them and within them. Erika noticed that Leandra jumped, and then the black woman scowled, her eyes flashing. The young girl just smiled and laughed, running over the rocks and sand with her hair flying like a golden banner behind her as she flung herself toward the old witch, her arms wrapping around the woman's neck.

Of an equal height, Agnes looped her arms around Erika, holding tight and firm, her old body still strong and powerful after more than a century of walking the earth. "Ah, child. We worried so. We knew Lori would find you, but by the time she and Jonathan reached where you had landed, you and this lady were already gone," Agnes murmured, her hand smoothing down Erika's hair. "And then, lass, you call me with this bit of news."

Erika turned and watched as her eyes met Leandra's over the distance. "She's not evil. I know what she did was, but she's not evil. I know too much about evil to not be able to see it," Erika said anxiously, holding tightly to Agnes' arm as the witches studied each her. Agnes narrowed her eyes, her pale, lined face taking on an eerie, otherworldly glow, her eyes gleaming like pale blue pearls in the moonlight.

"No...evil, she is not. But what she is, I've yet to decide. An unknown quantity, I dare say," Agnes murmured. "So powerful, so full of courage, pride. And very protective of you. She gives her heart quickly, and wholly." Sliding her eyes to Erika, she smiled. "Ahh, pet. None who loves you that truly can be so bad, can they? So what does she want?"

"To know about the Hunters. She doesn't understand them," Erika said, flushing as she looked back at Leandra and saw that the woman was indeed watching her very closely, very protectively. She paced back and forth on a small section beach like a caged panther, her long black braids swaying down her back as she moved.

"Hmmm. We are easy to misunderstand to the outside eye. But I see the mark of our enemy on her. They have worked strongly within her. This may be beyond what words can say, pet," Agnes murmured. With a sigh, she linked hands with

Erika and they walked together down the beach toward the other woman. "I feel so much anger from her, so much resentment."

"I kin hear ya well enough, old woman. And me anger is me own damn business," Leandra drawled, facing them with her arms folded across her chest and her legs planted wide apart. Lifting her chin high in the air, she said, "And me resentment as well. Though I don't tink I have any. De anger though, dat, well, dat I do have. And plenty of it. Since hearing me people say dey are ready to make me a mindless drone or kill me, since I no longer suit deir purposes."

"Good ears you have," Agnes mused, pursing her lips thoughtfully. *And not just the ones on your rather exotic head, either, pet.* Over the crashing of the waves, the woman shouldn't have been able to hear. Even a very refined witch-sense at this age most likely wouldn't have heard that. Sarel wouldn't have. Now, Lori might have. Though Lori wasn't a match for this witch, not this one.

Sarel, maybe. But not Lori, though she was not the soft, sweet innocent thing some mistook her for.

This lean, dangerous woman was a warrior through and through, from the top of her black, braided head, to the bottom of her black-booted feet, with a long wicked knife on her hip. The aura radiating from her flickered from gold to blue to white to red, enough to make Agnes wish she had a pair of sunglasses, so bright were the lights.

"Old woman, I've seen you before. With de big vampire, in Jamaica," Leandra said, her face closing up. "I know your face."

"I know many vampires," Agnes said with a smile. "Many. And I've been to Jamaica several times, though none in recent years. You'll have to be more specific than that, child." Though Agnes was quite certain she knew who she was facing…*so that is where you landed, child. Ah, Mal. We should have looked longer and much, much harder.*

"I tink ya know who I am," Leandra smirked, arching an eyebrow. "I may be a bit older now, but I would tink ya see wit more den your eyes, old woman."

Agnes laughed, the rich laugh carrying through the early morning air. "Oh my. I think I like you. So fiery, so proud." Her eyes sparkled with mirth. "Hmm, maybe I have an idea. I had wondered…what do you want of me, woman of the Scythe? I've no love for you. None at all. But I have Erika back at my side. And she looks whole, happy and uninjured. I can manage a few questions."

"Dis girl here," Leandra drawled, tossing her head at Erika, "insists I am wrong about de murderers you belong to. I want you to convince me I am wrong."

"Murderers, is that what we are?" Agnes mused, tapping a finger to her lips. "Hmm. We've been called vigilantes quite a bit. But not usually anything so harsh as murderers. How can it be murder to take the life of one who has ended the lives of others cruelly, coldly, brutally?"

"I don't care 'bout de scum you've slain. Dey deserve what you mete out. I care about de ones who refuse t' join ya. What 'bout dem? Ya take them away and dey are never seen again," Leandra snarled, tossing her braids back. "Young children, young men and women, ya don't care whether dey want to be one of ya or not. Ya take dem or ya kill dem."

Agnes frowned and pursed her lips. "My, my, my. You are definitely rather confused, aren't you?"

"Ya came huntin' me. If I didn't want t' be one of ya, ya would have killed me, too. Don't tell me that I am wrong—I can feel the lies just as well as you," Leandra hissed, starting to pace, her long body tensed and angry.

"Very well," Agnes said agreeably. Linking hands with Erika, she held a hand out to Leandra and smiled serenely. "I shall not tell you anything. You would not believe a word I told you. So I shall show you."

Agnes could not stop the laugh that bubbled up from her lips as Leandra cursed, long and loud. But she did clap her hands over Erika's ears.

Eli slid his eyes to Sarel's face. She was lost in deep thought, her eyes unfocused, faraway, her lips moving on occasion as though she were speaking. And he suspected she was. A faint scent clung to her skin that wasn't truly hers, and a magick moved through the air that wasn't hers either. The scent of lavender, powdered skin…Agnes.

Bloody good news, for once, I hope. He blew a harsh sigh out as he rolled over onto his side, laying his hand on the flat of her belly, stroking the smooth, warm skin there, focusing on the soft hum of voices he heard in the back of his mind. But he couldn't hear anything more than those voices. Not unless she wanted him to.

When her body went lax, he opened his eyes and lifted his head, staring into her golden-green eyes with an arched brow. "What did Agnes want?"

"She has Erika. She is safe," Sarel said, a shudder racking her body.

"Jon? Lori?"

"Still where the Scythe have settled in, they know she is gone. I suspect Lori wants to go in and destroy everything. She's learned too much of the Scythe." Sarel's eyes started to gleam. "Lori is no warrior. She can't handle a battle on her own—not even with Jonathan. But I can't reach her. She's blocked me."

"Lori isn't a child, or an inexperienced witch, sweet," Eli said, sitting up, looping his arms around his legs as he stared into the night. His eyes gleamed dully in the night as he pondered the way to tell her that her sister wasn't the child she still thought she was. "I've never doubted Lori's abilities as a witch, a Healer or one of my Hunters."

"She's not a Hunter."

"She is. She always has been. You just refuse to see. Bloody hell, Sarel, I trained her. Jonathan trained her. She's a damn fine witch—"

"She's a Healer." Sarel's mouth was set in mutinous lines as she glared up at him, folding her arms over her naked breasts.

"To be a Healer, she must first be a witch, and a damn fine one at that," Eli said with a frustrated sigh, flopping onto his back and flinging his arm over his eyes. This was an old, tired argument. "Your sister is a woman grown, a talented, powerful woman. She can take care of herself, handle herself, Sarel."

"No. I won't take that chance. Damn it, I'll have to go after her," Sarel muttered, sitting up and swinging her long, slim legs over the side of the bed.

Though the sun was moving closer to the horizon, it was still several hours before sundown. Eli eyed her naked back narrowly as she strode over to the closet, her rounded ass swaying from side to side as she gathered up dark, tough clothes. Hunting clothes.

"You plan to go alone."

"My sister, Eli," she said softly.

"Your sister isn't alone. Jonathan is with her. And if you *insist* on this, wait so that I can go with you. Mal can remain here and we will go out together," Eli said, sliding from the bed and moving up behind her, resting his hands on her shoulders.

"I can't trust my sister to one man. He's just a werewolf, Eli. And he barely tolerates her," Sarel snapped, shrugging Eli's hands off.

Eli bit off a harsh laugh. Her action, that small rejection of his touch, caused a hot, biting pain to lance through him. He turned away, stalking through the room and snagging a pair of pants. Donning them, he turned and glared at her, his eyes flashing eerily in the dim light of the windowless room. "How can such an intelligent woman be so very dim?" he asked drolly. "Jonathan would lay down his life for any woman, but he would slay every last dragon known to man for Lori. He has been in

178

love with her since he laid eyes on her. Rather odd that you are one of the few who do not realize it. And I wouldn't call him *just* a werewolf. That is like calling you *just* a witch. Don't make light of his gift. It's more powerful than you know."

Sarel, though, didn't really appear to be listening to him, Eli decided. She seemed to be focused on what he had said right after mentioning Jonathan slaying dragons for Lori. Something about the boy being in love with her sister. "You truly didn't know, sweet? Be honest—he has watched her like a bleeding hawk since she first stepped foot onto my lands. Hell, closer than that. She couldn't sneeze without him knowing about it."

"Then he's obsessed. That doesn't mean he is in love with her."

Eli shook his head. "No. He is in love with her. I know Jonathan. And I think you know him a bit better than you admit," he murmured, moving a little closer, waiting until she was staring into his eyes before he started to circle around her. "What is more, you know Lori. She is in love with him. Together they are quite powerful."

"Lori is young. She is sweet, she knows a lot of potions and she can close up cuts. She isn't a fighter," Sarel sneered, brushing past him. He felt her shiver, though, as her naked arm brushed his.

Eli shook his head.

Bloody hell.

Retreating to a corner, he watched as his little know-it-all finished gathering her belongings and then, just as she was getting ready to sling her pack over her shoulder, he lunged.

Judging the time, he figured he just needed to stall her for an hour. Then he could venture outside without danger and follow Sarel while she tracked her sister down. Not that Lori couldn't handle it. He suspected she could handle it very well.

But he wasn't so sure Sarel was ready to handle seeing her baby sister all grown up. And most likely pissed at Sarel's very condescending attitude.

Jonathan flopped onto his belly, burying his face in his arms, wanting to howl. He could smell her, hear her breathing, hear her heartbeat, all but feel the satin of her skin under his hands again. He should have pushed. Damn it, why in the hell was he being nice?

Because she was right, damn it. He had no fucking right to push her after months of being an ass.

Damn it, he wanted her. He wanted to spread her thighs wide and drive his cock deep inside her wet, waiting pussy, and hear her scream his name. He wanted to hear her moan that she loved him, tell her that he loved her, the way he had never said before.

A soft whimper reached his ears.

Faint. Very faint.

The stuttering skip of her heart. A broken little sigh. Shifting on the bed. More movement.

When the scream rent the air, he wasn't ready. Jackknifing up in the bedroll, he rolled onto his knees and was across the tent before the scream had even died on her lips. Pulling her into his arms, he scooped her onto his lap, murmuring her name with no thought to how dangerous it was to waken a nightmarish witch from her slumber. "Shhhh, shhhh, it's okay, baby, it's okay," he whispered against her damp brow. "Come on, come out of it, love. Come out of it." His hair spilled around them as he cupped one hand around her cheek, lifting her face to him as she tried to shy away. "Look at me, baby. Look at me."

Her body continued to tremble and shudder, her lips parting only to let another weak sob forth before she clamped her mouth closed as though she feared making another sound. Tears leaked from under her closed lashes, and Jonathan stroked them away with his thumb. Threading his fingers through her hair, he lowered his mouth to hers, pressing a gentle, soothing kiss to her lips. "Wake up, baby. Come on, wake up," he whispered.

A deep racking shudder tore through her and her eyes flew open, leaving her staring up at him, his face only inches from hers as he lifted his mouth from hers. "It's me, Lori, it's just me," he crooned as he rubbed his thumb gently across her lip. Sweeping one finger across her cheek and drying the tear tracks away, he lowered his brow to hers. "What were you dreaming about?"

The woman was as lovely as a faerie, with a soft, lilting voice — but malice filled every word, while her eyes were lit with the fires of hell. Lori stood staring from the shadows as Jonathan was dragged, bound and unconscious, into a deep, dark pit of a room in the lowest cavern in the network of caves.

They called her Mistress.

And she intended for Jonathan to as well.

He did not submit the way she wanted. With the gleam of madness and evil in her eyes, she told them to beat him to death, that the blood of his passing would work as well as his willing soul.

She intended to create a Dark Hunter of their own...somebody who could destroy the Hunters, somebody who could infiltrate.

A mimic.

And with her blood magick, Lori was sorely afraid it might even work. It nearly had, once before. They had almost succeeded in subverting a broken witch, a lost soul, who had too much darkness in his life, and in his heart.

But Jonathan didn't have darkness in his soul, or his heart. And the were never walked alone.

She fell to her knees, one hand at her mouth to hold back her screams as she saw his face, battered, bloodied and broken. Somebody grabbed him by his hair and forced him to look up at Mistress. She held his chin up with one dainty foot, turning it first one way, then the other, her lip poked out in a petulant scowl. "Stupid dog," she drawled. "You had such a handsome face and now it's ruined."

"Make him bleed," she said quietly, cocking her head as she pulled her foot back. Her voice was as calm as though she were saying, "I'll wear pink today". As she walked away, dozens and dozens of people launched themselves at Jonathan's inert, helpless body.

No! Lori shot to her feet and slammed her palm against a barrier that blocked her from them, light exploded from it as her hand connected.

This won't happen!

As she screamed, she heard the triumphant howl of a wolf.

And then Jonathan's voice, *Wake up, baby, come on...*

Her eyes opened and he was leaning over her, eyes gleaming faintly in the dark from his distress. His scent filled her head and she could taste him on her lips. *Damn it*, Lori thought desperately, that image of him nearly dead, bloodied and bruised, was burned on her mind. *I can't let it happen...*

Reaching up, she buried her fingers in his hair and slanted her lips against his, licking along the seam of his lips. Feeling them part as he took a deep, startled breath, she pushed her tongue inside his mouth when they did. Shifting, she straddled his lap and wrapped her arms around his neck, that long, gloriously silken hair of his spilling all around them like a dark cape. *Jonathan...*

A deep, warning growl rumbled in his chest. His hands clamped on her waist, fingers digging into the soft flesh there as he dragged her back and forth on the hard, thick ridge of his cock, even as he pulled his head away, dragging air into his lungs. "Aaahhh, sweet. Don't. You don't want this, not really. You're upset from the nightmare," he groaned. "If you do this now, you're gonna be madder than hell at us both in the morning."

Lori pushed up onto her knees, planting them into the ground, staring at him with stark, hungry eyes that still stung with tears. "No. If I don't do this *now*, I'm gonna be madder than hell at both of us. And I think I'll regret it for the rest of my life.

I'll make damn sure you do," she whispered roughly. Pulling back, she tugged the camisole over her head, freeing her breasts to the cool night air. She felt desperate to see his face as well as she knew he could see hers.

"*Illunmari*," she spoke, her voice throbbing, magick slithering through the air. Hot, burning little licks left her as it gathered there, hovering above them, the heat fading away until it was nothing but a luminous ball of light. Golden and soft, it highlighted the gleam in his eyes, and the sensual hungry curl of his mouth.

"I know what I want, no matter what dreams of blood run through my head," she murmured, leaning down, pressing her lips to his mouth. Against her naked breasts, she could feel the hard, muscled wall of his chest. He felt so hot, fiery, the scent of the woods and the earth coming from him as he banded one arm around her waist. The other hand buried in her hair, tugging her head back, arching her neck as he plundered her mouth hungrily.

When he pulled back briefly, Lori smiled serenely up at him. She reveled in the sight of his glowing eyes, tawny and gleaming like a wolf's in the night, as he growled, "Be certain, baby. You be very, very certain."

Lori chuckled. Sliding her hands down her torso, she cupped her breasts, rolling her nipples as she arched her back. "Hmmm...I'm certain that I've never wanted anything more. I'm certain...very, very certain."

Air flew from her lungs as Jonathan moved like lightning, rolling her onto her back, pinning her under his body and tearing her panties away. Lori was still trying to catch her breath, her eyes sliding down the lines of his lean, muscled body as his hands jerked away to free the button-fly of his jeans. Mouth dry as the desert, she licked her lips, reaching one hand out to trail her fingers over his flat belly, circling one over the dimple of his navel before his hands caught hers. Pinning them above her head, he wedged his thighs between hers.

"I won't wait this time," he warned her, growling. "I have to have you. Have to. I'll fuck you softer, slower, sweeter later."

Cream flooded her already aching pussy at his words. "Damn it, I don't care how you do it, I just want to feel you inside me," she whimpered, wrapping her legs around his waist and lifting her hips.

Lowering his head, he caught one swollen nipple in his mouth, and Lori mewled as the hot, wet cave of his mouth enveloped the tight, swollen bud. Tossing her head back and forth on the sleeping pad beneath her, Lori sank her nails into the hard muscles of his shoulders as he pushed the blunt rounded head of his cock against the entrance of her wet aching cleft. Trailing a path of hot, biting kisses in a line from her nipple to her mouth, he plunged his tongue deep inside. Lori groaned, swallowing down his taste, as he buried his thick, burning cock inside her.

Oh, the heat... She arched her back as he pierced her, burying himself to the hilt, his balls slapping against her ass as he drank down the scream that rose from her throat. The heat from a were's body was so intense just to touch, but to love... Lori whimpered as he pulled out, sinking back into the creamy wet sheath of her pussy.

When he finally freed her mouth, Lori's head fell back and she sucked in air. Whimpers replaced her frantic search for air as he shifted his grip on her hands. From holding one wrist in each hand, to pinning them both in one of his big hands, he reached down and circled his thumb tauntingly over the swollen bud of her clit.

"You're so tight, so sweet," he crooned against her mouth. "I can smell you...you're almost ripe, you know that? In a few more days, you'll be ovulating and I could fill that flat little belly with my baby." As he spoke, he circled his hips against the cradle formed by hers, riding higher on her body as he did so, and burying the head of his cock against the mouth of her womb. Lori couldn't stop the hungry moan that fell from her lips any more than she could stop her next breath. Her hands opened and closed convulsively, straining uselessly in his firm but painless grip.

Sobbing as he withdrew slowly, Lori screamed as he drove deeply back inside in one hard, heavy thrust. His hot, heavy length forged through the slick, swollen tissues that started to ripple and convulse around his invading length. "Scream again," he purred. "Do it. Scream again, and let me hear my name."

His name fell from her lips in long ragged sobs, and Jonathan felt the shudders that gripped her body as she started to come in hard, racking convulsions. Her snug little pussy tightened around his cock, he knew he was going to explode from the sheer, painfully sweet pleasure of it. Sinking his dick into her was like sinking it into a silk-swathed electrical outlet, and he was still buzzing from the shock. The scent of her sweet cream filled his head, making his mouth water and his gums ache as he hungered for a taste.

He should have tasted her—he would later.

But not now. Pulling out, he pushed back into her and felt the hungry press of her hands on his shoulders, her heels digging into his ass. The diamond-hard points of her nipples burned into his chest, and with a growl he dipped his head and caught one in his mouth, pulling it completely in and sucking deep. The soft, sweet taste of her skin flooded his mouth, the tight grip of her pussy hugged his cock. Shuddering, he rose onto his knees, gripping her hips as he slammed into her, staring down at the long, pale length of her body. His eyes trailed up the length of her torso—the berry red of her nipples, her pink mouth as her tongue trailed over her lips, her eyes gleaming, dazed and glassy.

"So damned pretty, so damned hot," he muttered. "I love you."

Lori gasped, shuddering and arching her back, her hands coming down and grasping on his wrists as she worked her hips against him, her eyes locking on his. "Jonathan—" her words broke off into a ragged scream as her vagina clenched on his cock in a slow, rhythmic series of convulsions, a flush working up from her breasts to her face.

Jonathan growled. Balls pulled tight against his body, he flexed his hands as his nails started to lengthen, his control shattering as his climax rushed up. Blood flooded his mouth as his teeth lengthened and fangs broke through his gums, lust calling to the animal inside him. The soft, silken, wet sheath clutched greedily around him yet again as he drove deep inside one last time and exploded inside her. Pumping her full of hot, creamy seed, he bent low over her body and sank his teeth into the soft fleshy pad of her shoulder.

The tangy sweet wash of her blood spilled down his throat, and her nails raked his back as she screamed out his name yet again.

Wrapping his arms around her, he rolled onto his back, cuddling her against his chest as he licked away the blood from the bite at her shoulder. "Damnation, I love you," he whispered.

"'Bout time you admitted it," Lori muttered, rubbing her cheek against his chest.

Chapter Ten

Lori reveled in the sweet aches of her body as she stood in the shadows of the woods. The wind tugged at her hair and dark clothes, as the moon rose over the lake. The water lapped at the rocky beach as Jonathan moved up behind her. "We won't be alone much longer."

Lori smiled slowly. "I know. I can feel her, too. She is not…happy." That was an understatement. The anger she felt pumping off Sarel was unreal. The anger, the fear—the *paranoia*—in Lori's opinion. "She's wrong. I don't care if you agree with her or not."

"I don't. Whether I want to put you in a tower is beside the point. You're not helpless," Jonathan said, forcing the words out through a tight throat. Moving up behind her, he rested his hands on her shoulders as she stared out over the empty space between them and the dark mouth of the cave. "You're not going to barrel headlong into danger like your sister would either. You're smarter than she and I combined. Smarter than all of us, I'd bet. And a Hunter, through and through."

The hair that stood up on her arms was all the warning she had before Eli purred, "Indeed. Like I'd allow somebody who couldn't take care of herself into my home. Unlike your stubborn sister, I've never had any doubts about you, sweet. Not one."

The slim-hipped, blond vamp strolled out of the woods, his golden hair glinting in the pale moonlight, his eyes as gold as doubloons. A small, amused smile curved his lips as he studied the way Jonathan's hands rested on Lori's shoulders. "Now your sister, though, that is a stubborn lady. Very stubborn, and very convinced she is right." His eyes moved to study the way the wind started whipping through the trees, and a sardonic smile curled his mouth. "No doubt she will be trying to peel the skin from my flesh for not taking what she calls 'her side'."

"Sides?"

Eli blinked. "As Hunter of the Council, Master of my lands, and as the man who loves the stubborn witch with all his heart, the side I take is my own, the side that will best protect us all in the end. She is just too arrogant to see it. Such a temper she has," he mused as the ground started to tremble.

Lori rolled her eyes. "Sarel likes to make her presence felt."

"Yes," Eli said drolly. "She does. Just know — regardless of what Sarel says, you stand your ground, Lori. You're more than she thinks."

The ground didn't actually shudder under her feet — though Lori wouldn't have been surprised if it had — as Sarel strode into the small clearing. Her flaming red hair was blowing back from her face, and her eyes were shooting sparks as she gave her husband a narrow look. "In a hurry?" she asked sweetly.

He lifted one broad shoulder and just smiled his feline smile at her, lowering sooty lashes over his eyes before looking back at Jon and Lori. "Wouldn't you like to say hello to your sister, pet?"

"No. I want to tell her to take her ass back to the house. This isn't something she can handle." Turning her flashing green eyes to Lori, Sarel smiled sharply and snapped, "Lori, take your cute little ass back to the house. You can't handle this."

Lori laughed. "Sarel, you have such a way with people." Turning her attention back to the cave, she closed her eyes and focused on the unrest, and the frenzied, hungry energy coming from deep within.

When the hand closed over her arm, Lori sighed. "Sarel, you need to get a grip. I'm not going anywhere. If you think otherwise…well, go check your arrogance at the door."

"Damn it, Lori. You are *not* a fighter," Sarel snarled, jerking her around.

Lori went with the move, meeting her sister's angry eyes with cool, blank ones. Reaching around, she caught Sarel's wrist, her fingers seeking out the nerves there and squeezing. "I fight when I need to. I'm staying."

Sarel's lips went white before she finally gasped and jerked her hand away. "Damn it, Lori. I can't lose you—"

Lori smiled. "I'm needed *here*. If I leave, we all lose. I've been pulled here for months," she said quietly, turning her attention back to the cave. She had been pulled here, to this spot, maybe for her entire life. "And if I leave, I lose what *I* need the most. *I* can't take that risk."

It was then that she felt it, a slight shift, a break in the air. Taking a deep breath, she looked to Jonathan. "It's time."

"Time for—" Sarel's words died in her throat as Jonathan fell to his knees, his head slumping forward as the muscles and bones in his body started to shift in preparation for the change. His hair rippled and flowed, blowing back from his body as the clothes shredded and fell. A rich musk—wild and earthy— poured from him as he lifted his eyes to meet hers.

"Don't...watch...me..." he rasped through gritted teeth as his face started to lengthen, a muzzle forming, hair changing to fur and flowing like water down over his body. The bones under his skin popped and reformed into a new, more powerful shape.

Eli's lids drooped, though the vampire knew Jonathan didn't give a damn about him or Sarel. Catching his wife's eye, he arched a golden brow, and she snarled but stalked toward him, her eyes full of biting fury and rage.

Lori crossed the space that separated her from her wolf, her eyes dark and watchful on his face. "I've watched you every day for the past seven years of my life, as much as I possibly could. Why wouldn't I watch you now?" Reaching up, she laced her fingers through his hair as the change took deeper hold, as his eyes went from dark, sinful brown to amber, and the bones in his legs broke and changed from human to werewolf. Covered with short, silken fur, his long rangy body crouched on the ground, his powerful head level with hers as he stared at her with glittering, unreadable eyes.

"I adore you, everything about you. Don't think that you have to hide the wolf from me," she murmured, stroking her hands down his silken pelt. "You're so soft, so silken. I've always wondered..."

A growl rumbled out of Jonathan's chest and his hands, large, tipped with ebony claws, closed convulsively over her arms. "Lori..."

"Shhh," she murmured. "Go. We don't have much time. They prepare, even now." Her lashes lowered, and she felt the bittersweet ache fill her heart. Just in case... "I adore you," she repeated. "You've always been my heart."

As Jonathan loped off into the woods, Lori rose, keeping her eyes on his gleaming dark hide, ignoring the ache in her heart. God willing...closing her eyes, she whispered a brief prayer.

Be willing...

"Since we're here, and you obviously intend to keep your ass here," Sarel said coldly. "Would you mind filling me in? Or am I gonna fight blind?"

Eli laughed. "Darling, you were going to do that anyway. Remember? You just tried to send her away."

Lori followed Jonathan through the bond that had formed between them when she had replaced the Scythe's mark with a mark of her own. As he ran through the tunnels on swift silent feet, following the scent of blood and magick, and frenzied, fucking bodies, Lori told Sarel and Eli what she knew, which was little.

"They mean to make a call to the Dark One," she said softly. "They had planned to subvert Jonathan somehow. But he can't be subverted. I don't know how they ever imagined it would work. Now they spill their own blood, and have spent the day in orgy. They call to him."

"They can't raise the devil, Lori," Sarel said, shaking her head.

"No, but they can try to invoke his power and harness it. People have before." Rubbing the flat of her palm against her chest, she turned and watched. And waited.

"What is the purpose of Jonathan going in there alone?" Eli asked, narrowing his eyes.

"A ruse," Lori said, honestly. She just didn't explain exactly how, or why it was intended to work. The same tactic had worked with Jonathan. The men would always be willing to protect their females, their mates. A bittersweet smile curved her lips up.

"To lead them all into a certain chamber," she said. "I'm going to collapse it. But I have to make sure they are all inside that one chamber before I do. They want Jonathan desperately enough to follow him to the ends of the earth. He's the bait."

"I don't want you going in there," Sarel said narrowly, striding forward.

"You can't do it. You can't get there fast enough," Lori said, blowing her a kiss. Eli was reaching for Sarel's hand even as Lori closed her eyes and felt the wind whipping past her…

"Love you, sis," she whispered. She wanted, desperately, to throw her arms around Sarel's neck. But if she did that, Sarel would know. She'd see. So she just settled for the whisper, and the knowledge that taking the band of the Scythe out was something that had to be done.

Leandra fell to the ground, reeling in shock, her head pounding. Her stomach clenched and heaved as bile tried to force its way up her throat. Swallowing the hot, sour taste, she pressed her forehead against the cool tile under her brow. *I won't be sick. I won't.*

She had done this to herself, damn it. She would damn well deal with it without humiliating herself.

All around her, wherever she was, she could feel waves of hostility battering at her finely tuned shields. Dragging a deep breath of vanilla and jasmine scented air in her lungs, she focused. The enclave of the vampire, the Hunter called Elijah Crawford, where she and her sis...no, where she and other murderers had plotted to kidnap Jonathan Wallace.

"Oh, child, you aren't a murderer. You were close, a time or two, weren't you?" Agnes murmured, lowering her ancient body. "Something always stopped you. You didn't aim as well as you thought. Something didn't feel right. The women who traveled with you, eh, they can't claim the same. And there is blood on your heart, that is true."

"Stop, old woman. Ya can't make me feel any better 'bout dis. Ya pulled me through de hearts and souls of too many men and woman to count. I know de truth now," Leandra said rawly, keeping her head down.

The raw hostility battering at her was making her edgy. She was used to animosity. Competition. Dislike. Fear. But not this righteous anger, this need for vengeance. She even knew why — she had led the attack that had killed two of their wolves, and so many of their traps had been set against them, all orchestrated by her.

And Erika. She had taken Erika.

Erika —

"Erika! Where's de girl, old woman? What did ya do with her?" Leandra demanded, sitting bolt upright, her golden eyes flashing, one hand flying out.

The words had not even died in the air, and Erika came flying out of the crowded room, before the blonde woman at her side could even react. "Leandra, don't be a goof. I'm fine!" the girl said, curling up against her side, wrapping her arms around Leandra's waist and snuggling against her. "I know Agnes did a poof on ya, but I was just *zap*...and here I was. Plopped right down next to Malachi, too — and he yelped."

"I did not," a dark, accented voice snapped.

"Did too," Erika said, grinning. "I wasn't supposed to tell."

"Children these days have no sense of honor."

That voice sent shivers down Leandra's spine—foreboding, fear...*hunger*...but mostly fear. Slowly, as he came around the room and into her line of view, she lifted her head and stared into his gaze. Watching his eyes, she waited. Over her head, he met Agnes' eyes and Leandra felt the unheard conversation taking place. "I could not care less that she fell into the wrong group," Malachi said silkily. Lowering his eyes to her face, he said, "What I want to know is where my friends are now. What good is your ass to me *now*? Have you any worth to us?"

But before she could answer, his eyes went vague and blank, and he turned around and left the room.

"She says they are just raising an energy level," Eli murmured, staring into the darkness.

The anger and fury that came pummeling back over the link between Eli and Malachi confirmed Eli's worst fears. "No. They want a blood sacrifice. They have somebody in mind. She's planning on swapping...herself for that victim. Then most likely, at the last moment, doing exactly what she said."

"Then why the lie? Why not just go in and do that without the misleading?"

Malachi's disbelief was felt clearly. "Do you really think Jonathan wouldn't have known what she was doing? Wouldn't have felt it? And stopped her?"

"So they had planned to sacrifice Erika," Eli said, shaking his head.

"And now Erika is safe, hale, and hearty. Her kidnapper became her hero. She—arrived here, just a little bit ago, quite suddenly. But I imagine Lori already knows she isn't there, and so does Jonathan. They have somebody else in mind. I hope whoever it is, this person is worth the risk that young fool witch is taking."

Eli forced himself to not ask questions. Erika was safe, that was important, how didn't matter. *"She's already gone inside. Tracking her is near impossible. Well, my friend...I am quite open to —*
"

Eli felt the magick burst as Lori reappeared. But it was unlike anything he had seen from her before. Her magick had always been quiet. Subtle. This was anything but.

In front of her, held by her magick, was a massive wolf. A still one — quiet, unmoving — but breathing.

Threading her fingers briefly through his fur, she whispered, "My heart, always." Then she let his body drift to the ground.

As she knelt beside him, she locked eyes with Eli, then Sarel. She placed her palms flat on the ground. "Safehold, keep them," she whispered eerily. "Until my word or death releases them..."

"Lori, *no*."

Sarel fell to her knees to try to counter the simple earthspell, but it was too late. The earth here knew Lori's blood, Lori's magick — that Sarel couldn't hope to copy. As Sarel tipped her head back and opened herself to her own magick, they watched a tear fall down Lori's cheek.

Jonathan felt her go. The little witch had tricked him.

The Wolf was trying, desperately, to work past the sleep spell she had thrown on him in the cave.

But it wasn't going to be easy.

And even then, the final spell, the earthspell...only two things would unlock that.

Little fool...why?

Malachi exploded through the door, his eyes blazing with flames of blue. "Our little witch, the sweet innocent Healer that the lot of you think is so bloody innocent, so fucking helpless, has gone and sacrificed herself so she can kill the Scythe. And the fools, the bloody braggarts are no smarter than their arrogant predecessors. So she'll likely be able to do it...but she'll die in the winning."

He had grief written in his eyes as he knelt in front of Agnes, taking her face in his hands. "The sweet lass will die.

They plan to kill, to sacrifice. If enough of them with magicked blood cry to Lucifer, they may be able to invoke his evil power and fill a dark army with it. They wanted to subvert Jonathan for this. But this…this is what they truly wanted all along. To have the power to infiltrate us, to find the weaker Hunters and fill them with darkness. To raise their own kind of Hunters. To breed their own Huntresses. Only the Scythe a millennia ago e'er came close."

Agnes gasped, her face pale. "We have to stop her," she whispered harshly.

Malachi lowered his lips to her brow and dropped his shielding. "No, love. We can't." Bitter self-hatred filled him. Because stopping her meant allowing them to succeed. He'd been prepared to die the last time. Would have this time, as well. Lori just beat him to it. Sliding his way into Agnes' mind was not easy. If she had not been wearied from her trials with the young witch who was now standing warily over them, Mal knew it never would have been possible.

As he pulled her under, into a gentle sleep, a tear fell.

He had thought he had already lost all of his self-respect.

How sad to realize he had been wrong.

Lifting his gaze, he met the amber eyes of the young witch Agnes had presented them with.

"I would tink dat a vampire as old as you would have lost so many people that one more witch would not matter," she said, smiling a bitter smile. "How wrong I am today."

Malachi opened his mouth to snarl at her.

But before he could, she was gone.

And he was left cursing himself for being a fool.

Should have known the little bitch was a bloody flyer.

Chapter Eleven

As Leandra came to rest on the land, she felt the touch of another witch on her earth. It was a powerful, healing touch, a good one, feeling much like her own, the magick meshing with hers, overlying it.

Laying one palm down, she listened to the whisper of the spell…*until my death or word releases them…*

"Such spelling on top of me spells," Leandra mused. "She must be a powerful ting."

Flexing her hand, letting her fingers dig into the earth, she whispered, "Not her death, but her *need*…"

The ground trembled as the two witch's spells battled. But Leandra had been there so long, battling the ill effects the bad magick had on land. Even though she hadn't understood why the land was taking ill, she had battled.

She thought she understood a bit now, though. The Scythe—the people she had lived with, worked with, lived for—were wrong, living against nature, and the land didn't like it.

With a brief sigh, she stood straight, feeling the wind whipping her braids around her shoulders as magick exploded through her. Before her heart could beat three more times, she was within the great chamber. Hiding within one of the recessed alcoves, retreating deep, her eyes locked on the center dais. Mistress waited with Marick, bound and struggling, staring at her with disbelieving eyes.

She so hated failure.

But there was also Jennifer, a young witchling they had brought in just a year ago, only twelve years old. Staring all around with wide, scared eyes, confusion written all over her face as she struggled against the two men who held her. Leandra withdrew further, whispering a silencing as she waited for the red-haired Healer to show herself.

Lori didn't make her unknown audience wait long.

The sight of another child down there sickened her. *Oh, no*...another baby. Her heart tore open as she studied the child. Her eyes wheeling around in terrified circles as she struggled against the men who held her.

Damn it. I don't have the time!

They had been fucking the day away. That and cutting into their own flesh.

The scents of so many frenzied copulating bodies, and so much spilled blood. First, one started to notice her...then another...then a few more. One man tried to grab her and drag her into an already crowded ménage a quatre. Purring roughly, he slid his hands down to cup her ass, "You waste time, *bebè*, wearing the clothes. *Veins ici*, let me have a taste."

"Taste this," she said sweetly. Slamming her hand against his chest, she released a bit of the illness she had felt from the land—the cold, barren impotent wasteland sinking into him, into his healthy, hungry body and changing it.

The shrieks of horror from his partners were joyful music to her ears as she continued her walk to the dais.

But it was no longer an unnoticed walk.

A blonde woman sat curled in the lap of a black-maned, Italian inherent who was driving his fingers into her pussy as they watched Lori approach. Lori felt a blush stain her cheeks as the woman screamed in climax. She was licking her lips like a satisfied cat as Lori leaped onto the dais.

"I don't know you, witch. You're a foolish thing, entering my territory. And on such a bad day—you'll be lucky if you only end up fucked within an inch of your life."

She had such a sweet, innocent voice, Lori mused.

And such evil in her eyes.

An empty smile curled Lori's lips. "I'm not too worried about that." Blinking slowly, she skimmed her gaze over the calming crowd. Oh, they were still busily fucking, but less screaming and moaning. More sighs, more were just holding still against their partners as they stared with blank, curious eyes at Lori. Trying to determine her place, what she meant to them.

"I bet you are the one who took one of my offerings. I must have an offering," the woman said, poking her lip out.

Arching a brow, Lori said, "Does that 'poor me, she took my toy' act really work?"

Red flags of rage appeared high on her cheeks. Lashing out with an angry hand, she hissed at Lori in Latin before settling back against the man, and wrapping her hand around his thick, heavy dick.

Lori felt the swipe of her magick, and only smiled as it barely even rippled her shields. Chuckling, she said, "It's going to take more than that."

Lori braced herself for the *more*.

Jonathan exploded out of the furred hide, into his human skin, with a furious roar. Grabbing Sarel's arms, he leaned down nose-to-nose and snarled, "Break the damn spell, Sarel!"

"I can't," she whispered softly. Her eyes, glassy with shock and tear-bright, met his. "I've been trying. I've got the warrior magicks. But the spells, the earth magicks—Lori has me beat. She is, by far, a more powerful witch in so many ways. And I never even knew…"

Jonathan felt her body wilt in his hands as Eli moved up behind her, wrapping his arms around his wife's waist. "Lori somehow knew what was being planned, Jonathan. She tricked you, and us as well. Lori is inside, alone. And we are stuck out here."

Jonathan felt his throat close up. "She is going to collapse the cave. From the inside."

"A brave mon, ya are."

That voice—Jonathan's head whipped up and he searched all around, though there was nobody else there with them. That voice, though. He had heard it. And this wasn't the first time. The first time he'd heard it had been only weeks ago, when he had taken that slice in his side. *"Dis is for my Mistress, wolf. Your pretty hide is what de lady wants, not your death."*

Eli's eyes were narrowed, the rim of gold flickering. Both he and Sarel had heard it as well.

"Just how brave are ya, though? Willing to walk into a death trap, I wonder?"

"What do you want, you evil bitch?" Jonathan hissed as his fangs broke through his gums, his rage calling to the wolf, his control in tatters.

"Your strength, your speed. I'm a channeler. I need a conduit. I cannot save de young witch alone. Come to me, Jonathan of de Council. I can save your lover, but I've wearied meself dis day. I need strength."

"It's a bloody trick," Elijah rasped, reaching out as Jonathan started to turn. "As your Master, I refuse to allow it. Bad enough we lose Lori—"

"I *can't* lose her," Jonathan snarled, grabbing Elijah's silk shirt, whirling and slamming the centuries-old vampire into a tree. The great oak shuddered under the impact. "She is my *life*. My heart and soul. If I lose her, I might as well die, too. So if this is a trick, it doesn't matter."

He was gone, shifting to full wolven form in heartbeats, running so fast, Eli could hardly track him with his eyes.

And when he tried to follow, Lori's shield spell stopped him. Sarel pounded against it with her fist. "The witch changed the spell. I can feel it. She changed it somehow," Sarel sobbed, resting her hands against the unseen wall as she slid to her knees.

Eli curled up behind her, wrapping his large, golden body around his wife's sobbing frame. "Take heart, love. Perhaps there is hope. Jonathan is the luckiest bastard I've ever known in my life," he murmured.

A channeler...how very odd...

Her other secret. The reason Leandra never seemed to fail, never seemed to tire, was because she always had a vast reserve of energy. Or so it seemed. Rarely did she rely on her energy reserves. She could always find energy from the land around her, or from her victims, the thugs she hunted and preyed upon on her own.

She had also siphoned energy from those in Scythe who were unworthy and unfit for the cause. Men like Marick...though she should have drained them all dry, including herself.

"Not de time, girl," she whispered harshly.

Though she heard no sound, she knew when the wolf was at her heels. She pivoted swiftly, knife in hand, just as he was shifting, and reaching for her with a big hand.

Staring at her with fury and rage in his dark, bottomless eyes, he smelled of the woods, and man. A light shone about him that was so true, so crystal-bright, that Leandra wanted to weep. "If ya kill me, ya cannot hope t' get her out of here alive," she whispered simply. "Even though I deserve me death." Then she held out her knife.

He backpedaled away from her and the blade, a look of disgust sliding through his eyes, across that golden face. The muscles in his chest and belly spasmed as he moved a hand in front of his face, shaking his head. "Keep your blade, witch. What do you want me for?"

"I need your hand."

He lowered his lashes. "Literally?"

Leandra chuckled. "No. Flesh to mine...just your flesh to mine, werewolf. And then be ready to fight. This won't go unnoticed," she whispered.

"And I'm here alone," he muttered.

She smiled. "Not for long. Her need, not her death."

Sarel fell forward as the wall of the spell disintegrated. Catching herself on her hands, she gasped as rocks dug into them. Her eyes narrowed and she rose to her feet. Elijah was already at the mouth of the cave.

"If she collapses it while we are in there..." Elijah murmured, looking back to her. "Will you please stay out here?"

"That is my baby sister in there. I thought once before that I had lost her. And I have a better than average chance of surviving a cave-in. Not as good as you, handsome, but better than average."

"She means for this to kill an army of witches and weres," he murmured, turning to stroke his hands down her back. "Please."

"I can't. Don't ask me," she said, cupping his face. Pressing her lips to his, she sent a brief prayer heavenward, and then strode into the dark maw. Eli closed his eyes briefly.

And then he followed her, his eyes on the shining dark-red banner of her hair.

* * * * *

Jonathan felt the heat of the witch's hand on his, and something rifling through him. And the Wolf, rousing, raised his head, studying the intruder. Jonathan prepared to battle the Wolf down—

But he only sighed at her presence, settling his muzzle on his paws as she siphoned the vast reserves a were held. "*A wise witch would take better care, girl,*" the wolf said lazily, his tongue lolling out.

Jonathan stiffened.

The woman only said, "Hush, you fool animal...d' ya wish me to leave marks all over your bearer?"

"If I thought you were likely to do that, do you think I'd be letting you touch him at all?" the Wolf asked.

The witch sighed as she reached up and cupped Jonathan's face with her free hand—not staring at his face, but at his chest, as though she could see into his heart. "He hardly understands ya a 'tall. After all dis time. He don't know what t' tink of ya. And ya don't help him, either, do ya now?"

"And do you think you understand me, child?"

"I am no Indian, but I understand a totem animal when I see one," she said, smirking. "That's a bit of what ya are at least. I can even see your aura, all over him."

With a shudder and a sigh, she took her hands away, flexing them. Blinking, she opened her eyes and stared up at Jonathan. "De Wolf laid his mark heavy on you. Such a rush of power I have never felt. And you don't even feel weak, I tink."

Jonathan stared into her glittering, gold eyes—into the face of the woman who had sliced him open and felt fine. "Are you the one who killed Brad?"

"No. But I did shoot your friend, the one who came home alive, t' tell ya what I had done with Erika and I did organize the whole ting. If ya wish to punish me, that is your right. But your lover does not have de time. She will bring de whole place down. In only seconds. And others, dey come. They felt me magick, and know I am here. As do your friends come."

Jonathan felt it as Eli and Sarel approached. Staring into her eyes, he said roughly, "If you fail to save her, you will know a death worse than any you have ever imagined."

She smiled sardonically. "I am imagining plenty already for meself. You will have to get in line," she said obliquely.

Jonathan was still staring at her as she winked out of sight.

Lori didn't plan on taking abuse or showing any false bravado. Staring into the sweet, blue eyes of the woman who called herself Mistress, she started to gather the energy that supported the bedrock beneath her. It was already weakened. Somebody had been trying to slowly heal the land, and had been doing a good job of it, but too many others were undermining her.

Collapse the cave, and flood it with fire. That would kill all of them. The energy she pulled from the bedrock would make one hell of a fireball. And it would incinerate her body completely, freeing Jonathan, Eli and Sarel right away. They would be able to get away in plenty of time to get Eli inside before full daylight.

"Why don't you tell me who you are, Red?" Mistress said, tossing her blonde curls back and stroking her hand down over her Adonis' cock as she shifted to straddle him, her back against his chest.

Lori smiled—a tiny, humorless smile. "Nobody too important."

The woman laughed, a deep, throaty chuckle as she slid down, arching her back. "You lie...you shine with power. It's too pure for my taste, but I love the challenge of corrupting that. Elias likes the innocent and he's a seductive bastard. Maybe I'll let him have you."

Closing her eyes, Lori whispered softly, "Not in this lifetime."

"What?"

"Mistress hates being told no," a soft, exotically accented voice whispered in her ear.

Lori didn't move a muscle, although the voice was as real as the couple fucking right in front of her. *"Ya know, girl, don't ya, that what ya plan is sure to kill ya?"*

Lori gave a tiny nod as she said easily to the lady in front of her, "I said, no thanks."

Coldly, "I wasn't offering. I was stating. You come into my territory and I'll do as I please. If I tell you to come over here and lick my pussy, you will."

Lori started to laugh.

Cupping her hands in front of her, she gathered the energy of the bedrock, taking it into her hands, and then inside of her as she laughed. "No. Not likely. You see, I came here to kill you. All of you. Hmm, and myself as well," she said as tears formed in her eyes. Answering whoever had been whispering into her ears.

A silvery sheen started to form in front of her. "I would have *liked* another way." Her throat started to tighten. "But you all can't leave this place. None of you can."

Opening her soul, she took the energy inside as the foundation of the cave started to shudder and the witch in front of her started to understand. "Stop!"

Her voice trembled as she tried to invoke the power of the earth.

But the earth wouldn't heed one who had gone against it for so long.

"Hmm...so ya did know."

"I feel no evil from you. If you are here to try and save me, then do not bother. Though my heart breaks for the child there. Save her, if you can. But do it now and get out. Because this cave is coming down."

"De girl is already gone."

Lori was barely aware of the girl flitting out of sight as more and more of the power of the earth sank into her. Her skin was too small to hold it all. Far too small. She ached with it, her skin stretched far too tight, and itched, and hurt, burning...all around her people started to scream. They were rushing closer and closer as somebody screeched, "Stop her, damn it!"

Jonathan shifted, exploding into his larger, wolfman form, swiping out with a clawed hand as two men rounded the corner—a wolf and a witch. Taking the throat of the wolf, he slammed the man into the wall as he started to shift, ripping with his claws before he could complete the change. The smell of blood on the air fueled his anger, his rage, and he turned to face the witch, only to see him facing off with Sarel.

Eli strolled up, his fangs sliding down past his lower lip, his golden eyes glowing in the dim chamber. "My lady wife will be greatly pissed if you interfere here, old boy," he said easily, though the heat of anger heated his voice.

Sarel's hand flew up only moments before the witch's volley of fire hit her in the face. She caught his flame with a shield that she flung back at him, wrapping him in a vortex that encircled him and ate at his flesh. She smiled coldly, striding past him, the wolf and the vampire at her side.

The ground was starting to tremble beneath their feet as they entered the next corridor.

"I hope, my love, that your sister is not in too big of a hurry," Eli murmured.

"I'm hoping that Jonathan's new friend is what she claims to be."

Jonathan said nothing as he followed the scent of Lori. He could taste her fear.

Leandra eased Jennifer's still body to the ground, stroking her hand down the side of her face and murmuring softly, "Not wakin' up now, ya hear?" Breathing a whisper of magick over the sleeping child, she stood and lifted her face to the sky. Feeling everything rush past her, she went flying through time and space, back inside the cave, just as Lori was forging the energy into fire.

She paused to whisper into the werewolf's ear, "I'm gonna get your woman now, turn around and get out of here. She's not gonna be...right after dis. De magick she is taking inside is too much. She will be needing your hand."

He stumbled as she allowed only a whisper of her body to form in front of him, nodding to the entrance. "De witch can put hold spells to hold anybody back. It won't hold me," she said, grinning widely. Nodding to Sarel, she added, "Don't bother with anything subtle. Big, flashy, dangerous. We don't need more din a few more minutes. And do it *now*, din get out."

She left them, flying through to hover behind Lori. The light around her had coalesced into a silver so bright and shining it nearly blinded Leandra, as she settled her feet on the ground. "Ya know dis is not your time, Lori," Leandra shouted over the roaring of the rocking, shuddering earth.

"I told you to get out of here. Where is the girl?"

"She is safe, unlike me and you." Evilly, Leandra leaned in and whispered, "An' ya friends. Dey broke thru dat spell ya set, Lori girl. And dey are trying to break thru me spells to get in de cave." *The end is what matters*, Leandra told herself.

Lori hissed, throwing her head back. "You bitch, what the hell…"

But the fire inside her had grown beyond what Lori could control. As it exploded, Leandra felt it. It was all the young Hunter could do to push it outside of her body, and that racked her with pain.

Wrapping her strong arms around Lori, Leandra felt her go limp. "Dere now," she crooned as she pulled them out. "Dat was all I needed. For you to let go for me. Your people are okay, hush now…"

Leandra settled down at the edge of the forest, stroking Lori's hair back, staring in bemusement at the streaks of white that now threaded it. "Ya went and had the mother of all highlighting treatments done, didn't ya, girl?" she murmured, shaking her head.

At her side, Jennifer slept on, her dark hair spilling around her pretty, young face. As she continued to stroke her dark hand through Lori's white-streaked hair, she sensed it as Jonathan, the vampire, and the witch's sister spilled out of the cave. Mere moments later, the fire started to boil up from the main chamber.

It lit up the darkness as the three Hunters came to kneel in front of her, staring at the woman lying cradled in her lap, almost afraid to look at her too closely.

The fire at their backs came almost too close. Jonathan could feel the heat of it as he stared at the three women in front of him. No…two women and a girl. He had no clue where the girl had come from.

The exotically beautiful witch looked up at him as she stroked her fingers through Lori's hair. *Her hair…*

It was streaked with white. Shot through with streaks of pure white. Closing his eyes, he sank to his knees and reached out, afraid to touch her.

"It is okay, mon. She is alive, son of de Wolf," the witch said quietly, a gentle smile on her face. The faint moonlight glimmered off the dark scythe mark on her face. "The fire was already burning inside, too much power, too much magick. I had to lie to her, let her tink ya were inside, coming after her, instead of running out to meet her. She pushed de fire out just in time, but it hurt, left a mark, and burned her inside." Stroking her fingers through Lori's hair, she whispered, "I don' know if her magick will ever be de same again. But she should be mostly fine."

Jonathan laid a hand on her breast, feeling the steady, slow pounding of her heart. *Alive…*

"Oh, God," he whispered brokenly, feeling a hot wash of tears rush to his eyes. "Thank You, God." He gently took Lori's limp body in his arms and cradled her against him, meeting the odd, amber eyes of the witch across from him. "Thank you."

They reflected the light of the moon back at him, like a cat's. "Mebbe He will be willin' to forgive at least a little of de tings I've done," she said dryly, folding her hands in her lap. Lifting her eyes, she stared up past Jonathan's shoulder, at Eli.

"Who are you?" Jonathan asked, forcing the words out through a thick, tight throat.

"Do ya always ask de names of your enemies before you take deir heads?" she asked calmly, drawing her knife from her hip and tossing it aside.

Jonathan's blood ran cold at the calm, easy way she spoke of her own death. And she truly expected it. He could see it in her eyes. Slowly, he shook his head, flashing fang as he spoke. "You saved the life of my mate. Whatever wrong you have done to me is cancelled out by that, and more. My life is yours. And any who try to take your life will have to face me."

Her lashes lowered over those exotic, almond-shaped eyes. "I'd rather die den live me life in some prison, wolf. If ya feel gratitude for your mate's life, then let me punishment be death."

Jonathan rubbed his cheek against Lori's hair, the white, silken streaks mingling with the streaks of red in a bizarre highlighted pattern. Keeping his hand pressed over her heart, Jonathan felt it pounding—reassuring himself that she was there, that she was alive and well.

"You will not die. Not be imprisoned. Not while I breathe."

Leandra followed the Hunters into Elijah's home. The members of his Enclave stared at her with suspicious, watchful eyes. Too many of them would know her, simply by her scent, the feel of her magick. She had the aura of wrongness to her, when she stood next to Lori. She knew—her soul was unclean.

Not evil, as the Mistress had been.

But unclean.

They would know.

What are ya doing here, girl? she asked herself, shaking her head. The wooden beads on the ends of her braids clacked, and she rubbed her hands together, flexing them. The soothing scent of jasmine rose to her nostrils and she breathed it in. Slowly, she lifted her lashes and met the gazes of those who stared at her.

"What have you brought us?" a long, lean vampire asked, his dark Italian eyes moving from the top of Leandra's head to the bottom of her leather-booted feet.

Lori, still tired, still weak, but cocky and calm, arched a brow and said, "Nobody brought you anything, Rafe. I think Sheila is more than you can handle, anyway."

Snickers filled the air and Kelsey said easily, "Sheila declared a few days ago she was rather tired of his...bullshit, is how she phrased it. With some more...definitive terms thrown in. For all to hear. Safe to say they are no longer speaking."

Leandra remained silent, pulling her eyes away from the vampire, not meeting the gaze of the other witch who had entered the conversation—not looking at any of the vampires or weres.

"You…"

Breathing in slowly, Leandra lifted her eyes and met the gaze of the man she had shot only seconds before she had taken Erika. She had never thought herself a coward—but staring into those pale-gray eyes was making her belly pitch and roll, making her cheeks flame, and she wanted to turn and flee.

The worst possible thing when she was surrounded by predators.

And witches far more powerful than she.

"Me," she said, lowering her head, slowly.

"Mike?"

Leandra didn't know where the whisper came from. It didn't matter.

All eyes moved to the were. His eyes were glowing, swirling with power and rage, as his fangs dropped, the scent of blood filling the air. He stalked through the room, his eyes on her face. And all other eyes followed him, tracking his movement.

Then settled on her.

Like they had one mind, connected to his. They all now knew.

"Elijah, why is she here?" one were asked.

A softer, cooler voice said, "She is here to die. Let me do it. The blood of a witch is a sweet prize."

Leandra refused to let her body shake, and she tried to keep her fear from showing.

Jonathan stepped in front of her. "No."

Mike continued to move closer, closer still, until he could reach out and touch her, his palm coming up and cupping her face, all under the watchful eye of the vampire and two witches at her back. Jonathan stood in front of her, separating them from the others.

"The one she hurt here the most was Mike. She didn't kill Brad. This will concern Mike and her. Not her and you," Jonathan said softly, a deep, threatening growl rumbling through his chest.

"She attacked us—"

Jonathan snarled, his eyes flashing at the were who had spoken, menace rolling from him. All of the wolves fell silent.

"Nice trick to silence the wolves, pup. It doesn't work on me," Rafe said darkly. "She is a threat to us. All of us. What are you gonna do to me, piss on my feet?"

"I'll rip your fucking throat out," Jonathan said, flexing a hand that displayed ebony claws. "Gladly, if you touch one hair on this woman's head. She saved the life of my mate. I'll destroy any person who thinks to harm her."

"Does one life saved equal the many evils she has done?" Rafe asked silkily, as he crossed the distance that separated him from Jonathan. Bloodlust, the need to end the life of the one who had served their tormentors filled his eyes, his face. His fangs had dropped and his dark eyes gleamed with red and gold pinwheels as he stood nose-to-nose with Jonathan.

"Rafe, you overstep yourself," Eli warned, his voice soft, but no less powerful as he moved out of the shadows. "The girl risked her life, not just once, but several times. And her freedom, as well. She knew what coming here meant, but she came nonetheless. Remember yourself."

Rafe narrowed his gaze, tearing his eyes away from Jonathan. Meeting Eli's look, he demanded, "Do you think I'm going to just sit here while this murdering bitch walks free among us?"

"The lass is no murderer."

Finally, she was able to tear her eyes away from Mike's mesmerizing gray gaze. Swallowing, the dry click in her throat audible to everybody around her, she dragged her eyes to the man who had spoken.

Malachi stared back from his perch on the bottom stair as people all around him parted, clearing a path between him and Leandra. "Oh, her soul isna the cleanest one I e'er saw, an' thas no lie. Aye, she has darkness in her soul, but it's her own torment. Not any true evil," he murmured, a smile curving that wide, sensual mouth. He studied her face, and Leandra felt her eyes sting with tears at the understanding, the sympathy she saw there. "An' her heart is a good one. Misled as bloody 'ell. But as true as the sunrise."

"You *can't* let them hurt her, Jonathan!"

Leandra gasped as the blonde whirlwind broke free, yet again, from the crowd, thrashing at the arms who tried to hold her. But the way she struggled, the only way to hold her was to hurt her. And none risked that. So Erika broke free of them and hurled herself at Leandra, throwing her arms around her waist and snuggling up against her side. "She protected me, and she loves me, even if she is a stupid witch," Erika said with the bluntness of childhood. "I don't care if she did have to kidnap me to figure out who she is supposed to be."

"And who is dat, Erika?" Leandra murmured, lowering her head to nuzzle the soft blonde hair, hugging Erika close.

"Well, one of us, of course," Erika said, sliding her eyes sideways to watch as Agnes came closer.

Agnes studied Leandra with solemn, serious eyes before turning to study the still angry, still hostile faces. "We went to Jamaica, Mal and I, fifteen years ago. To find a child. Her father was ready to sell her to the highest bidder so he could rape her while she was still a virgin."

Leandra closed her eyes, her shoulders slumping. A rough gasp next to her seemed to rake her skin as the angry muffled curse echoed in her ears. Blood rushed to her face. Damn that old witch. Inciting their pity. *His* pity.

"She got away, all on her own, and hid from us, eluded us, for weeks and months. We didn't search long enough, or hard enough. It's not that child's fault that she landed with some very, very evil people. If Mal and I had looked hard enough, or arrived sooner, things might not have played out like this."

As Agnes spoke, she moved around the large foyer studying the gathering of Hunters, some great, some very minor. Many were studying Leandra with looks akin to pity, while others continued to glare at her with outright hostility.

"She has wronged a few people here more than others. And those are the ones who will speak," Agnes said, sliding Erika a narrow look. "One has already made her opinions clear. And Jonathan was rather emphatic. He will rip out the throat—I believe, he said—of the person who touches Leandra. So, the only other person who needs to speak is Mike. Beyond that, none of you need to worry."

"Brad can't be consulted," Brielle snarled, rising from her crouch.

"She didn't kill Brad," Agnes said.

"I'm not innocent, old woman," Leandra said, rolling her eyes and stepping forward, away from Erika's clinging hands. "I did what I thought was right, at dat time. If me tinking was warped, den I will take me punishment. I do not hide behind children or old women. Or ancient vampires." Sliding Malachi a narrow glance, she faced the young inherent who had spoken. "I did many tings I am not proud of, wolf. I tink many of us have. I will take me punishment from whomever is man enough to dole it out. I just ask dat de person be worthy to hand out dat punishment."

"That would leave you out, Brielle."

That quiet, level voice came from Mike.

Leandra turned slowly, her eyes lifting and meeting his.

"Go on, witch. I won't ask for your life," he said softly. And then he turned on his heel and walked away.

"You don't have to leave," Lori said quietly, watching as Leandra finished plaiting her long ebony hair.

"Yes, I do. You tink I can stay here, wit so many people watchin' me wit such angry eyes?" Leandra asked. Tossing the last of the braids over her shoulder, she sighed. "Mebbe dat would be fittin' punishment—for me to never know another restful night of sleep."

Lori touched her fingers to Leandra's shoulder and gently said, "I suspect you'll be doing that to yourself." Her green eyes met Leandra's haunted ones, and Lori felt her heart squeeze. None but her could understand just how tortured this woman truly was. Even from the beginning, Leandra's heart had been pulled apart. Struggling to serve those she thought were right. But following the path her heart recognized as right.

"I hear da screams of da people I know da Scythe killed, people I could have saved. I closed my ears to them," Leandra whispered, staring blankly into the coming night as a tear rolled silently down her cheek. "I can't help but wonder to meself. Were dere others like Jennifer? She be fine, I know, at Excelsior. But were dere others, ones who wouldn't give over to evil? Did the Mistress have them killed?"

"Where will you go?" Lori asked, trying to distract her.

"Away," Leandra said absently. "Someplace where mebbe I can try to figure out how to forgive meself. If such a ting is possible. The good Lord knows nobody else ever will. But I, well, I have to live wit meself."

* * * * *

Lori was still standing there, her arms wrapped around herself, watching Leandra's tall proud profile as the black woman walked away, alone, from Eli's enclave. Malachi had hailed her briefly, and she had stared stonily into the night, shaking her head once or twice. He had brushed a gentle hand across her arm, an almost fatherly touch, before he moved aside.

Lori couldn't see her anymore.

"She'll be okay."

Jonathan's voice was a deep, hypnotic growl that sent shivers racing across her body. Lifting her eyes, she studied the moon as it rose higher in the sky. It would be full tomorrow.

Shiloh Walker

Earlier, she had glimpsed his eyes, and she had seen the near wildness that started to gleam in the eyes of the *were* when the full moon neared.

And the hunger. Complete and total hunger.

"She's never been okay," Lori said quietly. "This is actually the closest she's ever been. And that's the scariest thing."

"The scariest thing was sending a woman who had just kidnapped my baby to save the woman I love," Jonathan whispered from the doorway. "Why are you here? Instead of in my house?"

"Because it's your house," she said quietly, lifting one shoulder. "These are my rooms. We came home, so I came home."

"I want you in my bed. *Our* bed."

He was closer now, at her back. Lori shuddered as he lowered his head and kissed her neck, gripping her waist with his big, strong hands and dragging her back so that he could cuddle her ass against his cock. Folding his arms around her torso, trapping her arms against her body, he lowered his mouth to press it against her neck, scoring it with his teeth. "My mate. *Mine.*"

She felt enveloped by him, that large, lean body cuddling, protecting, guarding hers. Hungering for her…she could feel his hunger rolling off of him in waves.

Pressing the flat of his hand against her belly, he slid it down until he cupped her mound in his hand, stroking his finger back and forth over her clit, bringing a whimper to her lips. A startled scream rang in the room as Jonathan gripped the sarong styled pants at her hips and tore them to shreds, the paradise flowered material falling in pieces around her feet. Whirling her around, he took her shirt and pulled it over her head before grasping fistfuls of her hair, and lowering his face to bury his nose in the red and white wealth of it.

"My little redheaded hellcat has turned into a sweet little candy cane," he teased, smoothing his hands down the long line of her back, cupping her ass and lifting her against him. "Let's see if you still taste as sweet." Slanting his lips against her mouth, he pushed his tongue in, devouring her taste, swallowing her down hungrily as he pinned her back against the wall. Rocking his cock against her cleft, the rough material of his jeans abraded the sensitive flesh of her thighs.

"Moan for me...*scream*," Jonathan whispered as he lowered his head to take one swollen nipple into the hot cave of his mouth. Swirling his tongue over the hard crest, he rolled his eyes up to stare at her, the dark chocolate of his gaze shifting to a warm, burning gold. Against her belly, she could feel the hard, warm muscles of his chest—and he rocked against her, dragging his thick, rigid cock over her aching cleft time and again.

Lori felt a scream catch in her chest as she arched against him, her hands fisting in his hair. Bringing her legs up, she locked her heels just above the firm muscles of his ass. The cold wall bit into her back as he massaged her butt with his hands. Lori quivered as he breached the seam of her ass, probing the rosette with a blunt fingertip.

She felt the room whirling around her and blinked, dazed, realizing he had moved, positioning her on her knees by the bed. "Stay there," he ordered gruffly, running his hands over the rounded curve of her ass. "Damn, you've got the sweetest ass."

A hot flood of need washed through her and she lowered her brow to the cool floor, hardly able to support her body. She was shaking all over, fine little tremors ran through her entire body, and an aching emptiness filled her. Damn it, she needed him inside her. Her clit was pounding, pulsating, throbbing. *Ohhh...*

Jonathan pushed his thigh between hers, naked now.

And something slick, wet and warm pushed against her anus. Lori whimpered. "*Jonnie!*"

"This is mine," he whispered roughly. "You are mine. I will have every last part of you. Push down—" as he spoke, he pushed his finger inside, and Lori sobbed, arching back against the burning pain of his invasion. But as he entered her, he reached around, pinching her clit and stroking her, until she was rocking against his caress as he worked her ass. And then he pushed a second finger into the tight ring of muscle, nipping at her neck and groaning when she climaxed into his hand with a ragged scream.

Lori was still shaking when he pulled away and mounted her. Driving his cock into her aching pussy with one long, ruthless thrust, he gripped her hips and held her steady, as she screamed her way through a second orgasm. The ever tightening muscles in her sheath hugged greedily at his cock as he forged his way in and out of her creamy sheath.

"Damn it, that's it," he purred raggedly, rolling his hips and rocking against her as he seated himself completely inside her. "You're softer than silk, sweet and wet...I love it. *I love you.* My heart and soul."

Lori moaned as he bent over her, and whispered the last of the words against her ear, hugging her tightly. Holding still and deep inside her, repeating softly, "My heart and soul, damn it, I love you. I always have."

"Jonathan." Lori sank her teeth into her lip, her breath tearing in and out of her lungs as she struggled to breathe past the emotion lodged inside her. Reaching behind her, she wound one arm around his neck, burying her fingers in those long silken tresses falling around her. He wrapped one brawny forearm around her waist and pulled his cock out slowly, burrowing just as slowly back inside. "I love you..." her words ended on a ragged moan as he surged back in, his thick, burning-hot cock dragging over the wet, creamy tissues of her pussy. The curved end stroked over the nerve endings by the mouth of her womb *just right there,* and Lori arched back against him. She screamed as the room started to shake around her, lava pooling inside her loins, and heat exploding from the surface of her skin.

Tossing her head back, she screamed as he pulled out and drove back inside again—harder, and harder—pushing her hips lower and digging in with more force, his hands going to her buttocks and spreading her open. As if his gaze had actual weight, she could feel him staring at her as one hand left her hip, then returned, spreading a warm silky-slick substance all over her tight, puckered hole. Lori shivered as Jonathan started to probe insistently with his thumb as he rode her harder.

"You can use your magick to tease your body, baby," he murmured, his voice hot and smooth as whiskey as he pushed the tip of his thumb past the tight ring of muscle. "Do it…let me feel that."

Lori flushed, barely understanding, even as she felt some distant part of him reaching for her—not with his body—but with his soul. Wailing, she released the tenuous hold she had on her magick and let it pour through her, rolling over her skin, dancing down to stroke and tease her clit as Jonathan pulled out, leaving her.

"Play with yourself," he murmured, guiding one hand between her thighs even as a myriad of tiny, rainbow lights danced over her skin. The lights caressed her skin, kissing it, reflecting off him as they spun over and around her.

Jonathan settled back on his heels, his cock ruddy, wet and glistening from her cream. Stroking it absently as he studied her, a growl rumbling out of his chest as Lori trembled and sobbed. Her head rolled as the wild magick inside her ran free and loose over her aroused body. The exposed line of her ass, the opened folds of her sweet, wet cleft, the scent of her… Jonathan licked his lips as he picked up the lubricant, wanting to swallow her whole.

He shuddered as he slicked the silky substance over his sex and stared at the tiny, pink hole of her ass. Warming more of it in his hands, he rubbed the sweet little rosette teasingly. He steadied her as she jumped, and watched as it flowered open, groaning as the satiny confines gloved his fingers tightly.

Moving so that she was between his knees, he finger-fucked her ass and pussy with alternating hands, until she was rocking back and forth, her mouth desperately seeking his. And when she was begging, he moved behind her. Pulling his fingers from the clinging silk of her bottom, he spread her wide. Pushing against the tender, soft flesh, he watched as it gave way under his possession. *Tight...* "Damn it, you are *sweet*," he groaned, pushing relentlessly deeper as she froze beneath him.

Pulling out just a bit, he surged back in, shuddering as she involuntarily clenched the muscles in her buttocks around him. Her head fell low and Jonathan reached around, circling his fingers on her clitoris. Pulling out, he rocked against her with slow, steady motions until she was panting under him again. Then he started to push deeper.

Lori arched back, biting her lip against the burning, ever increasing pressure in her bottom. Her eyes teared and she whimpered involuntarily as Jonathan continued to push in, even as his fingers stroked and circled her clit. "Take a deep breath, baby and push down for me," he murmured, pulling out, just slightly rocking against her...*oh, that's nice*, Lori thought. Pushing back to meet him, she barely heard him as he repeated, "Push down for me," and she tried to focus on the exquisite sensations it caused as he stroked just barely into and out...*mmmm*...

Then he pulled out, just barely breaching her, his hands tightening on her hips. "Push. Down." His voice was low, rough, a deep, primal growl that called to everything female and primitive inside of her. Lori quivered and bowed her head, pushing as she lowered her torso and braced herself.

A hoarse scream filled the air as he filled her, seating himself inside her ass to the hilt. Jonathan filled her completely with a brutal, driving thrust that had her screaming with the glorious, sweetly painful pleasure even as she shuddered and tried to pull away from his restraining hands. Whimpering, she had to fight to keep from pulling away as he pulled out, then drove back in, again and again. The pressure was building to a crescendo that would surely be more than she could handle.

It broke, exploding over Lori in a wash of glorious, sweet pleasure and she pushed back, sobbing, "Again, damn it,

Jonathan, don't stop, *please*." Her nipples drew tight, her breaths became more and more ragged as she moved hungrily against him, under him. Taking more of his thrusts, and feeling the hungry, hard drives of his cock into her ass, the movement of his body against hers, she sought her climax, just as he sought his. They fell together, each pushing against the other and tensing, a long, eerie howl rising from Jonathan's mouth. Lori sobbed his name out as she collapsed, feeling the hot, scalding wash of his seed flooding her.

Long moments later, she was still trying to slow the sobbing breaths that raced in and out of her lungs, when he cradled her against him and gently lifted her to the bed. Easing her down against him, nuzzling her neck as he lifted the blankets over them, he murmured, "The next time I take you will be in our home, our bed. Say it, say yes."

Lori shuddered, opening her lips to agree to anything he wanted, but the words wouldn't come out quite that easily. "I haven't heard you ask me for anything yet," she said raggedly, her head falling forward, the streaked curls of golden-red and white mingling with his deep brunette locks on the pillow.

"Hmmm, you still don't know how to give an inch, baby, do you? First, I tell you to go away and you won't. Now I tell you to come to me, and you won't. You want me to ask," he said, with a muffled laugh of frustration. His voice deepened and he wrapped his arms around her, cuddling her against him. "I love everything about you, you adorable, stubborn, brave witch. Tell me you'll marry me and get it over with."

"I'll do better than that," she whispered, a smile curving her mouth. "I'll marry you…so we can get started. With our life."

Epilogue

It was the sound of wild magick, broken moans, and hot sex that drew her to Lori's rooms. Against her will, but damn it, if she didn't do it quick, others were going to be gathering up there soon. Or the whole house might shatter around them. Sarel felt the heat rush up her neck as she started down the hall toward Lori's rooms.

Lori's voice, high and keening, as she cried out Jonathan's name, came loud and clear through the door, and Sarel stopped. Whirling around she headed right back down, but then she heaved a sigh and hissed, "Bloody hell."

Her amused audience of one let a wolfish smile cross his face as he glided back into the shadows. He had been about to take care of it for her…but she was rather adorable, looking so embarrassed.

Sarel turned back and marched up to Lori's door, shoulders straight as a nun's, placed her hand flat against the wood and closed her eyes, not letting the fire and light that was seeping out from underneath distract her. And the miniature earthquake that followed didn't make her pause either as she settled a spell to block the sounds coming from the room.

Well, she works pretty good for a very embarrassed older sister, Ben mused as he slid out of the shadows and stood in the middle of the hall.

When she turned around, her cheeks were still flaming and she was swearing under her breath. He cocked a dark eyebrow at her and said, "Being Elijah Crawford's wife, I can't believe you've never heard people having sex before. I imagine you've even done it once or twice yourself."

Her eyes narrowed. "Leave me the hell alone, Cross."

"Aren't you grouchy?" he mused, as he forged a little ball of fire and started to toss it back and forth in his hands. "I had been planning on taking care of that for you. How was I to know you would insist on checking on *baby* sister so damn soon?"

"Go fuck yourself," Sarel suggested pithily.

He merely smiled at her, catching the fire in one hand, and pressing it between both palms until it was absorbed as he stared into her stormy eyes. "You witches are the oddest lot."

"You're a witch, too, Cross. Remember?"

A sad smile flickered across his face. "I don't know what I am, Sarel." Then he turned, walking away from the sounds of loving, and the suddenly understanding woman standing in front of him.

Ben had another witch to deal with.

The oddest of them all.

But first, he had to find her.

Enjoy this excerpt from
Her Wildest Dreams

Chapter One
February 2001

It's weird, the way a woman can go her whole life without ever really seeing herself. And the things that can flash through her mind when she's come face to face with a knife-welding punk out to snatch her purse, and end her life.

He was high; Alison had spent two years giving out Methadone at a clinic and she could spot high easily enough. Basically that meant her life wasn't worth the twenty dollars she had in her wallet — not to this guy.

Yet, in that moment — when seconds stretched out to a crawl — it wasn't any odd sentimental moment from childhood that rose to her memory, no poignant moment spent in a lover's arms.

Instead, she could see her reflection — as she had looked just twenty minutes before she had left the house to run to the bookstore — her nondescript brown hair pulled back in a loose ponytail, her glasses sliding down her nose, her long narrow face pale and listless.

The clothes she had on were baggy and simple — jeans and a flannel shirt — covered by a serviceable jacket of black wool. They hung on a frame so skinny, it could have belonged to a teenaged boy, not a twenty-six-year-old woman.

And that was what she saw.

Herself. Miserable, pathetic, lifeless.

Dimly, she heard footsteps and a shout.

With a jolt, reality snapped back into focus and her eyes, hidden behind huge plastic frames and lenses, narrowed, her mouth tightened into a grim line. She looped one wrist through the purse strap and drew the other one down, cocked back, the ball of her hand driving up—a trick she had learned long ago, back when she had still lived with her folks and one very protective older brother.

To her surprise, the boy—*God, was he even seventeen?*—went crashing down, shouting with shock. She was certain she had felt cartilage crunch under her hand, but the pain of that wouldn't faze somebody so obviously strung out. She drew her foot back, praying for forgiveness, and landed a kick square in his unprotected crotch.

That drew a howl from him...and a vicious curse. She dropped into a crouch she didn't even know she remembered, drawing her hands up, eyes darting around for a weapon.

But it wasn't necessary.

A body hurtled out from nowhere, tackling the boy who had rushed to his feet, taking him down. A large hand clipped the boy across the face, stunning him. Alison heard the clank of metal, followed by the quiet snick of handcuffs latching.

Her body had started to quiver and it took a long time to realize the voice addressing her was calling her by name. It took even longer to realize that voice was familiar.

Large hands closed over her shoulders and an irate voice demanded, "Girl, have you lost your mind?"

Slowly her lids lowered, then lifted once more and her gaze moved up, training on that face, her ears homing in on the rough, angry voice. It clicked and she smiled a dazed, rather dreamy smile.

"Why, Alexander O'Malley, how nice to see you," she murmured as her body went from subtle shivering to outright quaking in a matter of heartbeats. Her own heart started to kick, pounding heavily against the wall of her chest, causing her breath to catch in her throat.

His dark brown hair spilled onto his forehead, falling into his chocolate-brown eyes as he glared down at her in unsuppressed rage. His mouth — that sexy, sexy mouth she had always wanted one taste of — was grim and tight, his lean, tanned face stark with anger.

Her mind felt oddly disconnected as she stared at him, head cocked. Vicious, furious curses drew her attention away from Alex, but the angry narcotics detective barely even glanced at the struggling boy at his feet.

"Little idiot," he snapped out, giving her one final shake before drawing a cell phone from his pocket. She barely heard him barking into the phone. Instead, Alison focused on the battered boy who lay at their feet, moaning pitifully, crying and struggling to get up and away. Alex's feet were braced on either side of him and his glittering dark-brown gaze locked on the boy's face.

Alison's eyes were locked on the boys face too, widening as she realized some of the marks on him had come from her — the meekest, mildest woman ever to stroll through southern Indiana.

A warm hand closed on her face and she felt her chin being lifted. Staring into Alex's eyes, the fog that had started to envelope her brain thickened. "I think I might have broken his nose," she said calmly.

"You little idiot, he was about to slit your damn throat," Alex growled. "Why didn't you just give him your fucking purse?"

Her eyes dropped to the object in question and her lips pursed. "I really don't know." A frown marred her face as she looked back up at him and said quietly, "It wouldn't have mattered though. He would have killed me no matter what I did. And we both know it, Alex."

Alex paced the small office, watching the silent little figure huddled in the chair. Every now and then, Alison Ryan would sip from the cup of coffee she held, but for the most part, her eyes remained locked on the wall in front of her. He seriously doubted she was seeing anything, but he had to admit, she was much calmer than he ever would have thought.

It wouldn't have mattered though. He would have killed me no matter what I did. And we both know it, Alex.

Damn it. Fuck.

The bitch of it all? She was right. The boy was so fucking strung out, he would have killed her and it wouldn't have fazed him. Oh, he would have been sorry — once it was too late.

Too late — once Alex have had to go see quiet little Allie one last time, right before her coffin was closed. She had saved her own neck. A sick, hot little ball of nausea slid through his gut and Alex clenched his jaw. *Fuck.* He had known her since she was a kid. There was no way to describe the rage he had felt when he had raced upon the scene and seen the teenager flashing that knife, so close to her white neck.

But she had handled it. Who would have thought it? Alison Ryan. She was such a, well, *mouse*. It wasn't the nicest thing to say about his best friend's baby sister, but what else could he say? It was the truth.

Her pale little face was a bit paler than normal, but nothing that was worrying him.

The signs of shock had faded and she was calm. Geez, how long had he known her? Going on twenty-five years now. And he didn't think he had ever seen her upset. Alex seriously doubted she had the passion it took to get upset. So why was it surprising that she wasn't upset now? Hysterical, even?

Why, Alexander O'Malley, how nice to see you, she had said, pushing her glasses up and staring at him owlishly, like she hadn't almost been killed.

Little fool, he thought. For the fifteenth time.

Her ponytail had been tidied at some point, pulled back tightly from her face. Every now and then, her eyes would glance at the plain watch on her wrist, but she still hadn't said much. "Why don't I call your brother to come get you?"

In her soft, hesitant voice, she said, "Mike's out of town until next Saturday."

Alex pressed his fingers against his eyes and muttered, "Tahiti. I forgot."

Forgotten that he had stood up for Mike in his wedding only four days earlier? Alison smiled slightly. She didn't doubt it; Alex looked strained. And she doubted it had anything to do with what might have happened earlier. She set aside the half empty coffee cup and stood, folding her arms across her chest. "I can call a cab," she said. "I just need to get back to my car, anyway."

A cab. He stared at her, his pen falling from his hand. *A cab?* After damn near getting her throat slit, she was going to call a fucking cab? *Mike would kill me. Shit, I'd kill me.* "No," he said slowly, shaking his head and lowering his gaze back to the report. "No cab."

"I don't mind," she said softly. "It's late and—"

"No cab, Allie," he said in a steely voice. "I'll take you. I've got a few things to finish up and then I can take you home." He scowled. *Home? Alone?* "Is there a friend you could call? Go stay with?"

She frowned at him quizzically. "Why would I do that?"

"Because you almost got your throat slit?" he snapped and then mentally kicked his ass as her eyes fell away and her mouth twitched.

His date had called and cancelled at the last minute, which explained why he had been in the area. He had stopped to pick up a book and on the way out had seen Allie's car. He had almost turned around to go find her, to see if he could talk her into grabbing a bite with him, thinking it was better than going home alone.

Actually, even though it would end up without any sex, it was better than a date. Once you got her talking, Allie was adorable, funny, sharp-witted. And unmistakable.

He would have seen her in the store.

She hadn't been there. The worry hadn't even had a chance to settle in his gut when he heard the scuffle and the muttered curse from the small alley between the old bookstore and the run-down grocery and had known— just *known*—that the little twit was getting in trouble.

So instead of settling down with his book, dragging the shy kid sister of his best friend out for some food, or looking up another date, he was writing up a police report because the idiot was too stupid to realize it wasn't safe to walk from one store to the other—not in this neighborhood. Allie was a cop's sister, for crying out loud. *She* should know better.

"I'm sorry. Look, just give me a few minutes to wrap a few things up and then I can take you home, okay? Hang around a little while. You don't need to be alone just yet, okay?"

She nodded, slowly, hesitantly, and lowered herself back into the chair. Alex went to his desk and finished typing up the report. As he whipped the paper from the old typewriter he preferred, his eye caught sight of a file.

Hot damn. About time, he thought as satisfaction slid through his gut.

Eyes gleaming, he flipped it open. This was it, all right. What he had been waiting for.

Within five minutes of poring over the files, he had completely forgotten Alison was there.

After another thirty-five minutes had passed, Alison realized he had forgotten her. Biting back a sigh, she rose and made her way to the door on silent feet. Glancing back over her shoulder, she released the sigh. She was so forgettable. She knew damn well if she had been a criminal under arrest, or any other woman, she would never had made it out of that tiny office without Alex's sharp eyes catching her.

But her? Quiet, mousy little Alison Ryan? He didn't so much as glance up as she slid through the door. He still had his nose buried in the file as she made her way to the woman occupying the huge desk up front.

It hurt, but Alex had always had the ability to hurt her. Since she had spent the majority of her life dreaming about him, it was no surprise. At first, they had been the sweet romantic dreams of a girl, him sweeping her away, vowing to love her forever.

He was so damn sexy, so adorable, so hot...but it was more than that. Not that being six-feet-four with thick, curly brown hair, melted-chocolate eyes, and a flashing white smile didn't help. And his shoulders, that wide chest...tapering down to a flat, muscled belly and a tight ass that filled out a pair of jeans like nothing she had ever seen.

And of course there was always the front view—long, powerful legs, muscled thighs, a sizeable bulge that Allie eyed when she knew he wasn't looking. Which was often—he never really looked at her.

Oh, yeah, there was a lot about Alex's looks to fuel her dreams.

In her wildest dreams, they were both naked and sweaty and wrapped around each other, his dark body covering hers while he rode her hard. She had dreams where he bound her hands behind her and mounted her. Dreams where she knelt in front of him and licked and sucked on his penis like it was candy.

Now any time she dreamed about him, she woke up and cried, because the likelihood of him ever touching her was nonexistent. Alex was handsome, arrogant, living sex appeal, with broad shoulders, and arms and thighs heavy with muscle. His mouth was full and sensual and usually puckered with a scowl when he looked at her.

She'd had entire dreams spun around that mouth. Entire fantasies about the things he would do to her, that she would do to him. Things that made her blush almost as hotly as they made her burn. Things she was too damn clumsy to do, even if he was interested.

It wasn't just his looks, though—there was something about him that seemed to call to something inside of her.

About the author:

They always say to tell a little about yourself! I was born in Kentucky and have been reading avidly since I was six. At twelve, I discovered how much fun it was to write when I took a book that didn't end the way it should have ended, and I rewrote it. I've been writing since then.

About me now... hmm... I've been married since I was 19 to my high school sweetheart and we live in the midwest. Recently I made the plunge and turned to writing full-time and am looking for a part-time job so I can devote more time to my family—two adorable children who are growing way too fast, and my husband who doesn't see enough of me...

Shiloh welcomes mail from readers. You can write to her c/o Ellora's Cave Publishing at 1337 Commerce Drive, Suite 13, Stow OH 44224.

Why an electronic book?

We live in the Information Age—an exciting time in the history of human civilization in which technology rules supreme and continues to progress in leaps and bounds every minute of every hour of every day. For a multitude of reasons, more and more avid literary fans are opting to purchase e-books instead of paperbacks. The question to those not yet initiated to the world of electronic reading is simply: *why?*

1. *Price.* An electronic title at Ellora's Cave Publishing runs anywhere from 40-75% less than the cover price of the <u>exact same title</u> in paperback format. Why? Cold mathematics. It is less expensive to publish an e-book than it is to publish a paperback, so the savings are passed along to the consumer.

2. *Space.* Running out of room to house your paperback books? That is one worry you will never have with electronic novels. For a low one-time cost, you can purchase a handheld computer designed specifically for e-reading purposes. Many e-readers are larger than the average handheld, giving you plenty of screen room. Better yet, hundreds of titles can be stored within your new library—a single microchip. (Please note that Ellora's Cave does not endorse any specific brands. You can check our website at www.ellorascave.com for customer recommendations we make available to new consumers.)

3. *Mobility.* Because your new library now consists of only a microchip, your entire cache of books can be taken with you wherever you go.

4. *Personal preferences are accounted for.* Are the words you are currently reading too small? Too large? Too...**ANNOYING**? Paperback books cannot be modified according to personal preferences, but e-books can.

5. *Innovation.* The way you read a book is not the only advancement the Information Age has gifted the literary community with. There is also the factor of what you can read. Ellora's Cave Publishing will be introducing a new line of interactive titles that are available in e-book format only.

6. *Instant gratification.* Is it the middle of the night and all the bookstores are closed? Are you tired of waiting days—sometimes weeks—for online and offline bookstores to ship the novels you bought? Ellora's Cave Publishing sells instantaneous downloads 24 hours a day, 7 days a week, 365 days a year. Our e-book delivery system is 100% automated, meaning your order is filled as soon as you pay for it.

Those are a few of the top reasons why electronic novels are displacing paperbacks for many an avid reader. As always, Ellora's Cave Publishing welcomes your questions and comments. We invite you to email us at service@ellorascave.com or write to us directly at: 1337 Commerce Drive, Suite 13, Stow OH 44224.

Discover for yourself why readers can't get enough of the multiple award-winning publisher Ellora's Cave. Whether you prefer e-books or paperbacks, be sure to visit EC on the web at www.ellorascave.com for an erotic reading experience that will leave you breathless.

WWW.ELLORASCAVE.COM